*Mother c

MERCER
UNIVERSITY PRESS

Endowed by
Tom Watson Brown
and
The Watson-Brown Foundation, Inc.

Mother of Rain

A Novel

KAREN SPEARS ZACHARIAS

MERCER UNIVERSITY PRESS
MACON, GEORGIA

MUP/ P469

© 2013 Mercer University Press
1400 Coleman Avenue
Macon, Georgia 31207
All rights reserved

9 8 7 6 5 4 3

Books published by Mercer University Press are printed on acid-free paper that
meets the requirements of the American National Standard for Information
Sciences—Permanence of Paper for Printed Library Materials.

Mercer University Press is a member of Green Press Initiative
(greenpressinitiative.org), a nonprofit organization working to help publishers
and printers increase their use of recycled paper and decrease their use of fiber
derived from endangered forests. This book is printed on recycled paper.

ISBN   978-0-88146-448-1

Cataloging-in-Publication Data is available from the Library of Congress *great love for*

Gordon "Flash" Wofford, Tennessee;

Karen Mendenhall Clark, Georgia;

&

Peggy Stoneman Wright, Oregon

Previous Books

Benched: The Memoirs of Judge Rufe McCombs

After the Flag has Been Folded

Where's Your Jesus Now?

Will Jesus Buy Me a Double-Wide?

A Silence of Mockingbirds: The Memoir of a Murder

"Words Rise Up Out of the Country"

—engraving on Aunt Cil's headstone,

Christian Bend, Tennessee

Note to the Reader

As a young girl, I spent many a summer day in the care of Aunt Lucille "Cil" Shropshire Christian, in a Tennessee holler known as Christian Bend. This story whispers of my great affection for my cousin Lon, who was known among those mountain people as a "deaf mute." As a child, I was afraid of Lon because of his disability, but Lon was always good to those of us who lacked understanding. He was the first to teach me that admiration can be communicated without words.

Thirty miles up the road from where I live now, elders from the Cayuse, Umatilla and Walla Walla tribes are working diligently to preserve what is left of their nearly forgotten Sahaptin language and as its function as a keeper of their culture.

Ron Rash once told me that nature is our most universal language: "No matter where you go, a waterfall is a waterfall," Rash said. Those growing up far removed from waterways and waterfalls, and with no memory of the languages their elders spoke, may experience a cultural deafness.

My hope is that *Mother of Rain* will help restore the reverberations of the rivers and waterfalls, and the Appalachian voice of my father and my mother's people before it, like the Sahaptin language, is lost to future generations. A glossary is provided.

Mother of Rain

1

Burdy Luttrell

Auntie Tay was in Erwin the day they strung up the circus elephant.

"Listen here, Burdy, I wouldn't believe it none if I hadn't seen it with my own two eyeballs," Auntie Tay said. I feared she might blind herself pointing her two fingers up real close to her eyes the way she done. "It was a shame, but I reckon they had no other choice," Auntie explained. "That beast kilt a white man."

Cousin Hota and I scooched closer to the rocker where Auntie Tay sat barefoot, taking care not to git our fingers too close to the chair's slats. Whenever Auntie told a story, that rocker of hers would inch all the way acrost a floor, and over anything in its path.

"Why did she kill 'em? Tell us why!" Cousin Hota pleaded.

I dropped the jasmine leaves I was weaving into a necklace and looked up at Auntie. Bending over, she lifted the unfinished necklace out of my lap. "Pass me that, Burdy," she said, pointing to the pile of waxy leaves beside me. I handed them over. Tay was all the time telling me and Cousin Hota that idle hands make for the Devil's playground.

Auntie Tay's fingers folded the leaves into triangles as she continued her tale. She was all the time telling tales. Hota and I liked the stories of *our people* best. How we Melungeons, as she called us, came over the ridge to Christian Bend. How we Melungeons came from three tribes: the Cherokees, the Portyghees, and the Blackees.

But on that day, Auntie Tay didn't tell me and Hota about our people and their old ways. She only spoke of the white men that kilt the poor elephant.

"I'm telling you children, it ain't right to force an animal to live differently than Creator intended, and Creator didn't make elephants for city life. He made them for the wild, jes like some peoples," Auntie Tay said.

"You mean John the Baptist?" Cousin Hota asked. Hota was nine, two years younger than me, but he always placed first in the Bible quiz. "The Bible says John ate locust and honey and wore a loincloth."

"Maybe John the Baptist was Cherokee," I said.

Lifting her chin slightly, Auntie Tay stared off past a row of cedars, as if she was expecting the elephant's ghost to come trodding upriver, around Christian Bend.

"You children ever seen any elephants roaming these hills?"

"No, ma'am!" we answered, shaking our heads.

"No, and you won't neither. Elephants got hoofed feet but they ain't like deer. They ain't meant for these hills. They's supposed to be in Africa. Creator made them a big country 'cause they's big animals."

"How big?" I asked.

"Well, Burdy, I tell you. They's fatter than twenty cows."

"Nuh-uh!"

"Is too. They's fatter than twenty cows and fifty pigs."

"Can you eat 'em?" Hota asked.

"Might not taste so well. Elephant's hide is tougher than the skin on your heels. Arrows cain't tear it and bullets cain't pierce it. That's how come they's had to hang that creature."

"Didn't the tree limbs break?"

Auntie Tay dropped her head to her chest and laughed. "Tree? Burdy, you're a mess! There ain't no tree can hold an elephant. Not even the Giant Chestnut. They strung that poor creature up by a crane."

Yanking on Auntie's skirt, Hota asked, "But how come the elephant hurt the white man?"

"Well, now that's somethin' I didn't see. I jes heard tell of it when the townsmen told Father. The menfolk were gathered outside the feed store when Father and I got to town. Father told Ben Drummond if they kept standing around that way, Creator might turn them all into statues. That's when Old Ben told us the elephant stomped a white man to death after the fellow had taken the creature down to the watering canal following the circus show 'cause the beast was hot and thirsty."

"Did he have her on a leash?" Hota asked.

"Lordy, no! They ain't no man strong enough to lead an elephant on a leash. That beast weighed over 10,000 pounds. You might as well try to carry all the water from Horseshoe Falls in a straw basket as try to lead a creature like that. Cain't be done, no way, no how."

"I bet Samson could've done it!" Hota said. "Samson killed a lion with only his hands."

Pausing to consider his suggestion, Auntie Tay said, "Well, maybe Sampson could've, if Creator give him the powers to do it. The townsfolk would've been glad for the help, I tell you that. They's had a hard time of putting that creature down.

"They said the white man was guiding the elephant with a stick, like a shepherd boy, poking and prodding her along. Nobody knows how come the elephant to git so perturbed, but all of a sudden she whupped around and picked that white man up in her trunk like so"—and with that Auntie Tay folded her right arm up over itself—"and mashed him to the ground!" Her arm snapped out straight again. "Then, without any vexation at all, that creature stomped the white man's head flat as a melon under a tractor wheel!"

Hota and I gasped. I got the chicken skin.

"Did his brains mash out?"

"Mm-hm, sure did, Burdy." Auntie nodded. "Like a berry popped open."

My stomach cinched up at the thought of it.

"Old Ben said Sheriff grabbed his .45 and tried to kill the animal right then and there before it done stomped somebody else down, but the bullets bounced off the creature's hide like BB-shot off a boulder. She didn't even bleed.

"The circus manager told Sheriff he'd need some mighty big cannons if he intended to stop a crazed beast like that. He was afraid of the elephant his own self, but he couldn't let on none, or he'd be out of a job.

"So he picked up a stick and was able to coax the animal back to the fairgrounds, where he chained her to some posts. He was of two minds on what to do with her. If he let the townsfolk kill the elephant, he'd have to put out the money to git another. But if he didn't, the townsfolk might skin him alive. Sheriff made the decision for him. Said they'd electrocute the creature the next day. The circus manager figured out a way to make the towns-folk happy and make him some money. Everybody attending the matinee was invited to watch the elephant's electrocution." Auntie Tay drawled out that last word in a fashion that made me wish I lived in a place where it was always daylight and never dark.

"But I thought you said they hung her," Hota said.

"I did," Auntie replied. "I ain't got to that part yet."

"But how come people would pay to see a dangerous animal?" I asked. "Weren't they afeared of her after she stomped a man to death?"

"Well, Burdy, that's the confusing thing about people. They like dancing with the Devil. They pretend to be scared of him, like they don't want nothing to do with him, all the time they's flirting with him. Don't make no sense a'tall, but that's the truth as best I can tell.

"I know what that elephant done was wrong," Auntie continued, "stomping that white man thataway, and him only trying to git her some water. But I cain't he'p but feel sorry for her. There's something wrong with trying to make a being live contrary to its nature. That's all," Auntie said. "It ain't no wonder that animal got vexed enough to murder a white man."

There was something in Auntie Tay's tone that made me wonder if she'd fancied such a thing herself. Her hands were working lickety-split, folding those jasmine leaves, but Auntie Tay was staring far off, past the weathered fence posts and up the slope to the wild roses bursting white puffs of perfume along the church graveyard where her momma and daddy lay sleeping eternally.

"I ain't gonna lie to you. I hadn't never seen an elephant, so when Old Man Drummond asked Father and me to go with him and the others down to the rail yard, I was curious as a prowling cat.

"When we got there the poor thing was already chained up, and they was gitting ready to fry her with 50,000 volts of electricity. She was swaying nervously, from foot to foot, like you do, Burdy, when you gots to go pee and cain't.

"She knowed they was aiming to hurt her. You could see the fear in her eyes. But when they put the shocks to her, she threw back her head and let out a long whine and danced around on her hind feet. I'm sure it smarted, but it didn't come close to killing her. They really had a problem on their hands then. What do you do with a mad cow that weighs five tons?"

Hota shrugged. I shook my head. I hated making Father mad, and he didn't even weigh one ton as far as I knew.

"The train boss suggested they could mash her between two engines, but Sheriff said that would be too cruel, as if they's a kind way to kill such a creature," Auntie Tay said, clicking her tongue to the back of her teeth in a disapproving fashion.

"After that, they hauled out the crane, and one of the yard men ran up her spine, like he were climbing slanchwise up a mountain. He cinched a chain around her neck. She didn't give him no fight. I guess by then her fight was all give out.

"Then, a yard man hooked a boom to the chain, cranked the winch and up she went. That was a heap of flesh dangling. But only for a minute or two, because the elephant was so heavy the chain snapped in two like a twig. She came crashing down on her behinney and let out a whine that sounded like 100 trains whistling at once."

Hota looked at me. I stared back at him. Our jaws slacked like we'd jes seen the graves at the churchyard crack open and the dead dance a jig. We both looked up at Auntie Tay.

"The chain broke?" I asked.

"It sure did. Like peanut brittle, clean in two. I'm sure if she could've, that creature would've taken off running down Canal Street and jumped on the first boat back to Africa. But, poor thing, broke her back legs when she fell from that noose."

Auntie Tay leaned over and slipped the jasmine necklace over my head. I breathed in its sugared scent, hoping to calm the bees swarming around inside my belly. I was having a hard time catching my breath. I wasn't sure I wanted to hear any more of Auntie Tay's awful story. I kept thinking of that poor, poor elephant.

"I hate those white men!" I yelled. "They are evil! Evil! If I'd been that elephant, I would've stomped them all to death!"

"Me too!" Hota added.

"You children better calm down if you want me to finish," Auntie Tay said. "I cain't remember things rightly if you're going to make a bunch of racket." Auntie's chair was nearly spinning circles, she was rocking it so fast. Hota and I kept having to scooch out of her way.

"Seemed like the entire town was there. Thousands of people backed up against one another as that frightened creature slapped to the ground. Some folks started running and screaming. We was lucky nobody got crushed in the stampede. But we'd all kept a good distance from the elephant. That's probably what saved us."

Hota peeled a splintered reed from the rocker's back and used the tip to clean the grime from under his fingernails. "What did they do with the elephant after that?" he asked.

"Somebody got the yard man a heavier chain. One with links as big 'round as my fist," she said, holding out a clenched-up hand. "It took half a dozen men jes to git it around the elephant's neck. This time she couldn't fight them, even if she'd wanted to. All she could do was sit on her broken hind legs and cry as they noosed her up one last time and winched up the boom again. I could hear her bones crackle and crunch as they lynched her like a stiff-necked slave. It was the most gawd-awful sound." Auntie said.

I'd never seen a lynching, but I'd heard Ma and Daddy whisper about the time, before I was born, when Uncle Moses was cornered by some white men uptown who took him for a Blackee and threatened to hang him. Ma always said if it hadn't been for Uncle Moses's opal-blue eyes, they probably would've strung him up to the nearest tree. When I worked up the nerve to ask Ma about it, she explained, "We are a different people, Burdy, and there's some folks don't like different. They think everybody ought to be the same as them."

"Auntie Tay, have you ever seen a man hung?" I asked.

"No, child. Thank God, I ain't never seen such a thing," she replied. "But I cain't imagine it being much worse than what I seen in Erwin that day."

"How long did they leave the elephant strung up?" Hota asked.

"Long enough that folks had time to walk over to Wright's Grocery and git them a soda and still git back in time to watch the creature's carcass lowered into a pit they'd dug with steam shovels," Auntie said. "They buried her there in the rail yard, after they sawed off her tusks. Sometimes, even now, she comes to me in my dreams. I wake feeling guilty. I wanted to help her, but what could I do? I was jes a young girl, like you, Burdy."

Auntie Tay had been dead for years, and Cousin Hota had long ago moved off the mountain, but the story Tay told us as children haunted me as I witnessed the commotions going on at Zeb and Maizee Hurd's place.

Zeb had come to me right before he married Maizee and asked two favors of me: Could he rent the house on my property in exchange for some sweat equity? And, if so, would I be willing to help watch after his soon-to-be-wife who was expecting a child?

At the time, his request didn't seem too bothersome. Everybody around these parts knows that if it's a midwife you're needing or a healing of any sort—physical or spiritual—call me, Burdy Luttrell. But looking back now, I realize how foolish we'd all been. We believed we ought to be preparing for the baby coming, or the soldiers leaving, that night's supper or the next morning's breakfast, the summer garden or the winter snows. But the truth is we should've been concerning ourselves with the tribulations pressing in on us like autumn fog.

I promised Zeb I'd see after Maizee, and I tried my darndest, even after that Mashburn boy started coming around, but desire and promises don't make a person able. There are some wrongs in this life that only Creator can right. It appeared Maizee was one of 'em.

2

Maizee

A girl never forgets the day her momma dies. It was a Tuesday September 19, 1933. Up until then, Tuesdays were my favorite day of the week. Library days at school. Sometime before lunch, our fourth-grade teacher, Mrs. Chamberlain, would tell us to line up outside the door—"Keep your hands and feet to your-selves!"—then she would march us down to the library, where we had a whole hour to look through the books before it was time to march back.

I'd been waiting for a month or better to check out *Hitty*, a book about a magical wooden doll that traveled all over the world to foreign places like New Orleans. My bestest friend Eudie read the book first and couldn't quit talking about it. She kept trying to tell me all about Hitty and Phoebe, the girl who owned her, but I kept telling Eudie to please hush up because I wanted to read the book for myself and she was going to ruin it for me.

Eudie was nice enough to coax her brother into whittling us a couple of look-alike Hitty dolls. Eudie's brother was a real good whittler; he fashioned the dolls from the pictures drawed in the book and made 'em about half the size of a candle, the same as the real Hitty.

"He even carved 'em from witchwood, which is guaranteed to ward off the evil spirits, jes like Hitty says in the book," Eudie told me.

"If you don't hush telling me everything, I won't have no cause to read the book myself," I said in my most put-out voice, the one Momma said was plumb rude. But Momma was so pleased over the dolls, she helped me and Eudie paint 'em. We used Daddy's black shoe polish for the dolls' hair and Momma's red nail polish for their lips.

On the day before I found Momma in the backyard all pecked over like I done, I walked into my bedroom and found my doll leaning up against a pillow in Sunday-go-to-meeting clothes Momma sewed. The dress wasn't made from calico like the doll's was in the book, but it was pretty all the same.

She'd cut it from a blue feed sack with teensy bursts of what looked like red daisies all over it. She'd even sewed a matching dress for Eudie's doll. A way of saying thanks, Momma explained, "Since if it weren't for Eudie and her brother's generosity you wouldn't even have the doll."

I'd wrapped the dress for Eudie's doll in a napkin and carried it to school with me that morning. When I pulled it out and give it to Eudie right before the bell rang, she liked to have cried.

"I cain't believe your momma made this!" she said, pinching the tiny dress between her fingers and holding it straight out. "It's so beautiful!" Eudie switched it through the air like it was a dancing ghost-dress. She twirled on one foot, her golden hair swishing acrost her freckled face like hay in a hot summer's wind.

I couldn't wait to git home and tell Momma how much Eudie loved her present. And I was doubly excited because Mrs. Chamberlain said I was first in line on the waiting list. Finally it was my turn to check out *Hitty*. I knew Momma would want me to read it to her that very evening. Momma didn't read too good on account of her not gitting as much schooling as lucky me. She read picture books to me when I was little, but when I got big enough to read chapter books, I started reading to her.

Child of Light. That's what Momma called me. She'd go about the house dusting windowsills and tabletops singing,

"This child of light, this light of mine. I'm going to let my little light shine. Yes, this child, she's my sweet Maizee Delight!"

Sometimes Momma would give the song a hiccup-pause and walk over to wherever I was at—sitting on the davenport braiding potholders or writing out my memory verse for Sunday School—and she'd sit down beside me.

"Maizee Delight," she'd say, wrapping one arm around my shoulders, "listen here."

"But I *am* listening," I'd answer.

Then, Momma would place the other hand on top my head and commence to praying: *"Thank you, Jesus for this child. Send your angels to keep watch care over her."*

One night during supper, while she was peeling the skin off a baked yam, I asked her how come she always prayed thataway.

"How come Jesus got to send angels to keep watch care over me, Momma? Ain't that the job he give you?"

"Well, yes, Maizee. I reckon so," she said before blowing on the steaming tater. "Watch out! That's hot! But I cain't always be with you, so I need some he'p for those times when I ain't there, like when you're off playing at Eudie's house or when you've gone off to school."

"You're lucky your momma trusts Jesus enough to ask for his help," Daddy said. He mashed two clumps of butter over his taters with a fork. "I'm surprised your momma ain't enrolled herself in school so she can keep an eye on you."

"Hush now, Mr. Sam. Don't go putting ideas in Maizee's head."

Mr. Sam was what Momma called Daddy. Cal Sloane, who owned the hardware store, and Judge Madden called Daddy Mr. Daggett, by our last name, but not Momma. She called him by his first name—Sam—and added the Mister part out of respect, she said.

"The only person putting ideas in that girl's head is you, Nan," Daddy replied, shoveling a forkful of orange hotness in his mouth.

"Well," Momma said, smiling, "that's my job."

Momma and Daddy would spar like this forever and a day. It weren't true bickering. They didn't speak hatefulness the way some married folks do. This was their way of nudging up against each other with their heads, like young goats.

Eudie Norris didn't have a daddy. She lived in the rundown old house on the corner of Water and State streets. Eudie was my bestest friend in the entire world until I moved off to Christian Bend and met Wheedin, who then became my very bestest friend ever.

I guess it ain't right to say Eudie didn't have a daddy. I mean, a 'course she had a daddy. Every child has to have a daddy. Even I know that. What I mean to say is Eudie didn't know her daddy, didn't even know his name. And on account of that, Eudie was a bit scared of mine, but she loved Momma.

"I sware Maizee, you've got the prettiest momma in town," she said one afternoon while we was playing dress up with some clothes Momma give us.

"Shush!" I said. "Don't let Momma hear you sware." But I didn't correct Eudie on her opinion. My mother was the prettiest woman in all of Rogersville. Smallish, with teensy feet and an itty-bitty waist, Momma had dark hair that curled up snug against her head without her having to pin curl it the way Eudie's mother done. "Natural curl," Momma always said whenever anybody asked her, and sure as shooting, somebody asked her about it every fool time we went to the store.

Daddy was so tall he looked as if he was Momma's daddy instead of her husband. And skinny! "Lean as a string bean," Momma always said. But I could see where he might scare Eudie off. Daddy had a cross way about him. He was what some people called stern. "Mr. Sam's a serious man with a serious job. That's all," Momma explained. She was all the time defending Daddy.

A lot of people in town got real upset with Daddy after he arrested Loretta Hawkin's grandson for stealing a knife outta Cal Sloane's store and stabbing a ten-year-old boy in the stomach out of pure meanness, no other reason. The boy lived, but the puddle of his blood stains the sidewalk between the hardware store and the newspaper office to this very day.

Loretta used to be a Rogers, and it was some of her kin who settled this town that my father helped police. People could cuss Daddy all they wanted, he said, it don't matter who a person's grandpappy or grandmomma is—long as he's the lawman and they are breaking the law, they are going to jail for it. Momma said Daddy missed his calling. "Mr. Sam should've been a judge," she claimed.

I could appreciate Eudie's shyness around my father. When your daddy's a lawman, it's hard to figure out which side of him is the law and which side of him is a plain old daddy. He had all these rules, house laws, Momma called 'em.

Shoes had to be removed before coming into the house and placed to the left of the door, didn't matter which door or whose shoes. If I forgot and ran into the house with my shoes on, he would stop me before I got two feet inside.

"Back outside with you, young lady!" Daddy would say, pointing at my feet.

Beds could not be left unmade, ever, even if a friend came to spend the night. And no sleeping in past 7 a.m., even on Saturdays. "There's chores to be done," Daddy said.

My chores weren't hard. I had to sweep the front and back porch, clean up the chicken poop, and help Momma with anything she needed, but Momma wasn't stern like Daddy. She thought God invented childhood for playing, so she never needed me to do anything, and sometimes, if Daddy wasn't watching, she'd do my chores for me.

"But Momma, isn't that like being a lawbreaker?" I asked one morning as she cleaned up the chicken coop while I swept the back porch.

"What? You mean me doing your chores?"

"Yes, ma'am. Isn't that the same as breaking the law?"

Momma was bent over a shovel full of dirt and hardened poop. She didn't look up. "Helping people with their burdens isn't breaking the law, Maizee. There's no law that says we cain't help others. Fact is, God's law instructs us to help others whenever we can."

"So you're doing your duty by helping me, ma'am?"

"Yes, that's exactly what I'm doing," she said, smiling. "My duty, and let me tell you, it's a real dookey of a job."

"Momma!" I scolded. Slang-talk was the most forbidden of Daddy's house rules. He would've whupped me good if I'd dared say such a thing, not that I would have because I wouldn't have, not never. But that momma of mine had a devilish side to her. She wasn't mean, ever, but she could be naughty. She was all the time leaving her shoes to the right of the door jes to git Daddy's goat. He grew weary of gitting after her about it, so when he come home and took off his shoes, he'd move hers to the left of the door. I'd watch Momma smile as he did it, knowing all the while that she'd left them there on purpose.

"Why you gotta be so spiteful for, Nan?" Daddy asked, moving her shoes again. "Is it so hard to remember to put your shoes in the right place?"

"It ain't spite," Momma replied. "As long as I take my shoes off outside the house, what difference does it make whether I leave them to the right or the left of the door? Who says there's a right or wrong place for them?"

14

"I do! That's who!" Daddy said in his official police voice. That voice always scared me and Eudie, but it made Momma laugh.

Even though Eudie was uneasy around my daddy, she told me I was lucky to have two parents. Sometimes Eudie's momma would have to work an extra shift at the diner, and on those nights her momma wouldn't come home at all, and although he wasn't but fourteen, Eudie's brother would stay out all night on the nights her momma was gone. "That boy is out running the streets," Daddy said.

On those nights, sometimes two or three times a week, Eudie was left all by herself, with no grandparents or kin to care for her. When Daddy found out that she was staying by herself and her only nine, he told her to bring her pillow and come on down to our house. "A child that age got no business being all alone," Daddy said. "What if the house were to catch fire and her asleep?"

Momma said Mr. Sam was always worrying about the what-ifs of life. She claimed that worrying about the what-ifs of life was a waste of precious little time. I didn't comprehend what she was saying until the day I found her in the backyard. Then I came all too familiar with her meaning.

On that Tuesday, I took off my shoes and set them to the left of the door. Then I walked in, pulling that library book from my bag and opening it up to the first page, "In Which I Begin My Memoirs."

"Momma! Momma! I'm home!" I called out.

No one answered. I thought that was unsettling right off. Momma wouldn't go somewhere without waiting for me to git home from school first. I called out again while I continued reading the book: *"The antique shop is very still."*

Momma didn't return my greeting. Closing the book, I walked down the hall past my room to Momma and Daddy's room. The door was open. The patchwork quilt was pulled all even acrost the bed, jes the way Daddy liked it. The blinds, faded yellow, were drawn up halfway. Dust boogers floated through the afternoon sunlight.

I walked back down the hallway and into the kitchen. The breakfast dishes were warshed and turned upside down to dry on a dish towel. A glass of iced tea sat sweating on the red dinette table. Momma's Bible was open. That's when I figured out that Momma must've gone out back.

I wish now with all my heart that I'd never pushed open that screen door. I wish Hitty had give me a warning, the way she come to later when I needed it. But if she called to me from where she sat leaning against the pillow on my bed, warning me of some awful evil, I never heard her. I never heard anything, not even my own screams when I stepped out the back door and found Momma laying face up in the flowerbed between the bluebells and lilac bushes. Eudie told me later she could hear my screams all the way over at her house.

But I don't remember that myself. I don't remember much but the way those chickens kept pecking away at Momma till they weren't nothing left of her pretty blue eyes but bloody holes. I tried my best to shoo those devil chickens away. I picked up the biggest one and flung it acrost the yard, but she jes come flying back at me, right at my face, aiming to pluck out my eyes. I put my arms up, shielded my face, and started kicking at them. The neighbors called for Daddy, and by the time he got there in his police car with the horn blaring, I'd stomped to death three chickens and broke the wings of two more. I wish I'd kilt them all.

3

A brain bleed. That's what Doc Slater determined to have rendered Momma dead. One of them vessels that keeps the river of blood moving through the body got jammed, so the river clogged, and pretty soon the whole thing burst inside Momma's head and her blood flooded all over, only we couldn't see any of this because it all happened inside her skull.

"Did it hurt?" I asked Daddy when he told me how Momma died.

"Doc Slater ain't sure." My father walked over and sat down on the very edge of my bed. I was sitting cross-legged acrost it, not doing anything but staring off into nothingness. Daddy's nose and eyes were red, like he'd stood in the smoke of burning shumake and irritated them something fierce. His hands clutched his knees to keep his legs from shaking. "She might had a headache, or maybe not. Doc thinks she probably didn't feel nothing at all."

Well, I should hope to shout. Thank God for small favors. I could hear Momma's voice in my head. I was longing to ask Daddy if he thought Momma felt them chickens pecking on her thataway, but I decided some questions are better off left unasked. Falling between the lilac bushes and bluebells wouldn't have been such a bad place to die. Leastwise, the ground was soft there, if it hadn't been for what them hateful chickens did to my momma.

"I'm never going to eat drumsticks again! Not never!" I said, angrily crossing my arms over my chest. Daddy could tell I meant it, too, even though he and everybody else knew that fried drumsticks were near about my most favorite thing in the entire world to eat. It was a toss-up between fried drumsticks and Momma's banana pudding. It didn't matter since I wouldn't be gitting that choice now with Momma dead. It's funny the things you think about when somebody dies.

I cain't really remember too much of what happened after Daddy jumped outta his police car and came running around the back of the house, where I guess he laid witness to about the biggest mess he's ever seen, and being a lawman I imagine he's seen his share. There I was mid-stomp over one of the banty hens.

"Maizee! Don't!" Daddy hollered. I turned toward him, tears and snot running in one stream off my chin. Black and orange chicken feathers stuck in my hair and in the blood splats drying on my arms and legs. Daddy ran over, grabbed me around the waist, and swung me away from the chicken I was stomping.

"Lemme go! Lemme go!" I screamed, biting, slapping, and kicking at my own daddy like he was some awful stranger trying to carry me off.

But he didn't let me go. He held me tight, with all his might, till I quit screaming and kicking. By then neighbors were gathering. Somebody, I cain't remember who, took me from Daddy and carried me inside the house.

Daddy didn't try to change my mind about eating fried drumsticks, and he didn't tell me I was acting ugly. He didn't hold me and tell me everything would be okay, either, the way Momma would've surely done if it'd been Daddy who died. I was truly glad he didn't tell me that God needed Momma more than me, or anything stupid like that. I figured Daddy knew that when a girl's momma dies, there is nothing anybody can say or do to ease the hurt, so he didn't even bother. He never did git after me for killing them chickens. I think if I hadn't done it, he would've.

I don't know when Daddy took the notion to send me off to Christian Bend to live with Doc and Aunt Leela. I surely didn't see that a'coming. The grave tender wasn't done shoveling the dirt over Momma's casket before Daddy was asking Doc if he and Aunt Leela would raise me.

Daddy didn't know I was eavesdropping since I was standing off to one side with Eudie. She and her momma had come to pay their respects. Grabbing Eudie by the arm, I hushed her. "Listen."

"What is it?" she asked, her green eyes narrowing.

"Did you hear what Daddy jes said?"

"No, what?" Eudie turned and glanced over her shoulder at him.

"Don't do that!" I whispered. I could tell I was giving Eudie the willies, but she was too polite to say anything about how skittish I was behaving.

"Do what?"

"Don't look at Daddy! I cain't believe him! He asked Doc if I could come live up at Christian Bend!"

"Nu-huh!" Eudie shook her head. She was disbelieving Daddy's gall much as me.

"I'm telling you the gospel truth! I heard it my own self."

"What'd yer uncle say?"

"I ain't sure. I didn't hear that part."

Later that evening after Momma's burying, soon as all the company had gone home and all the food was put up, Daddy called me to the living room. Our kitchen was full of food. Goodly neighbors had started bringing plates piled with cornbread, biscuits, pies, sliced ham, pot roast—and fried chicken of all things—to the house soon as Mortician Preston came by with his shiny black car and carried Momma off. Daddy had changed out of his suit coat and back into his gray work slacks and shirt. He leaned in the doorway between the kitchen and the living room, his arms crossed, his head drooping. A drying towel was slung over his right shoulder. Momma's big suitcase sat on the rug next to her rocker, the one she used to rock me in when she sang the baby in me lullabies.

"Maizee, you need to pack up your belongings tonight."

"Where we going, sir?"

"*You* are going to live with your Aunt Leela and Doc."

"For how long, sir?"

"From now on," Daddy said, turning away so he didn't have to see my tears. He didn't know there wouldn't be any. Soon as I overheard him talking to Doc about gitting shed of me, I decided right then and there I would not cry for my daddy, and I always keep my word, even the word I give to my own self.

Momma's suitcase was tan with three red stripes around the middle. It snapped and locked shut, though a person has to have the key to lock it and I had no notion where that might be. For as long as I knew her, Momma never had any cause to use the thing. She kept it shoved 'neath her bed, up under the box springs.

Shiny pink material lined the case. It smelled of late summer camellias, dried on the bush. Momma's favorite flower. She kept a can of scented camellia talcum powder on her dresser. Every Sunday before church, she'd shake some into her hands and rub it on her neck. Once she put a teensy bit on the dip in my neck.

I stuck my whole head in the suitcase, took a deep breath, and held it long as I could. Then I did it again and again. I did it so many times I nearly passed out so I stopped. It didn't take me long to pack all my clothes and shoes; I didn't have but two pair of shoes, my good ones for church and school, and my play ones. I folded Hitty up in a pair of my best drawers, clean ones, mind you, and put her in one of the zippered pockets. I didn't zip it all the way closed, though, on account of Hitty needing some air. Mrs. Chamberlain taught us how trees are living things that breathe in bourbon dioxin or something like that, and breathe out oxygen, and since Hitty was made from wood I considered her a living, breathing being that needed air much as me.

I picked up the library book that I'd brought home the day I found Momma. I hadn't read past that first sentence, the one about the antique store being all quiet and still. Daddy was clanging around the kitchen. He was making a racket, trying to figure out where to put the dishes and pans. If it had been me making that much noise, he would've yelled out, "You're like a bull in a china shop! What you don't step on and break, you mess all over."

Daddy liked quiet when he come home from work. I suspect that's why he told Doc that he couldn't raise a girl child by himself. He depended on Momma to do the child-rearing. Without her around to tend after me, Daddy feared what trouble I might be. I packed the library book between two of my shirts. Then I marched into the kitchen.

"Daddy, sir?"

He about jumped out of his skin. I'd startled him bad.

"What?" Daddy asked, turning toward me. His eyebrows pinched together. He had Momma's cornbread skillet in one hand.

"Where is Momma's Bible, sir?"

"On her dresser. Why?"

"I want it. Can I have it to take with me?"

Daddy sat the skillet on the back of the stove, wiped his hands on the dish rag, and walked past me without saying nary a word. A minute later, he came back into the kitchen carrying Momma's black-leather Bible. Each page was edged in gold, like the china that President and Mrs. Roosevelt had at the White House. And Jesus' words were all red like his blood.

"Your momma loved her Bible very much, Maizee. I don't think in all the years we was together she ever missed a day's reading. I'm going to give this to you, but you have to promise me that you will treat it with the same respect and honor your momma did, okay?"

"Yes, sir."

"Don't sit anything on it and don't throw it around."

"No, sir. I won't."

"Try and live by it. Your momma would want that." Daddy's voice cracked. Grabbing hold of the corner of the kitchen table, he tried to steady himself. Pulling out a chair, he sat down. His head fell to his chest, and then my daddy did something I'll never forget for as long as I live. He started bawling. His skinny shoulders hunched into one heaving hump. He was clutching Momma's Bible between both hands. His tears warshed down over it.

I walked acrost the room to my daddy and rubbed his humped-up back. I didn't know what to say so I didn't say nothing.

"I'm sorry, Maizee," he said, sucking back a sob. "I don't know how I'm going to manage without your momma."

"It's okay, Daddy," I said, rubbing his back still. I knew it was a lie soon as I spoke it. Nothing was ever going to be okay now that Momma was dead. Daddy knew it, too, but sometimes a lie can seem like the best hope a person's got. Right then, me and Daddy needed some kind of hope.

Daddy stopped his crying and looked up at me. His grey eyes looked like thunderclouds. His cheeks were pink and shiny as the lining in Momma's suitcase. He reached over and patted my head, like I was his favorite puppy, and handed me the Bible.

"Thank you, sir," I said. As I took it in my hands, I swore right then to God on my momma's Bible that I wasn't going be any trouble to anybody, *ever*. I looked my father square-in-the-eyes and said, "I'll be a good girl, Daddy, I promise. I won't give Aunt Leela or Doc no trouble."

Daddy reached over and pulled me into a hug.

The next morning before heading off for the Holston Ferry, Daddy give me permission to run down to Eudie's. She was still sleeping, but her momma asked me to come in and told me to go on back to her room. The house smelled of coffee. I could hear it plurping on the stove.

I knocked on Eudie's door, then pushed it open.

"Morning, Maizee!" Eudie said, sitting up in bed. Her golden hair was pulled back in a fuzzy braid. "What are you doing here so early?"

"I've come to say good-bye. Here," I said, handing her a letter I wrote late last night. Eudie took the letter and jumped out of bed.

"No!" she said, grabbing me into a tight hug. "You cain't go, Maizee! You cain't. Come live with me! Momma will let you. I know she will."

"No. Your momma's got her hands full. Daddy would never allow it nohow," I said, squeezing Eudie tight. Then I stepped back. "I really gotta go." I turned away and ran out of Eudie's house and all three blocks home, but I did not cry. Not once, not then and not even later when Daddy stood lonely as a ghost, watching as the ferry pushed off from the bank of the Holston River, headed for Christian Bend.

Crying upset folks, and I'd promised on Momma's Bible to never be a bother to anyone, and I was good at keeping my promises. I could be stubborn that way.

4

Leela-Ma

I'd heard tell that by the time Maizee got home from school and found her stricken momma, the chickens had pecked over Nan so long there weren't nothing left of her blue eyes but bloodied holes.

I couldn't bear to think about the terror young Maizee witnessed that day. Mercy sakes. It made me sick at my stomach jes imagining it. I don't know how that child was able to close her eyes to the world again for fear of what might come and pluck at them in the dark, but as far as I knew, Maizee never suffered from haunted dreams. From the very first night she showed up at Christian Bend, she didn't cry out at night for want of anything, not father or mother, not hugs or water, nor God or his ministering angels.

Nan was laid to rest on the east side of the town cemetery. It wasn't a particularly good spot to spend eternity, overlooking the backside of Donnie's Market, but nobody was thinking about that then. Most folks was too shook up, wondering what would become of young Maizee.

As far as anyone in Christian Bend ever knew, Maizee didn't shed one tear for her dead momma, although everybody around these parts knew how much Nan had fussed over her only child. Until Maizee come along, it seemed as if our family line was cursed to end. Maizee was the only offspring between us four sisters, and her not borne till Nan was forty-two, and already in frail health.

Doc and I never told the young girl she needed to be strong, but whenever trials and tribulations came her way, Maizee sucked up all the sorrow and held onto it. Doc said it was as if there was this deep, dry well that Maizee was trying to fill. All her tears went inside her, down to the darkest part of her being. It's a terrible thing to see a child cry for a dead parent, but it's even more pitiful when the pain is so sharp that all a child can do is gasp for air. Maizee had been gasping for a long, long time. I was careful about prying the details from her of that last day with her momma. It was selfishness on my behalf, but I wasn't sure I wanted to know the truth of what Maizee seen when she walked out the back door, calling out for Nan, eager, I suspect, to tell her about the school day. It unnerved me that Maizee didn't cry at Nan's funeral, but Doc said all her tears were spent trying to quench that scorched soul of hers.

Sam pulled Doc aside right after the funeral and asked him if we'd be willing to take Maizee in, said he wasn't fit to care for no girl child. Sam knew we had room for his girl.

Our place sits right on the corner of Christian Bend, where the two roads cross over. It's kind of a low-lying spot, near a narrow, fenced-off pasture that runs down the property line alongside River Road.

The barn needs replacing, but Doc's never got around to it. There's a gaping hole on the west end of the roof, so when bad storms come up, the sod turns to mud inside the barn as well as outside. Doc said it didn't really matter since the ground was boggy anyways, the result of being the corner drain for all the runoff that trickles down the mountain slope and pours in from the gullies.

Doc's granddaddy built the original house. It sat high enough off the ground that snakes couldn't git in, and if need be, a grown man could bend over and crawl up under the house. When his granddaddy built it there weren't but two rooms: the kitchen and the sitting, sleeping room. But it was on a good piece of land, five acres, though three of them acres are in slope off to the east of the house. The slope's good for firewood, an evening hike, and the creatures who make their homes among the brush and rotting hickories, but not much else.

Doc's daddy built the barn down the drive. It'd have made more sense to build it out back to keep the hog smell from flowing into the house.

Doc's momma planted apple trees along the flats and harvested the garden his grandmomma first planted. We moved in with Doc's daddy after his momma died, when Doc was twenty-five and me eighteen. Mrs. Lawson died of rot gut, brought on from eating undercooked pork or venison badly cooked. Nobody was real sure.

Two years passed before Doc's daddy started courting Louise from up at Bulls Gap. It was a scandalous thing and all anybody talked about at Christian Bend, him being fifty-seven and her only nineteen. Weary of all the gossip, he up and moved off to Bulls Gap, married Louise, and give Doc the farm.

Doc tore down the old house and built us a fine home with four bedrooms. We'd hoped to fill the place up with children, but even though I was young, my womb was as hollow as a tree fallen by decay.

I don't know if Sam knew that Nan and I had spoken of the matter years before, when Maizee wasn't nothing more than a blanket heap herself. The pregnancy had been hard on Nan, her being so up there in years and all. Her feet swoll up so badly that she had to wrap and rewrap 'em all day long to keep the water pressed out. And if that weren't enough to contend with, her blood pressure was soaring. Doc Slater, the in-town doctor, confined her to bed that last month, but Nan never was one to take orders from nobody. She didn't slow down one bit, got up every morning and made hot biscuits and milk gravy. I didn't git to town but a couple of times that year, so it was real noticeable to me that Nan's arms and legs, usually tanned and muscular, were thin as willow branches.

"Nan, are you eating good?" I asked.

"I try but I ain't got much appetite," Nan replied.

"Looks to me like that baby is swiping every morsel. You'd better try harder or else your body ain't gonna have what it needs to nourish that young'un when the time comes."

That time came quicker than expected. Maizee was born a week later, three weeks early. But she was a healthy six pounds and not colicky at all. Nan never did regain the weight or the strength she'd lost carrying Maizee. Her feet continued to swell from time to time, and her blood pressure never did return to a level that suited Doc Slater. Nan had premonitions that she wouldn't live to see Maizee all growed up.

"I want you to promise me that you'll take care of my baby if I die," she said. I'd come to town to see my niece, who by then was already a couple of weeks old.

"Hush, Nan. Don't speak of such things," I answered. We were outside, picking sugar peas from the garden. I worried that one of the crows nearby could overhear Nan and was ready to carry that seed of fear and plant it on Satan's doorstep. Looking over my shoulder, I shivered.

"Promise me first, Leela. Promise me that you'll tend to my daughter."

"I promise."

We never spoke of it again, and I never would have broached the matter with Sam. I had prayed so long and so hard for a child of my own that I feared I might have had a hand in Nan's death. Maybe God had heard my tiresome supplications and answered them by offering me my sister's child. There could be no denying that despite my grief and guilt over Nan, I felt blessed beyond all measure to have Maizee as my own.

5

Maizee

The ferry ride took thirty minutes. I kept track on the watch Momma give me for my tenth birthday. Before me and Daddy left the house that morning, I took out the library book I'd packed the night before. I was feeling guilty. Was it stealing to keep the book? If I didn't keep it, I might never git the chance to read it. What if they didn't have a library at the school in Christian Bend? What if they didn't have a school? Maybe Aunt Leela was planning on teaching me herself. I couldn't leave the book with Daddy. He'd never return it. I decided to borry it till I came back to town again. Borrying wasn't the same as stealing.

Mr. Drennan, that's the ferry master, was what some people called rawboned. White whiskers poked out of his face like bristles on a new hairbrush. His teeth were yellow as buttercups. When he shouted out "All clear" and shoved away from the muddy bank, I refused to look at my daddy. It tore me up too badly, so I sat on Momma's suitcase and opened up my library book and started reading the part about Hitty sailing out of the Boston Harbor on a ship named the *Diana-Kate*. If the Holston Ferry had a fancy name like the *Diana-Kate*, I didn't know it. Far as I knew it was called the Holston Ferry.

A teeny frog, round as a nickel, plopped down beside my foot, liked to scared me to death, I'll tell you that. I was caught up pretending I was like Hitty, setting sail on some big adventure acrost the ocean, excepting the Holston smelled of slime and fish guts, not salt, sand, and wind.

We was about halfway acrost the river when I heard somebody shouting my name from far off: "MAIZEE! MAIZEE!"

I looked acrost at the bank where I'd last seen Daddy, but if he was there, I couldn't make him out.

"MAIZEE! MAIZEE!"

The calling seemed closer now, and not at all like it was coming from the banks, but from someplace else, and there was something else troubling. It was a girl's voice calling out my name. I tuned my ear to listen better, but it snapped to a stop so fast by the time we got to the other side of the river that I doubted I'd heard it at all.

Doc and Aunt Leela were waiting for me, though it was mid-morning, and Doc surely had sick people needing tending to. I ain't going to lie about it. Being sent off to Christian Bend by my own daddy was about the sorriest lowdown feeling in the whole wide world. Half the time I didn't know whether I ought to feel sorry for myself or whether I should hate Daddy for being such a weasel. He hadn't made the least little effort to care for me.

When Mr. Drennan nudged the ferry up to the dock, and I seen Aunt Leela clutching a bunch of ribbon-tied black-eyed Susans, and her and Doc waiting for me like I was the Queen of Sheba come for a royal visit, a warmness eased the loneliness and hate troubling me. It felt good to be expected, the way Momma did me when I come in from school. I didn't forgive Daddy right then for sending me off, but there was a part of me that knew he'd done a good thing.

Mr. Drennan held out a bony hand for me to grab hold of, a sign that his momma reared him up to be a gentleman. I took hold of his hand with my right one and grasped my book in the other. Mr. Drennan waited till I was safely on the dock before he handed my suitcase to my uncle.

"Thank you, sir," Doc said. "Appreciate all your help."

"You're welcome," Mr. Drennan said. "Always a pleasure to ferry such a pretty young lady acrost."

Lady? Nobody had ever called me a lady before. Lady Maizee. Maizee-Lady. It had a nice sound. I give Mr. Drennan one of my last-day-of-school smiles.

Aunt Leela, who was waiting right beside Doc, didn't look much like Momma. She had brown hair like Momma's, but a wide grey streak ran sidelong her face. Aunt Leela's face was long and hollowed out, but not in any scary way. I could tell from her freckles she was somebody who spent a lot of time outside. When I had both feet planted on the dock, Aunt Leela leaned over and hugged me.

"Welcome to Christian Bend, honey."

I liked her right away 'cause she smelled of fresh camellias, jes like Momma.

I hope I don't sound like a braggart when I say, for the most part, I am not moody. Even after all that mess with the chickens and Momma and all, I refused to dwell on it. But a person cain't help it when disturbing pictures come flooding back in their minds, the way the one of Momma all pecked over kept doing to me.

The Proverbs warn that we can be like dogs returning to our own vomit. There I'd be on a hot summer's afternoon, bent over a pot, paring knife in hand, skinning taters for supper, or spread acrost a blanket under a shade tree looking through a picture catalogue, and something would trigger a memory, and next thing I knew I'd see them awful chickens and Momma's empty eye sockets.

The first time it happened, about a month after I got to Christian Bend, I about jumped out of my skin. My heart started racing, and my knees got trembly. I felt sick to my stomach. Sweat pellets traced down the back of my neck.

Aunt Leela seen something was the matter. I was standing in the kitchen, trying to warsh up my dishes from dinner, but I had the shakes so bad I had to grip the sink. Aunt Leela come over and put a hand on my cheek.

"You okay, sweetie? You look awful peaked."

I nodded my head up and down, fearing what might happen if I tried to speak.

"You're clammy."

"Uh-huh," I said. Everything around me was circling the way it does after a girl's spent too much time on the merry-go-round. "I believe I need some air." Pushing open the screen door, I walked out to the backyard and found a wide-open spot. I lay on the grass, shut my eyes, and listened to the drumming of my heart. I stayed there so long I fell asleep.

When I woke up, Aunt Leela had supper on the table. She asked me if I was feeling well enough to eat.

"Yes, ma'am," I said.

Doc was uptown, hanging out at Cal Sloane's place, Aunt Leela said. She didn't ask me any more about the spell that come over me. Aunt Leela wasn't one to pry.

She'd fried the taters, along with some okra, and boiled up a mess of greens.

"Did your Momma ever tell you about the time she and Nickel Huffmaster nearly got locked up?"

"Locked up?" I was thinking of Daddy and the jail.

"In the church, overnight," Aunt Leela said, clearing the matter some.

"No, ma'am," I said, spooning a second helping of okra on my plate.

"W. B. Lyons used to be the head deacon at the Baptist church uptown, before your momma and Nickel found him in the baptismal licking grape juice off of Shari Dickerson's bare feet," Aunt Leela said, not blinking an eye. "Pass me the salt, please."

Handing over the shaker that looked like a raccoon, I was disbelieving what I was hearing.

"Come again?" I said, which was my way of asking Aunt Leela to explain her story. Momma would never have talked to me like I was a grown-up, the way Aunt Leela done, but I liked that my aunt spoke her mind in front of me. It made me feel older, smarter. I didn't have any idey why some man would want to lick any woman's nasty feet, but I could see why the other folks at church might not like someone using the Lord's baptismal as their personal playground.

"Your momma and Nickel found that bald-headed deacon down on all fours, fives if you include his belly, licking Shari's red toenails."

"You don't mean it!"

"Mercy sakes! I mean every word of it. Your momma and Nickel was supposed to meet Shari at four o'clock on a Friday to practice a duet for Revival Sunday, but they got dismissed from high school early on account of a thunderstorm knocking out all the power, so instead of going home first, they run the two blocks to the church in the rain.

"Your momma headed to the baptismal closet, with Nickel right on her heels, searching for towels to dry off. When they heard Shari's squealing, they hid behind the curtains and watched from the shadows as W. B. gave her a foot-warshing, so to speak."

"Ew!" I liked to have spit out the forkful of okra I was eating, but that didn't slow Aunt Leela down none, with her story or her eating. She jes kept right on.

"It was Pastor's day off, so nobody ever expected him to step up to the choir loft the way he done that very moment, looking for a hymnbook or something. If W. B. hadn't been half-deaf, and Shari squealing the way she was, they might have heard Pastor singing one of his favorite tunes."

Stopping for a minute to take a swallow of her iced tea, Aunt Leela then launched right into singing the same tune as if she was in that loft herself: *"Love lifted me! Love lifted me! When nothing else could help, Love lifted me.*

"As soon as they seen Pastor, your momma and Nickel shied away from the curtain and backed themselves straight into the storage closet and shut the door, which was locked. But they didn't know'd that until it was too late.

"It didn't take them long to figure out that the door was locked tight, and if they didn't want to spend the night in there they was going to need some help gitting out of that closet. But they bided their time till all the squallering passed. Pastor was giving W. B. a tongue-lashing fit for a Pharisee, while Miss Shari shoved her sticky feet back into her black pumps. Your momma waited till all the crying and carrying on settled down before pounding on the closet door and yelping for someone to let her and Nickel out."

Aunt Leela got to laughing so hard she got the hiccups, and then that got me so tickled that the food I was eating went straight up my nose and out my nostrils, which got Aunt Leela to laughing, hiccupping, and crying all at the same time.

By the time Doc come through the front door, pee was running in streams down my legs.

Early the next morning, before Rock Rooster climbed on the fence post and began his crowing, I heard that voice again.

"Maizee! Maizee!"

I opened my eyes to the purply darkness. For a minute I thought I was back in my old room, with Momma and Daddy sleeping acrost the hall, till the lace curtains blew against the foot of the bed rails, carrying in the dusky cool common to the mountains and the sweet stench of slop common to hogs. Then I remembered where I was and why, and what had woken me.

It was that girl's voice again. The one I heard when I first come over on the ferry. I turned over on my back, so I could put the pillow flat against my head and listen with both ears.

"Maizee! Maizee!"

I sat up. Shivers pricked my arms. The curtains sucked up against the window screen, taking my breath with it. Hitty was sitting up, too, propped upside a pillow in a nearby chair. The pillow was one Aunt Leela embroidered special. The shiny gold thread spelled out *"Big as God's morning sky."* It was part of a saying Aunt Leela taught me the first week I come to live at Christian Bend. I liked it so much I committed it to memory right away and recited it every night to Hitty, the way Aunt Leela done me.

"MAIZEE! MAIZEE!"

There was the voice again. There was no denying it this time. It sounded like a girl in some kind of awful trouble from afar, like maybe she was stuck in the bottom of the well and needed somebody to help pull her out.

I studied whether I ought to wake up Aunt Leela. What if some girl really had fallen into the well?

"What?" I whispered big as I dared. And again, "What?"

Nothing. Not one word. The only sounds was the soft hush of hickory leaves clapping and fingernail branches scratching acrost the tin roof.

Turning to Hitty, I said, "I'd rather have a ghost talk at me than to have to listen to that awful sound."

She giggled. Or so it seemed there in the dark by my lonesome.

Yanking the covers, I buried myself up underneath the pillow. Later, when I heard Rock Rooster crowing in the morning's light, I fell back to sleep.

Aunt Leela, thinking I was still suffering from whatever ailed me the day before, let me sleep till the sun was midway between daybreak and dinnertime. The first thing I done after I got dressed was run outside to the well. Taking care not to lean too far, I bent over the edge and yelled down, "Hello, Girlie! Are you there?"

It smelled of sobby wood and standing rain. I seen a daub of silver flash as I yanked on the bucket's rope and called out again. "Girlie! Girlie!"

All I seen was water skim catching sunlight. I blinked hard, then heard Aunt Leela calling me from the side yard where she was whacking weeds with a hooked blade. "Mercy sakes, Maizee! Git back away from the edge of that! You're gonna fall in! There's water in the pail on the porch. If you're thirsty git you a cup."

I didn't bother explaining to Aunt Leela that it wasn't water I was after, but I got me a drink anyway and studied the matter some. I got so stewed at Hitty for tricking me the way she done, I refused to play with her for a long, long time.

6

Burdy Luttrell leaned against the handle of her push mower and wiped her brow with a faded snot rag. Burdy, who was wearing one of Tibbis's old work shirts and a pair of dungarees, pulled her snuff can out of a pocket and put a pinch of the brown powder under her tongue. Wheedin's momma didn't go nowhere without her baccy, not even to mow the lawn.

Burdy's a squatty woman, no taller than the shortest sixth-grade boy. She has square-boned cheeks, a high forehead, and dark eyebrows arched high, like she's delighted with everything she sees. Her skin stays the color of tanned leather even in the dead of winter.

Leela-Ma always said God must've used cherry wood to carve out Burdy. He made her sturdy, built her to age well, to last through life's worst storm. Burdy has never cut her hair in all her born years. It falls in thick folds all the way to her hips. She has wisps of gray right around her face, but otherwise it's the rich brown of pecans, a wild contrast to those opal eyes of hers.

And despite all that amber juice from the baccy, Burdy's got good teeth. When she comes into church, or any other place, folks stop what they're doing jes to study on her. Doc says she has a presence that draws people to her. She ain't angelic-looking, but she is otherworldly.

"Wheedin! What's your dawg raising such a ruckus for?" Burdy hollered.

"I dunno."

"Well, git up off your behiney and go see to her. You was the one so all-fired bent on 'Got to have a dawg, got to have a dawg.'" Burdy shoved the mower clear of the mailbox post.

Rolling her oddball eyes at me, Wheedin stuck out her tongue at her momma, soon as Burdy turned away.

"I sware, you're the most gosh-awful girl!" I said. "I won't be surprised if one of these days God strikes you purple."

"Purple-schmurple," Wheedin taunted. "What'd God give me a tongue for if he didn't expect me to use it? C'mon, we better go see about Useless before Maw has a hissy fit."

Wheedin took her paintbrush and grabbed the one out of my hand and stuck 'em both in a cup of water. Burdy give Wheedin a box of watercolors for her twelfth birthday, along with the dawg. She'd asked me at school on Friday if I wanted to come over to her house on Saturday and paint with her. We spread our stuff out on the porch and were trying to paint pictures of the yellow and pink clumps of flowers growing 'longside the porch. I'd managed to git the clump part down since all the lines ran together.

The dawg's yelping grew so loud it hurt my ears.

"How come you to name your dawg Useless?" I asked, following after Wheedin.

"To spite Maw," she said. "When I told her I wanted a dawg for my birthday, she said dawgs are like old men—always chasing tail and scratching their hineys—useless. When I seen the puppy she brung me chase its tail, I figured might as well call 'im like it is."

Burdy got Useless from over at Mr. Doty's place. He lived up the road a piece and had nearly as many hounds as he did young'uns, and there was six of them with not much more than a year between each one.

Useless was standing on his hind legs, scratching the bark off a tree with his front paws. His hair was the color of tobacco cured. His long, flat ears were turned inside out. He was clearly bothered by something in that tree. Looking up, Wheedin and I seen a groundhog clinging to a crook in the branches. The hog was nearly as big as Useless.

"Wait here," Wheedin said and took off running.

"Where you going?" I hollered after her.

Wheedin ran through the back door and into her house. She came back lickety-split, carrying a shotgun.

"What are you doin'?" I asked, but Wheedin didn't take time to answer me. She come up beside me, raised the gun, took aim, and shot the hog out of that tree without a word of warning. Soon as it fell to the ground, Useless ran over and locked jaws on it, like he'd done gone and kilt the thing with his bare teeth.

Burdy came around the house quiet as an Indian scout. If that'd been me shooting off a gun, Aunt Leela would've hollered loud enough to raise the dead. Burdy studied the hog clinched up in Useless's mouth, then looked over at Wheedin gripping her gun and said, "Your daddy would be so proud of you. Go 'head and skin it and we'll have some good eats for supper. And Wheedin, git something and clean them blood splatters off the side of the house before they dry."

"Yes, ma'am," Wheedin answered.

I met Wheedin during Vacation Bible School week that first summer I come to live at Christian Bend. Aunt Leela was teaching, so I had to go. Everybody was sorted by their ages in the pews, little ones down front and bigger kids in the fourth pew back. Mrs. Lucy Shropshire led us all in a couple of songs, and then Preacher Blount went over some rules: no running in the hallways, bring pennies for our missionary friends, learn our memory verse, and be sure to invite all our lost friends. There would be a prize at the end of the week for the kid who brung the most friends.

Aunt Leela had to sit with the four- and five-year-old class, so I sat as close to the aisle as I could git in the fourth pew with the other big kids. The only time I looked up was when Lucy

Shropshire's eldest daughter, Charma, came over to welcome me and to tell me she'd be teaching our class that week.

Charma had orange hair and freckles on her cheeks that run together. One patch of freckles on her left arm that growed together resembled a turkey. Her eyes were the brown-green of tree moss. She had wide, straight white teeth, and when she smiled her right cheek dimpled. I thought she was about the prettiest girl I'd ever seen. I knew from Aunt Leela that Charma was about to be married to Sheriff Duncan's boy, Matt.

"So glad to have you with us this morning," she said as she reached out and patted my knee.

"Thank you," I whispered.

"Do you know where to go after this?"

"No, ma'am."

"We meet in the basement, at the back room on the right. Jes follow me, I'll show you."

"Yes, ma'am."

Preacher Blount called up a couple of kids who'd brung friends on that first day and give them each a pencil. Then, Mrs. Morris led us in a foot-stomping version of "Deep and Wide" before she turned us out for our classes.

I followed right behind Charma, down the stairs to the church basement, like she told me to do. The cooler air smelt of chalk dust. A couple of boys pushed right by me and into Charma. Grabbing one dark-haired fellow by the back of his overalls, she said, "No running, remember?"

"Yes ma'am," he said.

We were the first ones in the class.

"Take a seat anywhere," Charma said. "I've got to run back upstairs for a minute. I went off and left my Bible." She put down the bags of pinto beans, boxes of macaroni noodles, and jars of glue she was carrying onto the table and looked at me.

"Would you mind writing this memory verse on the chalkboard for me?"

"Yes, ma'am," I said. Charma handed me a piece of paper with the verse of the day, then turned to leave.

I picked up the chalk and wrote in my bestest script James 4:7: "Resist the devil and he will flee from you."

"That's real nice handwriting," said a girl standing in the door. She about scared me to death, I promise I jumped right into the chair nearest the front of the room. "I'm sorry," the girl said. "I didn't mean to frighten you."

She walked right over and pulled out a chair acrost the table from me. "My name's Wheedin Luttrell. What's yours?" Her hair, so long she could sit on it, was dark as the tail feathers on a mockingbird, but her eyes were an odd green-blue. Her skin was so dark that if I'd met her anywhere else but the white people's church, I'd have thought her to be a colored.

"Maizee Daggett," I answered.

"Who's your people?"

"Say what?"

More kids were piling into the classroom now, including those two boys Charma caught running in the stairwell. I didn't want everybody to know my business so I opened my Bible and made like I was searching for a memory verse.

"Who's your people? Your maw and pa?"

"Doc and Leela Lawson are my uncle and aunt," I whispered. I could feel my face redden.

"So you're the girl whose maw died?"

My lands! I couldn't believe how blunt that Wheedin girl was acting. It was a pity shame her momma never taught her no manners. I nodded my head, yes.

"Do you believe that?" Wheedin asked, pointing toward the chalkboard.

"Do what?"

"Do you believe that if you resist Satan he'll flee from you?"

I didn't rightly know anymore what was true and what wasn't, but I give Wheedin the answer I had been taught. "Momma always said if God's word said it, it must be so."

"Well, you're dumb as a stump," Wheedin said.

All the other kids laughed. I turned red as a 'mater.

"Maybe so," I answered, "but least I ain't got the manners of a mule same as you." I feared what Aunt Leela would say if she could hear me talking so ugly, but I didn't worry about what Wheedin thought—she was laughing.

Most folks would figure girls who got off to such a prickly start wouldn't git far, but me and Wheedin became fast friends. She asked me that very afternoon to go pearling with her at the Holston on Saturday.

"I'll have to check with Aunt Leela first," I said. I wasn't too sure what a person did when they went pearling, but I figured doing anything with Wheedin was sure to be lively. Aunt Leela said she didn't mind if I went, long as I got my chores done first.

She was different from Momma that way. Around Aunt Leela's house, the work was handed out evenly. I was expected to help out the same as if I were any other person. Before I came to Christian Bend I didn't know how to cook a lick. Now I could fix a whole meal if I had to. Cornbread was the first thing Aunt Leela taught me to make. On Wednesday last, I made a pound cake that didn't even fall.

I rose early Saturday and put on a t-shirt and pair of old coveralls Aunt Leela had dug up and cut off below the knee for summer wear. I pulled my curly hair back into a red hanky and told Hitty she was going to have to spend the whole day sitting in the chair without me to tend to her 'cause I had a new friend. She didn't say nothing. Jes put on that sulky face of hers and give me the silent treatment.

I was at the door and waiting when Wheedin come walking up the road to the house shortly before 8 a.m.

"Listen," Aunt Leela warned, when she eyed Wheedin, "that girl can git herself into some mischief. You best behave yourself, you hear me?"

"Yes, ma'am."

"I don't want to hear about you all gitting into any foolishness."

"No, ma'am."

"And you be careful at the river. That water can be powerful strong even when it might not look it."

"Yes, ma'am." I opened the door and greeted Wheedin, "I'm ready to go."

"Well c'mon then," Wheedin said. "G'morning Mrs. Lawson."

"Morning, Wheedin. How's your momma today?"

"She's good, ma'am. She was up in the garden, chasing away the critters when I lit out."

"Her hand must be healing up okay, then?"

Burdy had sliced off the tip of her little finger earlier that week while fooling around with an old saw belonging to her dead husband. I had no idey what she was doing with the saw. Wheedin said sometimes her momma likes to fool around in her daddy's old shop. Wheedin said her momma keeps the shop same as it was when her daddy was alive so that when his spirit returns he can still find everything. Aunt Leela says Wheedin's momma has been missing a button or two ever since she found Tibbis dead in the meadow. I don't rightly know what missing buttons has to do with anything, but the way Aunt Leela says it I can tell she don't mean it to be taken as praise.

"Yes, ma'am. She's all healed up. You know how Maw is about doctoring. She put some sort of salve on it and wrapped it up real good and two days later you couldn't even tell she'd cut herself, if it weren't that the one finger is stubbier than the others. Still got the nail though."

"Well, I'm glad to hear it," Aunt Leela said. "You tell her I've been praying for her."

"I will, ma'am."

"Now I've done warned Maizee, but you girls be careful down there on the river. Some of them sink holes are more dangerous than they look." Aunt Leela give me a sideways hug. "Y'all be back by dinner."

"Yes, ma'am!" we said together and took off running down the drive.

It was one of them clear summer days that makes the whole wide world seem cleaner, shinier. Even some of the rocks in the ditch alongside the road sparkled. Tangles of wild honeysuckle climbed the ditch to the edge of the woods. The air smelt of warm sap and cedar.

Wheedin was carrying a bucket with two pint-sized jars in it. She'd wrapped a rag between 'em to keep 'em from breaking.

"You ever been pearling before?" she asked.

"No." I couldn't muster up the gumption to tell her I hadn't the least idey what pearling was.

"Well, don't worry, I've been plenty. I got ten pearls already. Maw says she's going to bead them into a necklace for me when I git enough of 'em."

"You mean real pearls?"

"A'course they're real," Wheedin said. She looked at me in the Doubting Thomas way.

I hated that Wheedin had turned over my secret so quickly. I was hoping to fool her into thinking I was every bit as smart as her.

Laughing and shaking her head in that disbelieving way, Wheedin said, "Maw said town kids don't know the old ways."

"What old ways?" I asked, put out over that remark. It bugged the tar out of me that Wheedin might consider me dumb.

Wheedin laughed some more. "Don't worry about it," she said. "I'll teach you everything I know. By summer's end nobody'll ever be able to tell you weren't raised right here at Christian Bend."

I got my first lesson in mountain ways on the banks of the Holston that day as Wheedin taught me to stay away from the dark drop-offs in the river, where the currents run fast, and where snakes might hide. She showed me silvery popeye shiners, and how to use the jar as a looking glass to find mussels 'neath the riverbed. Wheedin taught me the names of different mussels—monkeyface, purple bean, rabbitsfoot, and comb-shells—and how their names come from the shape and color of the shells. The monkeyface was brown with streaks and bumps that looked like the ears and eyes of a monkey. The purple bean's shell was smooth and dark, purple on the inside.

Wheedin said when the Spanish came to Tennessee, the Indians give the Spanish a string of pearls that was three times as long as Doc was tall. She'd read that somewhere. She'd also read somewhere that mussels keep the river clear by breathing in the dirt and sand and cleaning it before spitting it out again. Mussels coat the grains of sand with some kind of shiny spit. The spit thickens and hardens and that's what makes the sand into a pearl. It takes years for one itsy pearl to take shape, and Wheedin had nearly a dozen of 'em.

She said her momma's people fry up the slimey innards of the mussels like okra and eat 'em.

"Ew, yuck!" I said. "I don't think I'd like 'em, even fried."

"Nah, they're good. I've eat 'em myself."

By noon we had twenty-five mussels in our pail. Some as big as my palm. We teamed up and carried the bucket back to Aunt Leela's.

"Mercy sakes! You two are a sight!" Aunt Leela said when we come around the bend with our haul. She probably smelt us before she seen us. Mud caked our feet and arms. We were giggling and carrying on. Aunt Leela was cleaning cobwebs off the windows with a broom. "Don't go in the house with them stinky clothes on. Strip 'em off by the back door and I'll git you both a clean change."

Aunt Leela stopped to shake the webs off the broom.

"We ain't ready to clean up yet, ma'am," I said. "We're going to check these shells for pearls." Wheedin and I sat the pail down in the tall grass near a fence post, away from the house.

"Alrighty, then," Aunt Leela said, heading on into the house. "I'll git you some clean clothes and you all change when you're ready."

Wheedin and I sat there in the grass for the next hour, cracking open the mussels, admiring the insides of their houses and searching for pearls. We each found one. Mine was big as my thumbnail. It was a whitish-pink, round on the bottom and almost pointy at the top.

"It looks like a big tear," I said.

"Maw's people believed pearls are Creator's tears," Wheedin said.

"What do they say he's crying over?"

"Us," Wheedin said, her dark eyebrows raised, her blue-green eyes aflame. "Creator cries for us and for what we've done to ourselves."

7

Zebulon

From the first day I seen Maizee, sitting between Doc and Leela-Ma in the second pew at the Freewill Baptist Church, she stirred something in me I'd never known before.

She wasn't but ten or eleven; I cain't recall exactly. I'd jes finished up eighth grade. I'd overheard Shug Mosely in the church foyer tell his wife that Doc Lawson and Leela-Ma had taken in her niece after the girl's momma up and died. Newcomers on the mountain was always big news. I didn't think anything of it at the time, but that was before I seen her.

Maizee was wearing a pink dress. It had a white collar with flowers sewn in the corners. Her hair, black as a moonless midnight, rippled like the Holston. Even when Maizee was sitting still as a board, her hair seemed to keep moving. She'd clipped it up on the sides, directly above her ears, with two bobby pins to hold back its thickness.

Her skin was white as a morning cloud. There wasn't one freckle, one mole, one blemish of any sort marring it. And when she smiled, which she did the moment she seen me staring at her all gap-mouthed, my stomach flopped every whichaway like a trout on a string. I was smitten with Maizee from then on.

She didn't know it, of course. A boy cain't be going off after a girl like a lop-eared dog. That's the surest way to git kicked aside. I didn't even speak to her till she turned thirteen, and even then it was only a "Hello" in passing. My daddy always said that romance is like whittling. If you try to hurry it along, you end up with something you never intended. I wanted Maizee in the worst way, so the wait never seemed too burdensome.

8

Maizee

There's a commandment about loving the Lord God with all your heart, mind, body, and soul. I never understood such a love as that until the day Zeb kissed me under the old chestnut on Horseshoe Ridge. I decided right then if it was wrong, God was jes gonna have to forgive me for it without expecting any repentance on my behalf. I wasn't the least bit sorry about kissing Zeb. I'd been aching after it for a long time.

Zeb said he fell in love with me the first day he seen me sitting in church. He claimed I was wearing a pink dress with roses on the collar. I remember the dress but I don't remember meeting him. I think Doc and Leela-Ma introduced me to practically everybody who lived in Christian Bend, so I'm sure we must've least seen each other.

I do remember the first time Zeb Hurd spoke to me. I was thirteen, so he had to be fifteen or sixteen. Ida Mosely had half-a-dozen rows of beans all come in at once, due to all the hot weather we'd been having. Mrs. Ida said her back wouldn't tolerate the picking and canning both, and asked me and Wheedin if we'd be sweet enough to come help her pick her beans. If us picked 'em, she'd put on bells and dance at our weddings.

Me and Wheedin weren't the least bit interested in seeing Mrs. Ida dance at any weddings. Wheedin said it was a pitiful shame enough the way Mrs. Ida's hips jiggled when she walked.

"Shoot, if she put a bell on, people might figure her for a cow for sure," Wheedin said.

Wheedin had an awful mean streak to her mouth. Whenever I acted shocked over something she said, Wheedin would narrow her eyes at me and say, "You was thinking the same thing as me. Only difference between us is I say what I think."

She was right. I usually was, but a person ought not go around saying every blasted thing that comes to their mind. Leela-Ma said Wheedin had more mouth than a monkey's got tail. Wheedin was never one to shy away from helping folks though. We was up at Mrs. Ida's before eight o'clock on Saturday, picking them beans for her. By noon, we had finished two rows each.

"It must be ninety degrees in the shade," Wheedin said, sweat dripping from up underneath her arms and her neck.

"You look jes like a field hand," I said, dropping another apron load of beans into the bucket.

"Well, Missy, you ain't gonna win no beauty contests yo'self," Wheedin said. "You got dirt an inch thick in yo' neck."

Standing over the bucket of beans, I wiped my neck with the back of my hand. All I managed to do was streak soil on my neck and hand. "Here, try this," came a voice from behind me. I about peed my britches before turning to see what fool fellow had done snuck up on me like that.

There was Zebulon Hurd, holding out a hanky and looking ever so bashful. "Didn't mean to sneak up on you," he said.

I know it sounds quare to those who never had it happen, but I believed from that minute on me and Zeb would marry. I was glad God had made him such a handsome fellow. Zeb wasn't tall, but he stood head and shoulders over me. He had wide shoulders, lean waist and legs, and thick, tanned arms. His eyes were the color of brown sugar, melted. I'd never seen eyes like his. They looked like drops of caramel. That's what I told Wheedin later, but wished I hadn't after the way she teased me about it forever and a day. But what attracted me more'n Zeb's eyes was the sprinkle of freckles acrost his nose and his slow smile.

"That's aw'right," I said, taking his hanky and wiping my neck and the backs of my hands. "I scare easy."

Me and Wheedin hadn't seen hide nor hair of Mrs. Ida since she give us a couple of buckets from the barn and sent us out to pick beans. Zeb explained that Shug had hired him to do some odd chores around the place and that Mrs. Ida had been the one to send him up to the garden to fetch the full pails of beans so's she could git started on the canning. Wheedin said Mrs. Ida was more'n likely looking for some way to spend the afternoon sitting in the shade, and breaking beans would be the ticket for it.

Zeb give me and Wheedin a smile, picked up the full pails, and said he'd be right back after he emptied them.

"Mm-hm," Wheedin said, shaking her head and clicking her tongue.

"What?" I asked.

"Nothin'. I didn't say nothin'."

"Well, what's all that mm-hmming about?"

"You got it bad."

"Got what?" I asked, bending over to pick beans from the bottom up. I figured I'd have an apron full by the time Zeb got back.

"I seen the way he was looking at you," Wheedin replied. "You seen it too."

I had, but I wasn't about to confess it to her.

"I sware your head is full of horse poot, Wheedin Luttrell."

"Swaring's a sin," she said, clicking her tongue again.

"Since when did you git so religious?"

"Didn't I tell you? I've been seeing visions and such. I saw one jes a minute ago, right here in this garden."

"Really? And what was this vision of yours?"

"You and Zeb k-i-s-s-i-n-g." Wheedin made some sort of swooning motion as she mocked me.

I picked up a dirt clod and threw it at her feet.

It was true. Whenever I seen Zeb at church, or down on the Holston fishing, or riding in the truck with Shug Mosely, I felt a heat hotter than the sun that beat down on me and Wheedin the day we picked them beans. Only this heat rose up out of my belly, and it didn't matter how much cold water I drank or how many wet rags I pressed to my head, nothing helped ease it.

Not even kissing Kade Mashburn.

I knew my first and last kiss belonged to Zeb. I didn't know how or when it would happen, but I knew it was bound to. Which is how come I got so mad when Kade Mashburn grabbed and kissed me.

Harvest is such a pretty time, what with the leafy maples, burning bushes, and possumhaw turning the hills gold and red. The air cool and sweet as a ripe plum. Doc and I spent all Saturday morning carving pumpkins, while Leela-Ma warshed and baked the seeds.

"Tell me the story of Jack again," I asked, pleading with Doc to tell me the story he told every Halloween.

"Oh, you don't want to hear that old tale again," he said. "You've heard it half-a-dozen times." Doc took out his pocketknife and cut a saucer-sized lid into a pumpkin.

"Please," I begged.

"Now, Maizee, you know I cain't stand it when you beg," Doc said.

"*Please,*" I pestered. Doc wasn't related to Momma except by marriage, but sometimes it seemed to me that him and her were more blood kin than Leela-Ma and Momma. Doc spoilt me, jes like Momma used to.

"Aw, aw'right," he said, giving in the way I knew he would. "Jack was a troublemaker, always gitting himself into some mischief, embarrassing his family and hisself. One night as the Devil was passing under a hemlock, ol' Jack tricked him up in the tree. Then Jack carved a cross into the tree's trunk, trapping that ol' Devil and making him mad as a hornet. Never a good idea," Doc said, smiling and pulling out the pumpkin's stringy guts.

"What happened next?"

"Ol' Jack said he'd make a deal with the Devil—that's never a good idea either. Jack told the Devil he'd let him out of the tree if he would promise to never tempt him again. You see, Jack was figuring all that tempting was to blame for putting him at crossways with his own family. The Devil agreed and Jack let him down. But after Jack died, he couldn't git into heaven on account of all his foolish ways, and that ol' Devil wouldn't let him into hell. The Devil did take some pity on Jack though. He give him one little flame to warm himself by. Jack put it inside a hollowed-out pumpkin to protect it."

"And that's how come we have jack-o'-lanterns," I said, chiming in.

"Well, that's how I always heard tell it," Doc said.

When we finished with the carving, Doc and I sat our pumpkins out on the porch, three on each side of the steps. Leela-Ma got the seeds salted and baked and made a couple of pies to carry over to the harvest party later that evening.

Everybody and his brother wanted to take the hayride, so there was a couple of trucks hauling people up and down the dirt roads. Shug Mosely hauled around the adults who wanted to go, and Zeb and Poke Mosely drove the youth of the church. Wheedin and I stood in the back right corner of the truck, away from everyone else, so we'd be the first to see any ghosts.

Wheedin was the only person I'd dare tell about the time when I heared some girl's voice, and how I suspected it came from the doll Eudie's brother carved me. I knew Wheedin wouldn't think I was crazy, 'cause I didn't tell her about it till after the night she confessed her dead daddy would sometimes come sit on her bed and talk with her. Me and Wheedin believed in ghosts 'cause we'd both been visited by 'em.

We was standing in the corner whispering about those things, and breathing in the sweet scent of hay, when Kade Mashburn cozied up next to us. Wheedin had told me two weeks ago Sunday that she'd heared from Poke that Kade was sweet on me. Kade had pretty red hair and dancing eyes, but I wasn't interested in nobody but Zeb, and I didn't need to tell Wheedin that; she'd known it since that day in Mrs. Ida's garden.

"You girls ain't feared of ghosts, are you?" Kade asked. "'Cause if you are, don't worry. I got tricks to scare away any haints."

"I bet you do," Wheedin said, nudging me in the ribs.

"Care to see one?" Kade leaned in so close we was practically nose to nose. I could feel his breath on my lips.

"No, thank you," I said, turning my face from his. The light of the full moon cast shadows that made Kade look more devilish than was his nature. It sent shivers down my arms.

Somebody started singing "Dem bones, dem bones, dem dry bones" and we all chimed in, laughing and carrying on, and I forgot about Kade Mashburn till we pulled up at Shug's place and started piling out of the truck for the bonfire. Wheedin had gone over to help some of the younger kids off the truck, giving Kade a chance to press in beside me. He was much taller than me and had long arms. He reached out and grabbed me with 'em as I tried to dodge my way past him. Then, without a word, Kade ducked down and kissed me right on the lips!

I was so mad I felt like slapping Kade upside the head, and probably would've except I didn't want to cause a scene. So I spit at Kade's feet, wiped my lips with the back of my hand, and pushed past him.

Zeb, who was standing at the back edge of the truck bed helping folks climb down, seen what I done. "You need some help there, Maizee?" he asked, offering me his hand. I grabbed hold of it and jumped so hard from the truck, I nearly knocked the both of us over. Zeb caught me, held on to me till I got my bearings, and whispered, "I hope when I go to kiss you, you don't spit at me."

I smiled and run off to find Wheedin.

Zeb waited nearly a year before he finally kissed me. We were playing a game of hide-n-seek with the Mosely brothers and Wheedin.

I was hiding at the top of Horseshoe Ridge, behind the giant chestnut, which was big around as some houses, when Zeb come up from behind and tackled me. We tumbled along the ground, till we came to rest with him laying atop me. Zeb was worried my giggling would give him away, so he reached up and "shushed" me with his hand. When I yanked his hand away, he pressed his lips to mine, which was exactly what I'd been aching for.

I made no effort to resist Zeb and would have gladly spent the entire evening kissing him underneath that grandfather chestnut if it hadn't been for Wheedin interrupting us, with some remark about this supposed to be a game of hide-n-seek. I was tempted to tell her she ought to take a flying leap off the ridge and leave us alone, but I didn't want to ruin such a magical moment by acting ugly.

9

Zebulon

Horseshoe Falls was mine and Maizee's special place. I'd first played up there as kids with the Mosely boys, pretending we were Indians fighting over the giant chestnut that sat atop the ridge. At well over 100 feet tall, the tree was a sure-fire route to the lap of the Great Spirit, or so we boasted.

We boys told ourselves that chewing the bark of the chestnut could make us stronger than the town kids, who didn't know anything about trees and their powers. Town kids couldn't tell a chestnut from a redbud. Maizee was standing under the grandfather chestnut the first time I kissed her.

A group of us kids headed up to the falls to cool down one hot August evening following a homecoming. People from as far away as Kingsport and Knoxville returned to the mountain for the event. We spent the day listening to Preacher Blount carry on about the Second Coming of Christ. Then everybody gathered 'round back for a picnic that lasted clean through the afternoon.

When all the grown-ups started decorating the graves in the church cemetery and talking about people long since dead, me and Maizee snuck off with the Mosely brothers and Burdy Luttrell's daughter, Wheedin, who was in the same grade as Maizee. They'd been friends since Maizee arrived on the mountain. Maizee always said it's because Wheedin knew what it felt like to be an outsider, too.

Wheedin had coal-black hair that hung past her hips, and the same dark skin and opal-blue eyes as her momma. The church altar was stained with the salty tears of young boys confessing to impure thoughts of Wheedin, but her charms were lost on me.

After I kissed Maizee under that towering chestnut, it seemed like everwhich spirit had made the tree grow took hold of me. Urges I'd never felt before sprouted up. I felt exposed, as if my skin done peeled away like bark.

We were playing a game of hide-n-seek at the time. I was *It*. Base was the rock at the bottom of the falls. I came acrost Maizee, my first victim, crouching behind the chestnut, and I tackled her. She laughed as we tumbled acrost the soft earth. I put my hand over her mouth to hush her.

"Ssshhh! You'll give me away," I whispered. She reached up and yanked my hand down. So I pressed my lips over hers. An act of self-defense, I later claimed. Instead of pushing me away, Maizee yielded her tongue, warm and soft as a roasted marshmallow. The sweetness of that kiss lingers in my mouth still.

I could've strangled Wheedin when she snuck up on us.

"My Lawd! I thought we was playing hide-n-seek, not hide-n-hump," Wheedin said, leaning back against the tree. I jumped to my feet. Maizee did the same.

"I'm sorry. I didn't mean to interrupt anything," Wheedin said.

"Sure you did," Maizee replied. "Why else aren't you hiding?"

Wheedin protested, "I was hiding, right over there." She pointed to a boulder nearby. "But I sat so long on the ground waiting to git found that my seat was starting to git damp. Now I know what was taking Mr. *It* so long to find me." She flashed Maizee a knowing smile. Maizee did not return it.

"Hush-up, Wheedin! And if you tell anyone about this, I sware I'll go straight to your momma and tell her what you and Poke Mosely did in his daddy's barn!"

That wiped the grin right off Wheedin's face.

Maizee and I returned to Horseshoe Falls many times after that, but we never did invite Wheedin along again.

I'd spent the better part of a spring day working Shug Mosely's fields. I was hot, sweaty, and bone-tired, but Maizee insisted on packing a picnic supper and hiking up to the falls.

"C'mon, Zeb. We ain't been up there since last summer's homecoming. This is the best time of year at the falls."

I couldn't argue Maizee on that. Horseshoe Falls were at their grandest when the redbuds bloomed. During the early run-off, the waters sounded jes like a thousand horses thundering down the mountainside, which is how come they got that name.

Maizee and I had been officially courting. I'd asked permission from Doc. I got the impression that Leela-Ma wasn't too keen on Maizee and me courting, but Doc said not to worry about it, that if it were left up to Leela, Maizee would be doomed a spinster woman.

We spread a blanket under the ridge, far enough away from the falls that we wouldn't git sprayed and so we wouldn't have to yell at each other to be heard. I was about to starve, having not eaten anything since breakfast, so for the first half hour I shoveled food as Maizee rattled on about the garden she and Leela-Ma were planting, the trip into town she and Wheedin were planning, and the sick folks she'd visited with Doc.

"Doc showed me how to make up a poultice with garlic and lemon leaves. He says it's as good as lung balm at lifting the croup right out of a child. Did you know that?"

"No."

"Yes, sir. Garlic can help heal the cracks like the ones on your heels, too." Maizee pointed to my bare feet. My boots were caked in muck from Shug's barn. I'd taken them off and placed them on a nearby rock, away from the food. I apologized for my stinky feet. Maizee pinched her nose and laughed.

"As bad as my feet smell, they are a mite better smelling than my boots," I said.

"You ought to try soaking your feet at night in a tub of warm water and walnut leaves, then scrubbing them with the pulp from a garlic."

"What's the walnut leaves for?"

"There's an oil in the leaves that helps in the healing process," Maizee said. She broke the sugar cookie she was eating in two and handed me half.

"Is that so?" A couple of chipmunks were loitering nearby, eager for any crumb tossed their way. I threw the cookie at 'em. They scrambled after it.

"Mm-hm, it is."

"Well, I don't git it. Wouldn't the garlic make my feet reek, maybe worse than they do now?"

"I suppose, maybe," Maizee answered. Then, cutting her eyes my way, she added, "But they wouldn't be all cracked and peeling the way they are now. You should try it."

"I'll tell you what I'm going to try," I said, jumping up and stripping off my shirt, "that pool of water over there!"

"You must've had a heat stroke today 'cause your plumb brain dead," Maizee said. "You'll freeze your behiney off in that water. It's ice cold. You're liable to catch the croup."

"Well, if I do, I know jes the doctoring team who can fix me up," I said, yanking off my jeans.

Maizee whistled. "I sware, Zeb, you've got the best set of legs on the mountain. I'd kill for calves like yourn."

"Calves? Why, take a look at this!" I said, bending over and flexing my muscles for her.

Maizee waved me off. "Go on with you."

I dashed off and plunged into the pool beneath the falls. "Aw, shit!" Maizee was right. The plunge nearly sucked the air out of me. Scrambling back for the muddy bank, I pronounced, "The water's colder than a witch's tit."

Maizee stood ready with the blanket and a smug smile. "I tried to warn you. But you're a hardheaded man, Zebulon Hurd. Cain't be told nothing. Have to learn it all for yourself."

She threw the blanket over my shoulders and wrapped it around me.

"C'mere, woman," I said, drawing her close, "and warm me up."

Dang if she didn't do exactly as I'd ordered her. Maizee unbuttoned her dress and let it slip to her feet. Then, she stepped out of her slip and pressed herself up against me. Her skin was hot as a fry cake. Touching her nearly pained me, but it was a good pleasure and one I wasn't about to stop.

There had been other times when we'd strip down to our skivvies and lie next to each other, pressing up against each other, wishing for more but never trying. This time was different though. Neither of us wanted to stop.

"I'm gitting you all wet," I whispered.

"I don't mind," Maizee said, and she ran her tongue up my neck, under my ear, lapping up the rivulets falling from my head.

I shivered, not from the cold as much as from the heat stirring. I swooped over and cradled Maizee up into my arms. She gave out a yelp.

"Hold on tight," I said. Maizee wrapped her arms around my neck and burrowed in. Her hair smelled of sunshine. I carried her to the top of the ridge before putting her down. "Packing me all that way in your bare feet, jes like a real warrior would've done," Maizee said.

We spread the blanket over the soft, damp ground. Then, as the protective chestnut kept watch, Maizee and I moved to the rhythm of the water thundering down the mountainside.

10

Leela-Ma

Every Thursday morning during the late spring of 1940, me and half a dozen other women gathered in the basement of the Freewill Baptist Church to piece a quilt together. Spring mornings are best spent outdoors, hacking through clumps of clover, poking seeds into miniature volcanic mounds, all the while mulling on the eruption of green shoots to follow. But we gave up those bright mornings to stitch together blocks of scraps. Pale pinks from the Sunday dresses some had made their daughters, along with the soft sage leftovers of aprons, tablecloths, and curtains we'd sewn.

If we'd known earlier that Maizee was gitting married, we'd have set up the frame beside the coal stove and worked through the winter, but we didn't know. Maizee didn't know herself that she was with child until that Spring. Her monthlies weren't regular, so missing one or two didn't seem out of the ordinary, but that wasn't the first clue. She knew she was pregnant when she couldn't keep down the biscuits and fried eggs she had for breakfast. She no more than got the last bite down than the whole thing came back up.

She rushed over to the pail in the sink, the one I used for drawing up water from the well, and puked right into it. This wasn't no easy queasiness, not like when the flu crept up on a person, causing feverish muscles and a heavy head. This was a violent turning, like somebody twisted Maizee's innards till all the gut seams threatened to come undone.

When the puking wrenched her again the next morning, I held a wet rag to Maizee's forehead, pulled back her wavy hair, and asked, "You carrying a child?"

Maizee didn't answer, too shamed to admit to what she did in the dark places, as if the denying of such things could undo what was already done. She had never been one to lie to herself or to me. But Maizee thought anybody who considered public confession good for the soul had to be a dern fool. What good on God's green earth would come from talking about such things? That's how come Maizee rarely spoke of her own momma after Nan passed, or the daddy who up and left her.

Maizee knew sooner or later she'd have to pay the devil for the deed she and Zeb done. Looked like the sooner was now. The tightness forming under her belly betrayed her pride. I was sitting on the edge of my bed, unweaving my long gray braid, when Maizee came in and sat down beside me one evening. A lone kerosene lamp next to the bed cast long shadows against the front wall.

"Zeb's asked me to marry him," Maizee said, rubbing her sweaty palms down her thighs. Her ankles jittered up and down. Taking the hairbrush from my bedside table, I ran it back over my scalp and through my waist-length hair.

"Guess you best do that then," I said.

A church wedding was out of the question. Still, the women of the church had loved Maizee since she first came to live with me and Doc. Doc wasn't his given name. His Christian name was Luke. He wasn't school-trained like the doctors uptown. Doc had learned his craft from other mountain healers. Still, he knew doctoring as well as any.

We gifted the quilt to Maizee during a blessing ceremony at Embry Mae Cooper's place the week before she and Zeb married. Maizee sat in a ladder-back chair while the other women, holding hands, formed a circle around her. That quilt was the only wedding gift Maizee received that wasn't either canned, frozen, or preserved in some fashion until eaten.

"The Bible says that faith is the things hoped for, things not yet seen," I said as I placed the tissue-wrapped gift in Maizee's lap. "We hope the best for you and Zeb."

Although she never was one to indulge much in hope and daydreaming, Maizee allowed her heart that one moment. Her eyes, the faint blue of morning light, filled with tears, but she fought them back, willing them not to fall over the beautiful quilt spread out between us.

"I don't know what to say 'cept thank you all," Maizee said. Double circles of sage and pink crossed over each other, creating interlocking rings. She ran her fingers acrost those rings, marveling over each teensy pull of thread and the work it represented. "It's the prettiest thing I've ever seen."

I stepped back into the circle and asked Embry Mae to lead us all in a word of prayer. There was no mention of the growing mound kicking and twisting inside of Maizee, no out-loud prayers for the baby yet unborn, but there were plenty of silent ones.

Maizee turned seventeen the week she married Zebulon Hurd. He was twenty-one. Me and Doc stood in as witnesses to the civil ceremony at the courthouse in town. Maizee wore a black skirt and white eyelet blouse. Zeb wore gray slacks and a button-down shirt. They got married on Monday, June 3, 1940, the same day the Germans surrounded Dunkirk, although no one up Christian Bend way or uptown way knew anything about what was happening in Europe. Later, though, there was some folks who claimed it to be a sure sign of the trouble to follow.

11

Maizee

I held on to the ways of the mountain that Wheedin taught me, and to the pearl I found in the mussel. The day I married Zebulon Hurd, I wore it around my neck. Grasping it between my fingers, I recited my vows, promising to love, honor, cherish, and obey Zeb, always.

I cried throughout my wedding. I suspect Leela-Ma thought I was crying over having to git married the way I done, being with child and all. But fact is, I was crying mostly because so many blessings had come my way after Momma's death—my friendship with Wheedin, my life at Christian Bend, my marriage to Zeb.

Sure, I was crying in part for my momma. I missed her more on my wedding day than any day since I'd found her dead in the back yard. I missed Daddy too, and the life we should've had, if Momma had lived. Doc had called Daddy, told him I was gitting married, invited him over, but Daddy refused. Said he had to work, but Doc didn't believe him. I overheard him and Leela-Ma talking over a coffee the morning of my marrying day.

"He cain't stand to see her. She looks too much like her momma," Doc said. "That's how come he don't come. She reminds him of Nan. It's too much for him."

"What about her?" Leela-Ma replied. "Why doesn't he ever think of her first?"

"I don't know."

Standing there beside Zeb, I couldn't git out of my mind that some of life's greatest treasures are born of great sorrow. I understood in that moment how it is that God's tears turn to pearls. But happy as I was, I couldn't shake the troubling feeling creeping over me. The feeling that God was at that very moment filling the Holston River with tears. I wasn't sure if his were tears of sorrow or of joy, or maybe a bit of both, like mine.

12

Burdy Luttrell

The first I knowed of the trouble happened shortly after Maizee and Zeb moved onto my property in early June of '40. By then, her belly bore the soft curve of a ripened pear. Grannywomen like me don't need a conjure ball to know when a girl is in that way.

Maizee's presence was always a contrary thing. She brought happiness for Doc and Leela, who never conceived a child of their own, but Maizee was cursed with the shadow common to motherless children. It was as if the devil himself had his sights set on her. Maizee was an easy mark for hard times.

I believe Satan does such a thing—handpicks souls that he will fight tooth and nail over. If he cain't make them his own, he'll mess with 'em so bad that they'll forget the devil is their real enemy, and pretty soon, they're fighting with anybody who crosses their path, including they own selves. Maizee fought him something fierce, but it wasn't enough.

Even as a grown woman, Maizee was a frailish thing, not itty-bitty, but she looked like a strong wind could snap her in half. Her beauty didn't burst like daffodils the way Wheedin's did. Her's was more like a half-moon, a shy radiance that slipped up on a person.

The first sign of Maizee's trouble showed itself in the early afternoon on July 3. I remember the date because it was a Wednesday, my warsh day. I'd stripped the bed, warshed the sheets, and was outside hanging them when I heard the screen door slam at Zeb and Maizee's place. Not paying it much mind, I snapped a pillowcase to the line between two clothespins. It was only mid-morning, but the sun was already hot as blazes. As I reached for the second pillowcase Maizee come up behind me, quiet as a flea.

"Lawd, girl!" I hollered. "Don't sneak up on me like that!"

As soon as I'd spit them words out, I wished I could swallow 'em back. The girl standing before me was a picture of midnight fright. Maizee's hair, usually neatly groomed, was brittle and knotted. She was pale as a possum's underbelly. Her hands were shaking, lips quivering. Her eyes were dark empty caverns.

Leaning forward over her swollen belly, she whispered, "Burdy, I know what the problem is."

I looked around her. "Problem?" I asked. "What kind of problem, Maizee? Is something wrong with Zeb?"

She shook her head from side to side.

"Leela?"

"No," she answered, whispering still. Maizee rubbed her cheeks and her forehead in a worrisome fashion. "I know why I cain't git nothing to eat. I cain't git into the kitchen."

That last remark seemed as out of place as red hair on a frog, but Maizee said it as plainly as if she was reciting the books of the B-I-B-L-E. I reached over and took hold of her elbows and held her still for a moment. I look hard into her eyes. They didn't look right.

Zeb had stopped by the house last Monday while I was sitting out on the porch enjoying the evening cool. He mentioned then that he was worried about Maizee, but I didn't think nothing of it. A man's got a right to worry when his wife is plump with child. I told him I'd be sure to keep an eye on her during the days when he was working over at Shug Mosely's place. But Zeb didn't give an indication of anything unnatural being wrong. Seeing her thisaway, it looked to me like Maizee had gone and misplaced her mind somewhere.

"Why cain't you git into the kitchen?" I asked.

"Zeb's sitting at the table, reading."

"Cain't you walk around him?"

Maizee shook her head back and forth in that way dogs do when they come up out of the river and are trying to clear their ears. Then, bending over, she picked up a sheet and folded it over the line. I shoved a clothespin down on one corner while she held the other. I handed her a wooden pin and she put it snug over the sheet. The air smelled of sunshine and soap. We worked quietly, taking in that brain-cleansing perfume until all the laundry was on the line.

"I got some biscuits and bacon leftover from breakfast," I said. "Why don't you come in and I'll fix you a plate. I'll even git out some apple butter."

"I'd like that very much," Maizee replied softly.

I knew she wouldn't decline. Maizee loved apple butter. When she and Wheedin were younger, they'd sneak a jar from the pantry and climb up to the pool at Horseshoe Falls with that jar stuffed inside the bib of Wheedin's coveralls. They'd sit on the large rock and pour the apple butter out into the palms of their hands and lap it up like weaned kittens until every bit of it was clean gone. Then they'd warsh the jar in the pool till it was sparkling, carry it home and put it back on the shelf, all the while pretending like I wasn't going to notice an empty jar. I'd not only noticed the missing butter, I'd followed them up the trail a time or two jes to watch them do it.

There was nothing I loved better than watching those two girls and the messes they got into. They didn't need to swipe the apple butter. I'd gladly have given it to them. But I let them git away with it, because every sinner knows stolen food taste the best and any meal shared with a friend is good.

Maizee pulled out a chair and sat at the table. Tibbis had carved the table for our fifth anniversary after a strong wind blew over one of the aging black cherries behind the house.

"How come Zeb's home?" I asked as I put a couple of biscuits on a plate and set them in front of Maizee.

"Zeb's not home," she replied. Maizee cut a biscuit open and slathered apple butter over both halves.

"I thought you said he was sitting in the kitchen reading."

Maizee fiddled with her food, then said, "Did I? I don't remember saying that. He left early this morning for Shug's place. They're cutting the far field today. Said he wouldn't be home before dark."

I poured myself a glass of iced tea and Maizee a glass of cold milk and sat down acrost from her. I seen flickers of light in Maizee's eyes that had not been there earlier when she was speaking foolishness.

"Have you heard from Wheedin lately?" I asked.

"She sent me a letter last week. Said she liked her job and her place but missed me."

"I'll bet."

My girl had moved off to South Carolina, and she hadn't been back to the mountain since she blew her arm off during a brawl she had with Poke Mosely a year ago when the two of them were shacking up.

Wheedin tried to put all the blame on Poke, but I knew better. Wheedin was my only child, but I wasn't amused by her faults. She was a slave to a bad temper. Poke loved Wheedin more than a good man ought to love a selfish woman, so he went along with her claim that the shooting was an accident.

He told Sheriff Duncan that he'd asked Wheedin to fetch him the sawed-off special from the hall closet so he could shoot a fox that had gotten into the chicken coop and killed two of his hens. Poke said Wheedin tripped coming off the porch, and fell on the loaded gun. It discharged and blew her left arm clean off, all the way to the socket hole.

Sheriff didn't doubt for one minute that Wheedin fell off the porch, but the likely truth was that she and Poke had been arguing over one thing or another, and Wheedin was chasing him outta the house when she fell on that gun. Sheriff said he couldn't find a speck of evidence of any fox in the chicken coop, and that made him suspicious of the whole affair.

Any other man would've been tempted to leave Wheedin there to die in the curdle of her own blood after being chased by a hot-tempered girl with a tampered shotgun, but, like I said, Poke was a good man. He staunched the bleeding and got Wheedin to the town doctor, who sawed off her stub and sewed her up good and tight. Then Poke brought her back to my house to recoup, but soon as she figured out how to hook and unhook her bra with one hand, Wheedin left Christian Bend. I didn't even try to stop her. People with good sense don't step in front of freight trains when the engines are churning.

Wheedin had a friend who worked at the Hog's Snout Bar in Columbia, who had offered Wheedin a place to stay. Jobs were plentiful there because of the university. Wheedin got a job at the library answering phones and putting books away, and a month later, she had her own room at a boarding house.

"It's real pretty, Ma," Wheedin said in her first letter home. "Got me a picture window that looks right out on the Congaree River, which is really nice but not like the Holston at all. The Congaree has a bunch of boulders rising up like river creatures."

I've never seen any river except the Holston. I'm as familiar with its flows as I am my own. Most every spring the river swells up so high it warshes right over the road to Christian Bend. When that happens, the ferry still carries people from bank to bank, but from there they have to slosh through ankle-high waters home, or wherever it is they're headed. At dusk a person can wander down to the bend and watch the sun plop into the Holston, like a new penny in an old fountain. I've walked down there many an afternoon jes to wish upon the setting of it.

Maizee finished off the biscuits, the bacon, the last bit of apple butter, and the glass of milk.

"I've got some pound cake leftover from Sunday's lunch. You want a slice?"

"No, thank you, Burdy," Maizee said. "We're all full now." She rubbed her belly hump.

"Honey, would you like me to give your hair a warshing? I could git those tangles out and wrap it in a braid for you."

"I'd *love* that!" Maizee said. "If you're sure. I don't want to trouble you, Miz Burdy, but I do have a hard time warshing my hair with this big ol' lump in the way."

I carried one of the kitchen chairs to the back porch. Maizee sat down and I wrapped her shoulders with a towel. Then I grabbed a pail of rainwater from where it sat under the gutter.

"Nothing gits tangles out better," I said, pouring a cupful over Maizee's scalp. She was leaning backwards, with her neck resting on the chair and her feet stretched out in front of her. The sun had warmed up the water, so Maizee didn't even flinch as I soaked her head.

"When I was pregnant with Wheedin, Tibbis would warsh my hair for me thisaway," I said.

"He would?" Maizee asked. "I don't think I've ever seen a man shampoo a woman's head."

"Tibbis always was his own boss. He was never partial to anyone's idea of how a man ought to act. He did whatever he had a compulsion to do, and he didn't care what nobody else thought of him. I reckon it's a good thing he was that way or he'd likely never have married me."

"How come you to say that?" Maizee asked, pulling the edge of the towel to wipe at the water dripping in her eyes.

"Wasn't nobody here on this mountain that wanted Tibbis to marry me."

"Whyever not?"

13

People couldn't figure out why Tibbis wanted to marry a Melungeon like me. Mountain folks were suspicious of our dark-skinned kin who came over from Snake Hollow Ridge. They warned their children, "Behave or the Melungeons will come and carry you off!" Those children and their parents feared our people, so they made up awful names, which they threw at us like rotting fruit—mountain Melungeons, half-breeds, or worser yet, ridge-niggers.

Daddy, Ma, and Auntie Tay fled over the ridge from Snake Hollow before I was weaned. Ma would never say why her and Daddy left their clan and come acrost the ridge to Christian Bend, but Auntie told Cousin Hota, who told me one night when we was kids laying out under the hickory in the backyard counting stars. I was up to 142, but Hota couldn't see faraway too good, so I think he brought the matter up to mess up my counting.

"I know a secret," Hota said.

"So," I replied, keeping my eyes on the night sky. "I know lots of stuff I don't tell you."

"Yeah, betcha don't know this."

"If you're going to tell me about Emma Hawkins's brother, I already heard. Emma told me yesterday that Marlin got Mahaley Rogers pregnant."

Mahaley Rogers was a town girl. Her daddy was mayor of Rogersville, which was named after some kin of his. Mahaley's daddy got so fired up he kicked her outta the house; so now she was living at the Hawkins's place. Which meant Emma had to share her room with Mahaley, and Emma wasn't none too happy about it.

"That's not what I was going to tell you," Hota said. "My secret ain't about somebody's else's family. It's about ours. Besides, I didn't know Emma's brother had done that."

"One hundred and forty-three," I said, pointing to one of the stars forming the Little Bear's tail. "Well, don't you go saying nothing about it. Emma is sure to know who told you, and I got enough problems with her without you stirring up more."

"I ain't going to say nothing," Hota replied. "But I know why your daddy and ma left Snake Hollow."

I quit counting the stars and leaned up on one elbow, so I could face Hota. "You do?"

Hota nodded. "Tay told me."

"She didn't."

"Did too!" Hota cried.

I rolled onto my back, pretended to count the stars again, trying to act like I didn't give a care about anything Hota had to say.

He jumped up.

"Where you headed?" I asked.

"Inside to git me another piece of berry pie."

"Dern you, Hota. I cain't believe you're going to go off and leave me hanging like the Big Dipper. I thought we was best friends. Best friends supposed to tell each other everything."

"If you don't tell me your secrets, why should I tell you mine?"

"Don't git sore jes because I didn't tell you about Marlin and Mahaley. I swore to Emma I wouldn't say nothing. She made me put my hand on the Bible and sware it."

"You swore on the Bible?" Hota asked.

I could tell by his tone he was disbelieving me. I nodded.

"I cain't believe you'd sware on the Bible, and then break a promise to God," he said.

"I know. I know," I said. "I wouldn't've, but Emma made me. You know how ornery she can be. And I never would've told you if you hadn't gone and tempted me."

"Don't go blaming me!" Hota said. "I was only trying to tell you something you oughta know."

"Then why don't you jes spit it out."

Hota sat back down beside me. "Your daddy's daddy shot Mamaw."

I sat up. "Come again?"

"You heard me, Burdy. I said your daddy's daddy shot Mamaw, and that's how come your daddy brung your ma and mine over the ridge."

"Did Papaw kill her?"

"Yep," Hota said, nodding. I couldn't see his eyes for the darkness out, but I knew Hota was telling me the truth. Ma always said a lie has short legs; it cain't git too far. Hota knew I'd find him out if he was lying to me.

"How come he kilt her?" I asked.

"Momma said it was an accident," Hota explained. "She said Papaw Bowlins and Mamaw was arguing on account of her drinking and not tending to his supper. Papaw didn't mean to kill nobody, but Mamaw ended up dead all the same. Your daddy was so upset over it he took you and your ma and mine and left Snake Hollow for good."

Hota might as well walloped me with a hickory stick. I couldn't hardly catch my breath. I'd often wondered how come Daddy never mentioned his people, and the only time I'd been around Ma's kin were at summer gatherings. I knew we had people at Snake Hollow, but Christian Bend was the only home I knew.

Daddy wasn't much one for talking about kin or anything. Sometimes Ma would speak of Snake Hollow and her growing up days. Mostly when we were out berry picking, or scouring for roots. Ma wasn't a healer woman by divination, but she knew which roots could cure and she taught me what she knowed: ague-weed for fever; snakeroot for the bites of mad dogs; Dutchman-pipe for spasms, so on and so forth.

I was born with the healer's mark, a dark-tinged handprint on my right side. Ma said it looked like God grabbed me around the waist after dipping his hand in the juice of bloodroot. The day I turned ten, Ma gave me a small silver cross. "You're marked for a purpose, Burdy," she said, placing the crucifix in my hand. "You're meant to heal people and perform miracles in the Jesus way."

Ma didn't say nothing about the *curse of knowing* which almost always accompanies the gift of healing. The knowing of when an ailing person would die no matter what cures I offered 'em. Sometimes the knowing came to me in my sleep, like it did winter before last, on the night before Mrs. Betty's firstborn died.

Her poor boy had been sick with the croup for days. I'd crushed up hawkweed and made a syrup to soothe Baby Boone's throat and open up his breathing tube. It was working well enough that I'd left Mrs. Betty to tend to Boone herself around suppertime. But that night I dreamed Boone coughed himself purple, and when I woke I knowed he was dead.

The curse of knowing ain't the same as the seer's gift. I cain't read tea leaves or coffee grinds the way Auntie Tay could. People was all the time coming up to her place and asking her to read their futures. Mostly young girls wanting to know about some fella they favored. Auntie Tay was quick to tell 'em to hold off if she seen they was about to drive their ducks to a bad market. But then Auntie Tay was gitting paid in butterbeans and frogskins to say what she seen.

I didn't say nothing to Ma or anyone else, not even Hota, about this knowing of mine. It didn't seem right to talk about such things. I feared I'd sound haughty, the way some preachers sound when they go around claiming God give them a message "jes for you." I figured God knew me well enough, he could speak directly to me if he had something important to say.

Because of our Melungeon ancestry, there wasn't nary a soul in Christian Bend who counted on Tibbis Luttrell taking up with the likes of me. Tibbis's family were some of the first people to settle this mountain, and they owned a good chunk of it. And even though Ma and Daddy had come acrost the ridge when I wasn't yet weaned, a lot of folks still considered us outlanders. Tibbis was expected to marry one of the fair-skinned locals— somebody like Emma Hawkins.

I'm over it now, but there'd been a time when I hated Emma with every fiber in my being. She was everything I wasn't—blonde, freckled, and round of cheek and bone. Mostly I hated her because she wasn't a mixed mutt like me.

With age, I've come to favor my peculiarities, but as a youngster my looks frazzled me. I wanted skin white as a dogwood blossoms and eyes as blue as bachelor buttons, not the skin of a walnut or eyes the blue-green of Indian bead. What I wanted worse than anything was to look like Emma.

As a teenager, during the summers, when the sun could tan a turnip, I took to wearing long sleeves and coveralls. Sometimes I'd tie a scarf over my jaw and nose like a robber, to keep 'em from browning more. Sweat would ripple in the bends around my nose, elbows, and knees the way the Holston does around Christian Bend.

Ma would shake her head and say, "Child, are you stricken with a brain fever? What are you doing putting on all them clothes in this heat?"

But she had grown up on the ridge, where she was kin to nearly everyone, in a place where folks all favored each other. Ma didn't know what it was like to stand out. And I was too shamed to tell her the ugly names some of the kids called me; how they didn't want to play with a ridge-nigger; how they was all the time telling me to take a bath and warsh the dirt off.

I might never have gotten over all that if Tibbis hadn't loved me the way he did. But when someone loves you the way Tibbis loved me, harboring hate takes work. We had an easy love, one that grew out of a shared childhood.

My daddy worked for his, seeing to all the things Mr. Luttrell didn't have time for, like fixing fences, plowing, calving, and butchering. I tagged along with my daddy and Tibbis with his. I cain't remember a time when we didn't know each other.

On my twelfth birthday, Tibbis taught me how take a worm, fold it end to end, and snap a fishhook through its gut.

"You ain't squeamish like other girls, Burdy," he said, after I baited my fifth worm of the day. "You're like one of them pictures I seen of men with hoofed feet and hairy behinds. Take off your pants and let me make sure you're a girl and not some fuzzy-butt animal."

"Aw'right," I replied. "As long as you promise to kiss it."

Tibbis and I sparred with each other in a good-natured fashion, the way puppies born from the same litter do. I don't know if there came a moment when we fell in love; seemed to me we'd grown up loving each other.

Mr. Luttrell didn't pay much mind to Tibbis and me spending time together, but his momma wasn't the least bit shy about letting on how upset she was about it. Janny Luttrell was a woman torn. She'd studied to be a teacher at some university in Georgia but gave that up to marry Mr. Luttrell. Tibbis used to say that his momma should've been in the Army since giving orders is what she did best.

When we was kids, Miz Janny was congenial in that way that well-off people often are to those who ain't. She'd ask after my folks and tell me to give them her regards. Something she wouldn't have done if they was standing right there at her front door. Miz Janny didn't think it was right for people of color to mix. She was all the time working the differences between our families into a conversation.

She came out on the porch one afternoon when me and Tibbis was sitting there, doing nothing, jes talking, which is the best thing to do on a midday in summer's heat.

"Burdy, I was cleaning out my pantry today and came acrost a sack of nigger toes that somebody gave us. I don't remember who. We have no use for them, so I'm sending them home with you," she said. "I'm sure your momma will put them to good use."

Miz Janny handed me the poke of nuts.

I didn't say nothing. Not even thank you. Ain't no use in trying to convince people of changing their ways when they already got their minds made up, and Miz Janny had made it clear that God never intended for fair-haired boys like Tibbis to mix with dark-skinned girls like me.

Miz Janny became more agitated once it became clear to everyone in sight that Tibbis and I were more than good friends. She liked to have had a heart attack one Sunday when Tibbis invited me over for dinner. But, angry as she might be, Miz Janny could never stay cross with her boy. Instead, she took it all out on me. Passing the bowl of green beans over to Mr. Luttrell, she said, "Your people aren't like all those other gypsies, are they, Burdy?"

"*Momma!*" Tibbis said. "Don't be rude!"

"Your people don't move around like gypsies, do they?"

"I couldn't say," I replied, taking a biscuit off a plate. "I don't know any gypsies."

"Oh, I'm sorry," Miz Janny said. "I thought your people—what is it they call themselves?"

"Melungeons," I said.

"Oh, I always git that clan confused with gypsies."

"I'll bet," Tibbis said.

Two days after that warsh day when Maizee came by the house talking nonsense about not being able to git into her kitchen, I made the trek up to Tibbis's grave house and told him all about Maizee's strange behavior. I took along a beer, some smokes, and a bowl of beautyberries I'd picked fresh. I never went to Tibbis's grave without an offering of some sort. It was my way of tending after him.

Doc had helped me build Tibbis's grave house. Grave shelters weren't common to Christian Bend, but Ma built one for Daddy after he died. And when Ma died, Auntie Tay built one for her. "Building a wooden house or roof over the grave was part of the ways of our people," Auntie Tay explained.

Wheedin wasn't but seven, and me only twenty-five, when I found Tibbis dead in the meadow about a mile south of Horseshoe Falls, where the mountain laurel grows so thick. It was going on dusk when I found him, face up toward the sun, like he'd decided to lie down to nap between the bushes. He'd hiked up there in the morning, shortly after he finished off the oatmeal I'd fixed. Tibbis said he was going to go check on some timber on the other side of the meadow. He said he'd be back before dinner, but when he didn't show up for dinner or supper, I begun to fret.

Wheedin was too little for such a hike, so I carried her over to Shug Mosely's house and asked Ida to keep watch over her for awhile.

"Tibbis went off to the woods this morning and I ain't seen hide nor hair of him since," I said. "Do you mind watching over Wheedin for a bit?"

"Not at all, Burdy," Ida said. "You're welcome to take our mare. She's out in the barn."

"I believe I will borry Rose, if you're sure you won't be needing her."

"Go ahead, take her," Ida said. "I ain't going nowhere with all these young'uns."

Tibbis had a couple of horses, but one was too green and the other too aged. I'd have been better off walking than taking either of 'em. Rose was surefooted on the slope.

It was early October. The air smelled well scrubbed. The leaves on the hickories and chestnuts were the yellow of newborn chicks. The trek up to Horseshoe Falls was jeweled with the purples of ironweed and of Joe Pye weed. As I approached the falls, I expected I might find Tibbis with a twisted ankle, a broken leg, something that could have slowed him down, but I never expected for one minute I'd find him dead. When I spotted him acrost the meadow, along the path, I jumped off the horse and run over to him, screaming, "TIBBIS! TIBBIS!"

He didn't answer. Jes laid there, his green eyes staring at the heavens above. I shook his shoulders, slapped his face, pounded on his chest. Nothing. Tibbis didn't even let go a sigh. He was stone-cold dead.

I searched his head for bullet holes, bruises, anything to give me a sign of what had felled him. But it wasn't till I rolled him over that I seen what done it—an arrow, snapped in two, half of it still stuck in-between Tibbis's shoulder blades. I don't remember the rest of the day or most of the year that followed. I know from what Ida told me that Rose carried me back to her place.

"You was half outta your mind," Ida has told me a dozen times since.

Shug and some of the men fetched Tibbis from the meadow, and Sheriff Duncan tracked down the boy who killed my husband.

Jimmie Price was a shitepoke town kid, from up at Johnson City. He'd gotten into some kind of trouble right before the school year ended, and his folks had sent him off to Christian Bend to summer with his Papaw Algie. When the new school year rolled around, Jimmie refused to go back to Johnson City.

Algie didn't mind the boy staying on. He'd lived alone since Rozzela, his wife, died some years back. She'd been bitten by a timber rattler while picking lettuce in the garden. Up until I discovered Tibbis dead in the meadow, the only thing I knew about Jimmie Price I heard from Doc Lawson. Doc had stopped by the house in August and told Tibbis and me that old man Algie had found his grandson struttin' around the yard jaybird nekkid on the Fourth of July, shooting at mountain boomers with a rifle. When his Papaw Algie asked him what in Jehoshaphat's name he thought he was doing, running around nekkid in broad daylight, Jimmy replied, "It's hot." Doc laughed as he told us that story, but none of us thought it was anything other than the antics of a young buck.

When Sheriff Duncan asked Jimmie why he killed Tibbis, Jimmie answered flatly, "To watch him die." Jimmie wasn't but a kid when he kilt Tibbis, so he was sent to a detention home and let out when he was twenty-one. Last I heared he was living up in Nashville, playing guitar in the juke joints. I buried Tibbis in the meadow, not far from where I'd found him, near the woods he loved so well and close enough by that he could hear the thunder of Horseshoe Falls.

Even though he was long dead, I figured Tibbis would be the best one to help me sort out matters concerning Maizee. Placing the offering I brung in the spot where I thought his heart might rest, I said, "Go easy on the smokes. You know they ain't good for you."

I could imagine Tibbis laughing. His green eyes crinkling. That lone dimple high on his right cheekbone. Tibbis would be forever handsome, he'd died so young. Wheedin was now the age I'd been when I birthed her. Soon enough she'd be the age Tibbis was when he passed. It weren't right.

"This ain't the way our life was supposed to turn out," I said. It weren't the first time Tibbis had heard that complaint. He responded the same as he'd always done—he ignored me.

So I went to telling him about how Maizee had come by the house, talking nonsense about not being able to git into the kitchen, and how I'd warshed her hair the way he had mine when I was pregnant, and how Zeb had asked me to keep an eye on Maizee. Even when he was alive, Tibbis was always a good listener, rarely prone to interrupting me, no matter how much I carried on. Like most men, he'd gotten even better at it over the years.

Wrapping up my concerns, I told Tibbis, "Maizee ain't right. Something's bad wrong and I don't believe this baby is going to make everything straight." I'd rose up, dusted myself off, and was about to walk away when I heard Tibbis say clear as if he was standing next to me, "Tell Zeb and Maizee to beware the arrow that flies by day."

"You're one to talk," I said. Then I bent over and took back the bowl of beautyberries I brung. No sense wasting good food on sour company.

14

Maizee

I don't remember the exact day when I started hearing the voice again, but when it come back it didn't come alone. I was heavy pregnant, I recall that for sure. Zeb and me ain't been married but for a short while, maybe a month.

We were living in a house behind Burdy Luttrell's place. She give it to us cheap on account of Zeb doing some chores around her property. It was a nice place, with a small porch, and a window over the kitchen sink. Having a window over the sink helped pass the task of dishwarshing. Leela-Ma used to stand at her sink, which faced the corner at Christian Bend, and recite the Psalms: "I will lift up mine eyes unto the hills, from whence comes my help. My help comes from the Lord, who made heaven and earth."

I could see the tree line that led up to Horseshoe Falls from my window. Leela-Ma helped me make curtains for all the windows, blue-checkered ones for the kitchen and sitting room, and solid white ones for the bedroom. She give me a yellow vase to sit on the dinette table, and made some pretty yellow pillows for the sitting room. Leela-Ma claimed yellow could cheer the most troubled soul. I knowed she was praying for mine.

It shames me to say I was with child when Zeb and I married. Doc and Leela-Ma would've loved better 'n anything to have me married proper in the church, before God and all our friends. I hated disappointing them when they'd done nothing but look after me in loving ways.

But I was so swollen with child when Zeb and me married that there was no denying what deeds me and Zeb had done in the dark. I should've waited, saved myself for marriage, the way God and Preacher Blount expected. But the trouble is, I'd been aching after Zeb for so long that it seemed as though I'd been waiting all my life for the comfort that come to me when I was wrapped in his arms. It's hard to feel bad about something that good, but I managed. Guilt come easy to me ever since Momma died.

The voices knew that about me. Fact is, the voices knew pretty much everything about me. They shadowed me during the day and haunted my sleep at night. I could hear 'em even when I was dead asleep. I heared 'em best then, that's how come I got to where I couldn't sleep much.

They called out to me jes like that day when I left Daddy and come acrost the Holston on the ferry.

"MAIZEE! MAIZEE!"

They'd call softly at first, but if I didn't sit upright and answer 'em, they'd git sore and talk at me in ugly voices. They'd whisper things about my baby, things too awful to repeat. I didn't tell Zeb, or anyone else. It wasn't that I didn't trust him. It was me I didn't trust. I couldn't be sure if I truly was hearing things or if I was imagining 'em.

Zeb knew something was disturbing me, especially after that night when he heared me crying in my sleep.

"Maizee, honey," Zeb said, shaking me. "Wake up. Wake up."

I turned over on my side and faced him. My pillow was wet with tears.

"Honey, what's the matter?" Zeb's whole face was pinched with worriment. "Are you hurting somewhere?" He run his hand softly acrost my belly.

"I'm aw'right," I said. "Jes a bad dream, that's all."

"Wanna tell me about it?" Zeb asked, rising up from his pillow on one elbow, so he could study my face better.

I closed my eyes and shook my head from side to side.

"You sure?"

"Mm-hm." I wasn't about to tell Zeb that I dreamt I'd given birth to a baby whose eyes were missing. I don't mean the baby's eyes were empty sockets. I dreamt that our baby was born with a beautiful smile and turned-up nose and nothing else. Like it had an extra forehead where its eyes ought to be.

From that morning on, I was sickly with the notion that our baby would be born misshapen. Maybe the dream was a warning from God. I hoped if I could figure out what it was I'd done to disappoint God; I could fix things before my time come and nobody would ever know the difference.

On those evenings when I couldn't sleep, I'd wait till I knew for sure Zeb was asleep—I could tell by the way his jaw went slack—and I'd git out of bed and go into the sitting room to pray and read my Bible. I committed to memory the verse from Matthew about the heart's defilement: "For out of the heart proceed evil thoughts, murders, adulteries, fornicators, thefts, false witness, blasphemies."

I begged God to restore to me a clean heart, and to please, please not punish my baby for my sins. In return, I promised to purge my life from every evil deed or thought and to submit my will to God's, for always and forever, amen. Sometimes, I'd git to crying so hard, I could feel my belly tighten. I feared that might cause the baby harm, so I began to sing hymns and songs of praise, like the Scriptures commanded: "Speak to yourself in psalms and hymns and spiritual songs, singing and making melody in your heart to the Lord."

I'd sing the old songs, the ones folks always called out whenever Mrs. Kerry Morris asked the congregation for their favorites. Songs like "Count Your Blessings" and "'Tis So Sweet to Trust in Jesus," and when the voices got really loud, I'd sing "Power in the Blood."

It helped some. As long as I was singing, I couldn't hear nobody's voice but my own. But only a crazy person would go around singing all day long. A person's got to be silent some of the time. Trouble was, I couldn't find that silent time. As soon as I stopped singing or reciting Bible verses to myself, the voices would return. There was noise in my head all the time.

Weren't long ago, a walk in the woods could quiet my soul better 'n anything. Better even than sitting all by my lonesome in the church. I kept telling myself if I could hike up to Horseshoe Falls, I could git rid of the noise in my head. I mentioned it to Zeb over dinner one night.

"I'll be glad when this baby comes so we can hike up the mountain. I ain't been up to the falls all summer long."

Zeb pulled apart his cornbread and said, "Soon as this baby is born, and you're able, I'll take you up the ridge. I'll carry you if I have to."

"Don't you worry about me," I said, laughing at Zeb's ridiculous remark. "I'm pregnant, not crippled. I'll be able-bodied enough to carry myself up the mountain, but I'll let you pack the baby, if you like."

"My pleasure," Zeb said, grinning proudly.

That night I dreamt our baby was born without any arms or legs. We put him in a poke and carried him wherever we went. When I woke the next morning, the voices told me to stay out of the kitchen, or else, they warned, my dream would come true.

Zeb was gone off to work. I sat on the edge of the davenport, reading my Bible, praying, asking God to make the voices go away. But it seemed the more I prayed, the noisier they got. I told myself there was nobody there but me and the baby kicking inside me. And Jesus, in my heart.

Your wicked heart, the voices corrected me.

I put my hands over my ears and said out loud, "I'm going into the kitchen and fix myself something to eat."

"You cain't," a voice said.

"How come?" I asked.

"Because Zeb won't let you," he answered.

"Zeb ain't even here!" I cried out.

"Sure, he is. Look and see," the voice thundered.

And sure enough, I seen Zeb sitting at the table, reading. Onliest he'd pulled the table over so it blocked off the kitchen. I would never be able to git past him, unless he pulled the table outta my way.

"Zeb?" I said. "I need something to drink. I'm thirsty and hungry."

He didn't say nothing. Didn't even look up from whatever it was he was reading. That angered me. Here I am, heavy with child, tired and worn out from entertaining all these voices talking at me all the time, and Zeb hasn't got the courtesy to git outta my way so I can git myself something to eat.

My chest hurt from the anger erupting inside me. I started to pray again. Anger's a sin, so I couldn't be angry. So I asked Jesus to take away the anger, to give me patience, to restore in me a clean heart. I asked forgiveness for all my rebellious ways. I asked Jesus to forgive Zeb his selfishness and that got me right back where I started—angry at Zeb.

The voices were laughing at me now, mocking me for praying. I ran out of the house, away from the laughter. I might've tried to run straight up the mountain if Burdy hadn't been outside hanging up the warsh.

The thing is, when the voices come to you, part of you knows something is the matter with you. That part of you wants to tell people. But the other part of you knows you cain't tell folks what's happening because they'll git that pitiful soul look in their eyes and, if they are the religious sort, they'll make it their mission in life to fix you.

Burdy wasn't like that. She had the healer's mark on her; a sure sign that she was one of God's anointed. If anybody could cure a person, Burdy Luttrell and her roots could. I knew I could tell Burdy about the voices and she'd help me, but whenever I tried to tell her, the voices started shouting all together inside my head. They was so awful loud. I couldn't make out everything they was saying. They said I was trash. That Daddy had never loved me. That Zeb didn't. That my baby was deformed. That I was a whore, unfit to be a mother. That the worms infesting my heart were this very minute trying to crawl out my nose, my ears, my unmentionable.

No wonder Burdy about jumped outta her skin when I came upon her hanging out her sheets. Seeing all them worms crawling over a person's body the way they were me would likely trouble most anyone. I'd done scared Burdy so bad, I feared coming right out and telling her about all the voices. I mentioned the trouble I was having gitting into the kitchen on account of Zeb pushing the table over so that it blocked off the entryway, but Burdy looked so confused, I couldn't bear burdening her with any more. So I helped her hang the laundry and she fed me some apple butter and biscuits.

Seemed like my head cleared some. Burdy offered to warsh my hair and fix it. I know it looked something gosh-awful, what with them worms knotting it up the way they done. When Burdy poured that rainwater over my head, it was like being baptized. A peace warshed over me, silencing all that noise. I could've fallen to sleep right there, with Burdy cradling my head between her healing hands.

That head-warshing cured me good. After Burdy plaited my hair, I went home and fixed a good supper. I made a salad with lettuce and onions I got from the garden. I salted and peppered some pork chops and fried 'em up, along with some taters I cut. And I cooked a mess of greens.

I got one of Momma's tablecloths that Leela-Ma give me and spread it over the table. I fiddled with it till the embroidered corners hung evenly. I picked some of the wild pink roses growing up alongside the house and put them in the yellow vase. Then I took down the good plates I got from Zeb, the ones with the blue willow pattern. They'd been his momma's, but she died the year before we was married.

Mrs. Hurd, Zeb's momma, had a bad sore on her right shin that wouldn't scab over. Gangrene set in and eat up her leg, lickety-split. Doc Slater said the only way to stop the infection was to cut her leg off, but before he could do that, the infection spread to her system and kilt her. Zeb said it was jes as well, since his momma wasn't the kind of woman who'd sit still for nothing.

The day after we married, Zeb wrapped up one of the cup and saucer sets from the dishes really fancy, with ribbon, and give it to me with a card that he wrote himself: "My love for you is deeper than the roots of the willow tree planted by the river of living waters."

He give me the present as we sat eating grits and eggs on our first morning together as husband and wife. I held the cup in my hand and twisted and turned it every whichaway, admiring all the tiny blue pictures.

"Oh, Zeb! It's so, so…delicate!"

Reaching acrost the table, Zeb took my hand into his and said, "All them pictures tell a story."

"They do? What is it?"

"Well, I'm not sure I can remember all of it, but it goes something like this." Zeb took the cup into his hands. "There was a princess from China who fell in love with a hillbilly. The two would sneak off and met underneath the willow tree near her rich daddy's mansion—"

"Hey, whoa! They got hillbillies in China?" I asked, giving Zeb the stink eye.

"Yeah, sure. Every place got their own hillbillies," Zeb answered. "You wanna hear the rest of the story?"

"Yes, sir."

"See this here tree?"

"Yes, sir."

"That's the one they met under. When the rich daddy found out about his daughter's hillbilly boyfriend, he built a fence around the place and told the hillbilly to keep away from his daughter." Zeb pointed to the zig-zagged fence.

"Looks like he could've built that a little straighter if you ask me," I said.

"Yeah, kind of makes you wonder who the real hillbilly was, huh?" Zeb said, twisting the cup around in his hand. "The rich daddy then promised his daughter to another man. When the hillbilly found out, he jumped the fence and grabbed the girl, and run off."

"Aw, Zeb, that's such a sweet story. You'd do that for me, wouldn't you?"

"What? Jump a fence?"

"Steal me away?"

"A' course I would. Shoot, I'm pretty sure I could step over a fence no bigger than that," he said. "But the story doesn't end there."

"It doesn't?"

"Naw. See these two birds?"

"Yes, sir."

"When the rich daddy found out, he chased the couple down and had the feller killed, then the girl killed herself. Some Chinese god took pity on the couple and resurrected them as lovebirds."

"Gawd, Zeb, that's awful!"

"Jes a few minutes ago you said it was sweet."

"Well, that's before I knew you were going to kill everybody off."

"Whoa, Nellie! I didn't kill anybody off. I was only telling you the story behind the pictures."

"Well, you've nearly spoilt the gift," I said, whining. "Now every time I look at these dishes I'll be sad, not only about your momma but about some Chinese hillbilly and his gal."

Zeb rose up out of his chair and come around to where I was sitting. Pulling me to my feet, he held me close for a moment. "Here's what I want you to remember every time you handle one of these dishes." Then Zeb pressed his warm lips to mine and kissed me gently. Lifting my hair off my neck, Zeb kissed it too. "Remember the tree where the lovers met, down by the water, and all the good memories we've made at Horseshoe Falls under the giant chestnut."

One more kiss from Zeb and I plumb near forgot all about the sad Chinese hillbilly.

15

My water broke in mid-morning on the first day of August. Burdy, Doc, and Leela-Ma were all with me when Rain was born. Zeb, who'd been off with Shug somewhere, showed up sometime later.

From the top of his curly dark hair to the tips of his pointy toes, Rain was perfect. There was not one flaw on him. No double forehead. No limbs missing. Not even a birthmark or mole. His features were so fine, he was pretty enough to be a girl. When Leela-Ma got him all cleaned up, she wrapped him in a blanket and handed him to me.

"I made that blanket special for the baby Doc and me never had," Leela-Ma said.

The blanket, made from well-worn blocks of denim, was soft as kitten fur. Leela-Ma had trimmed it out in an ivory satin.

"I'll embroider Rain's initials on it if you like."

"I'd like that very much," I said. Leela-Ma seemed to have aged over the past few months. The folds over her eyes were full. I noticed creases around her smile, and there were even some furrows in her forehead and her eyebrows were graying.

"Leela-Ma," I said, touching her forearm.

"Yes, honey?"

"You would've made a wonderful mother. I'm sorry you never had a baby of your own."

Tears filled Leela-Ma's eyes. Her lips tightened. She swallowed hard and nodded her head in a knowing way. "I appreciate that," she said, bending over to kiss my cheek. "But today's a day of rejoicing. *You* have a beautiful and healthy baby boy for me and Doc to love and enjoy. Now give me that baby back for a minute. I know Doc is eager to hold 'im."

Cuddling my son up close, I sucked in his sweet breath. Zeb and I had decided that whether the baby was a boy or girl, we was going to name it Rain after the water thundering off Horseshoe Ridge, under the shelter of the grandfather chestnut. I hoped naming him Rain would guarantee him a measure of power and protection. What I didn't suspect was how much Rain would be needing such favor.

"Rain is the perfect name," I said. "He smells fresh like the air after a storm." I kissed him on the cheek and handed him back to Leela-Ma.

Leela-Ma barely walked out the bedroom when Zeb come through the front door. I heard him yelling, "I have a boy? A son?"

Zeb knocked gently on the door.

"What's the matter with you?" Burdy said. "This is your bedroom, Zeb. Git your tail in here and see about your wife." She swung the door wide open. "I should've known you'd show up soon as all the work was done." Burdy was trying to act all huffed up, but she was smiling all the same.

"Now, Burdy," Zeb said, "you know good and well if I'd gotten here any earlier you'd have been kicking my hiney outta here."

"Probably so," Burdy said. "But you done denied me that right. So don't go trying to sweet-talk me now that I'm perturbed with you."

Zeb grabbed Burdy into a bear hug as she tried to push on past him. "Well, mad or not, you're still gitting a hug from me. Thanks so much for taking such good care of my wife and son." Zeb kissed her smack on the lips.

"Go on with you now!" Burdy said sternly.

"You don't have to tell me twice. I know better than to try and hang onto a wildcat," Zeb said, giving me a wink.

Burdy shut the door behind her, and Zeb walked acrost the

room and sat down on the bed. "How you feeling?" he asked.

"I'm a little worn out."

"Well you sure don't look it. You're pretty as ever. Prettier than the first day I laid eyes on you." Zeb kissed my hand, my forehead, my eyes, then my lips. "Thank you, honey, for our son. He's beautiful."

"He is, isn't he?"

"A real fine boy. The spittin' image of his momma." Zeb leaned his forehead against mine. "I'm sorry I wasn't here sooner."

"It's aw'right. I know you were working. There wasn't nothing you could do anyway."

"I know, but I hate that I wasn't here for you."

"I had plenty of help. Burdy came over soon as I told her, and she called for Doc and Leela-Ma."

"So what you're telling me is that you didn't really need me? That you're capable of doing this all by yourself? You are stubborn as a mule, Maizee Delight."

"Well, I cain't quite do it *all* by myself," I said, kissing Zeb long and slow.

"You got a middle name picked out?" Zeb asked.

"I'm partial to Zebulon, myself."

"Rain Zebulon? Nah. I was thinking maybe we ought to name him Rain Lawson Hurd."

My heart nearly stopped. If I'd ever had any doubts about the goodness of Zeb's soul, the matter was settled right then. "Why, honey, I think that's a fine, fine name. A perfect name for our perfect son. And it's such a sweet way to honor Doc and Leela-Ma."

Zeb smiled. "Aw'righty, then. It's settled. Unless, of course, you think we ought to name him after Burdy? We could call him Rain Burdy Hurd. It's kinda of catchy, don't cha think?"

"Rain Burdy Hurd? I think it sounds like a hog call."

16

It weren't long after Rain was born that I began to fret about the graves rising from the government lakes. For years, government men had been coming into the valleys and building dams. They'd built one uptown where the Holston joined with the French Broad River.

Them government people knew what would happen when they plugged up the river—they'd flood entire towns—so they came in and offered people money for their land and told 'em to move what dead they could to new cemeteries.

It was plumb awful the way they treated people, making 'em move from the land that held the sweat, blood, and bones of their mothers and fathers, grandmothers and grandfathers, and for some, their daughters and sons. Hundreds of folks had to find themselves a new home, and twice as many of the dead were forced to move.

Burdy said some of her kin's graves upriver never did git moved because the government men said they didn't have to move the bones of Injuns or half-breeds. Burdy figured that's how come when late summer come 'round, some of the gravestones started rising.

"The spirits are angry," Burdy said. "It's disrespectful to drown the dead the way they done."

I don't know what it was about them graves rising up thataway. It ain't like I'd seen any stones poking up from the waters. I hadn't been upriver, but something about the whole situation unnerved me. I got to where I didn't want to be around water a'tall. I didn't want to draw it. Didn't want to bathe in it. Didn't want to do the dishes or the warsh. Didn't want to even drink it. I got to where I could go nearly till noon before I'd take a sip of it, and only then one spoonful at a time.

My mind wasn't working properly. I'd always loved being near the water. I liked the holy silence of still waters and the all-over tingly feeling that bathing in the falls give me. I liked the sweetness of cold water drawn from the well and supped from a tin cup. I liked the power that come with taking a dirty tater or carrot and plunging it into a pan of soapy water and scrubbing it till it was clean as a new soul. And I loved rinsing my hair till it squeaked between my fingers.

Preacher Blount give a message about how we ought to take control of our minds and bring them under obedience, not of the flesh but of the spirit, so I began to pray for deliverance. The voices, they kept telling me that God couldn't hear me, that He wasn't listening. Preacher Blount said to expect fiery arrows from the Devil, and that the only way to be victorious in the battle for the mind was to stand firm on the Word of God.

So whenever I felt afraid, which I did near 'bout all the time, I would pray and read my Bible. Whenever I got to dwelling on those stones rising from the water, I'd turn in my Bible to Psalms 77:

> The waters saw thee, O God,
> the waters saw thee; they were afraid:
> the depths also were troubled.
> The clouds poured out water:
> the skies sent out a sound:
> thine arrows also went abroad.
> The voice of thy thunder was in the heaven:
> the lightnings lightened the world:
> the earth trembled and shook.
> Thy way is in the sea,
> and thy path in the great waters,
> and thy footsteps are not known.

I'd read it over and over again, and begged for God to deliver me, but all that praying didn't do me one lick of good. The only time I'd go near water was to tend after Rain. One Saturday, a month or so after Rain was born, Zeb asked if I wanted to hike up to the falls and go berry picking.

I thought about it long and hard. It was a real pretty day and I hadn't seen the falls in such a long time. The weather hadn't turned yet, so the hickories and oaks were still summer green. But I told Zeb no, maybe we could go tomorrow, after church. "I jes ain't up to a hike today." Then, I laid on the davenport, reading my Bible and praying.

Zeb said he couldn't understand why I wanted to lay around like that, staring off into nothingness the way I done, but he didn't know about the visions I had of sad souls rising up in resurrection clothes soiled from the sludge in them government lakes. Their hair slicked with slime, rotting fish coming out their mouths. Slivers of fish guts seeping from their eyes as they cried out to the Lord. No amount of praying took away the visions of those people.

The dinner hour came and went. I fixed Rain a bottle and give it to him. I'd told Zeb to go on up to the falls without me and he had, with a bucket and a promise to bring home some berries. I put Rain down for his afternoon nap and was about to lie back down myself when I remembered something.

Hitty.

She was made from witchwood, which all the old people, even Burdy, claimed could ward off the evil spirits. Since my prayers seem hindered, for whatever reason, maybe Hitty'd fix things. If she'd been able to keep the *Diana-Kate* from capsizing in that awful storm, the way the book said she had, surely she'd be able to help me weather this storm.

All I had to do was find her. I'd left Hitty at Leela-Ma's when I got married. I hated to wake Rain, but I needed Hitty.

Besides, it was a short walk to Leela-Ma's. Rain could nap when we got back.

"Leela? Leela-Ma!" I said, walking through Leela-Ma's house with Rain tucked up snug against me.

"Back here," she answered. Leela-Ma called to me from her backyard.

I kicked open the screen door and nearly sent Martha's big, black-feathered rump flying. Unbeknownst to me, Martha was up on the porch, clucking at the screen door. That hen always scared me some. She liked to follow me around too closely. Leela-Ma said it was because Martha didn't have no chicks of her own. She'd sit all day long on an empty nest, hoping for an offspring, despite all proof to the contrary. Leela-Ma and Martha was kindred spirits that way. Leela-Ma and Doc treated them chickens and the rooster like family members.

Martha was the boss. Then there was Gloria. As a chick, Gloria's head got caught in the lid of the box that held her and the rest of the chicks. By the time Doc found her stuck, Gloria had the dropsy. She was limp from beak to tailfeathers. Thinking she'd killed the poor thing, Leela-Ma prayed over the chick, and when she opened her eyes—Glory! Halleluiah!—Gloria was holding up her own head and chirping up a storm. Sometimes I wished Leela-Ma had been there to pray over Momma that day I found her in the backyard.

Leela-Ma was standing over a burn barrel, stripping bark off a small hickory.

"Whatcha doin'?"

"Need me a new broom," Leela-Ma said. "Wore my other one clean out." Piece by piece, she split and frayed the ends of the sapling.

"Where's Doc?"

"He's over at the church. Deacons prayer meeting."

"I forgot," I said, shifting Rain from one shoulder to the other.

Leela-Ma put down the hickory and reached for Rain. "Here, pass me that baby," she said. I handed her my son. Rain took a fistful of my hair with him.

"He's gonna snatch me bald one of these days."

"Looks like it," Leela-Ma said, uncurling his tiny fingers from my stringy hair, which hadn't been warshed in I don't know how long. "Where's Zeb?"

"Up at the falls, berry pickin."

"How come you ain't up there with him?" Leela-Ma knew how much I loved Horseshoe Ridge.

"I didn't feel up to going," I said. It wasn't exactly the whole truth, but it weren't a bald-face lie, either.

"Oh," Leela-Ma said. She cuddled Rain and studied on me for a minute or two. "If you don't have time to tend to your hair, maybe I ought to cut it for you."

A soft wind blew down from the mountain. Leaves fluttered over us like the wings of a thousand dragonflies. Leela-Ma's offer was her comment on my unkempt appearance. She was too nice to come right out and tell me I needed a bath. It wasn't like I didn't know it myself. I was the first one to smell me coming. I didn't like it none, but when you're afeared of something, common sense goes right out the window. I figured best jes let her comment pass.

"Leela-Ma, do you remember that whittled doll I brung with me when I come to live with you and Doc?"

She shook her head. "Cain't say that I do. Why?"

"I was wanting to take it back over to the house."

"There might be a box of your belongings in the attic, next to the boxes where Doc keeps his daddy's things. I can have Doc climb up there and git it for you after supper if you like."

"I'd sure appreciate it."

"You got time to come in and sit a spell?"

"No, ma'am. I need to be gitting back home and fixing Zeb some supper."

Leela-Ma kissed the top of Rain's dark head and passed him back to me. "Well, then."

"Tell Doc if he cain't find the box not to worry about it," I said, turning to leave.

"If he finds it, I'll have him bring it over tonight," Leela-Ma said. "And, Maizee, if you change your mind about that haircut, it won't take me longer an hour to fix you up real pretty. Lots of new mommas cut their hair short. It's easier to take care of."

I smiled and give Leela-Ma a kiss on the cheek. "Yes, ma'am."

Doc knocked on the door soon as I'd gotten the table cleared.

"I ain't interrupting supper am I?" Doc asked. He was holding a box under his left arm.

"No, sir," Zeb said, greeting him. "C'mon on in. We're finished. Here, let me take that." Doc passed the box over to Zeb, who sat it down on the floor by the davenport.

"Leela said you was needing this box of your things, Maizee."

"I appreciate you carrying it all the way over here, Doc, but you didn't have to do that. I could've come back up to the house to git it."

"It weren't no problem," he said, taking out a handkerchief and wiping his upper lip. "I hope it's got what you were looking for."

Hitty was wrapped in an embroidered pillowcase and stuck at the bottom of the box. I couldn't remember exactly when I'd packed her away, but I believe it was the same year Kade Mashburn kissed me. I remembered that because I figured any girl old enough to be kissed was too old to be fooling with dolls anymore.

"What is that?" Zeb asked when I slipped Hitty from the pillowcase.

"A wooden doll."

"Where'd you git her?"

"I had a girlfriend, Eudie, from when I went to school uptown. Her brother made us both one the year Momma died."

Hitty didn't look any worse for the wear. Her blue dress was a little faded and she smelled musty, but there wasn't a drawn-on hair out of place. Her book, the one I'd borrowed from the school library, was stuffed in a corner of the box, underneath the pillowcase. I never had taken it back to the school. I opened it up to the middle, the part where Amos said, "I sware that doll acts plumb witched to me."

Zeb took Hitty from my hands and turned her over in his. "I can make you a real nice doll, if you like."

"No," I said. "I don't want another doll. This one is special."

"Special in what way?" Zeb asked.

"She's carved from witchwood—mountain ash," I replied.

"I'll make you one from hickory or pine, or even chestnut. I'll even make you one with legs and arms that move."

"I done told you I don't want another doll, Zeb. The old people say that witchwood wards off evil spirits." I yanked Hitty back from Zeb and held her up against my heart, as if she was some sort of protective armor.

17

Leela-Ma

After Zeb and Maizee married, they moved into a rental acrost River Road and up the corner from the church. The house sat out behind the Widow Luttrell's place. Zeb got the rent forgive because he helped the Widow Luttrell out around the farm. He kept the grass mowed, pruned the trees back, fed the hogs and butchered them.

Truth be told, I've never cared much for the Widow Luttrell. Burdy Luttrell is a contrary woman. She has the markings of darkie and probably would pass for one if not for her eyes. They're the color of opals, an unusual greenish-blue, even for a white woman, which Burdy definitely is not. She's a half-bred, part Cherokee, part colored, part Portyghee. She come from that Melungeon clan from over Newman's Ridge.

She climbs these hills this time every year, and again in the spring, scouring the earth for roots, mushrooms, and berries, and Lord knows what else. There's talk that she uses these things to help the people she likes and hex those she don't. Whenever Sheriff Duncan finds a couple of dead cattle or deer with their hearts and innards cut out, which he comes acrost at least once a year, rumors fly that it's Burdy Luttrell doing the slaughtering. It's not of me to repeat these things, so I held my tongue and my fears when Zeb moved Maizee to that house on Burdy's land.

It was a smallish place, but nice enough. There was a sitting room big enough for a couple of rockers, a bedroom off of that, and a kitchen. The kitchen was as big as the bedroom and sitting room combined. They heated the place with a coal stove, and

Maizee cooked on a wood stove. The outhouse sat to the far right and back beyond the house. A good piece to walk at dark.

Doc counted the talk about Widow Luttrell as pure nonsense. He was good friends with Burdy's husband, Tibbis. They'd grown up together, gotten into all sorts of foolishness when they was young, hunted together, butchered together, and went to church together. Sometimes Burdy would come with Tibbis to church, but she didn't start until their daughter, Wheedin, got to be of learning age.

Like Doc, Burdy has healing powers, but devoted folk won't call her for help. They're scared of her witch doctoring because it's rumored her gift was bestowed upon her by her dead ancestors, whereas Doc received his anointing from Jesus the day he got saved. What these folks don't know is that Doc often seeks Burdy's advice on ways to treat the ailing. She's wise about the roots and cures.

18

Burdy Luttrell

Maizee was in good spirits after I warshed and braided her hair and sent her home with a belly full of biscuits and apple butter. But I suspected that wasn't the end of the matter, and it turns out I was right. I hate it when I'm right about all the wrong things.

Weren't long after Rain was born, maybe five or six weeks, Zeb pounded at my back door near 'bout midnight. Grabbing a housedress from where I'd flung it over the bedpost, I pulled it on, snapped it shut, and called out, "Hold on! I'm a'coming!"

Zeb was breathing hard, like he'd run clear to the Holston Crossing and back again. "I'm sorry to bother you so late, Burdy, but something's bad wrong with Maizee," he said between pants. "Can you come see about her?"

"Calm down, Zeb, and tell me what's wrong." I needed time to clear my head.

Zeb rubbed his forehead in that way men do when they're facing something they cain't wrap their mind around. He looked like he'd jes come in off the fields. He had on his work boots, jeans, and blue work shirt. He smelled of mown hay.

"Maizee ain't been sleeping good," he said.

"That ain't unusual for a new mother," I replied.

"I know, I know," he added. "But, Burdy, it isn't that she ain't sleeping good. Maizee ain't slept one wink in the past three nights. She walks the floor between the bedroom and living room all night long. When she ain't pacing, she's staring. Jes standing and staring at Rain in his bed."

Zeb leaned up against the wood stove, bracing himself in case the earth cracked and rumbled, I reckon.

"When I got home tonight, Maizee was holding Rain and pacing," he said. "I tried to take the baby, to git her to sit down and rest, but Maizee clutched him so tight I thought she might squeeze the life right outta him. She's sulled up. Ain't said one word all night long."

Zeb's hazel eyes were fogged with worry. His jaw clenched tight as a bear trap.

"Worst of all, she seems bewitched," he said. "I cain't describe it good, but she's got this quare look, like somebody took an eraser and wiped her clean of any remembrances. Like maybe Maizee's gone off somewhere and a haint took up house inside her."

I didn't make mention of it, but Zeb looked like he was on the tail end of misery hisself.

"Let me grab my pouch," I said. "I believe I got something that'll help."

I stored all my healing powders and roots in mason jars on a shelf in the back of the pantry. The cool, dry air helped keep the medicines fresh. I took care to tape labels to each jar so I didn't git 'em mixed up. I searched for whippoorwill's shoes or lady's slipper as some call it. I found it without much trouble, and placed some of it in the beaded pouch Ma gave me shortly before she died. I also grabbed a jar of the monkey rum distilled from sorghum cane.

"Here," I said, handing the jar to Zeb, "take a swig of this. It'll help settle you."

Zeb didn't argy with me. He took the jar, unscrewed the lid in a twist, and chugged down a quarter of it in one gulp. He put the lid back on and offered it back to me.

"You keep it," I said. "You might be needing it when I ain't around."

"Thank ya, ma'am," he said as he stepped outside and held open the screen door for me.

We walked acrost the yard in silence. The katydids were making a racket, like toddlers banging on pans with spoons. Yellow light poured like bottled sunshine from the sitting room. I seen Maizee's shadow pass over the front porch. Zeb took the steps in one stride. I followed in three. He pushed open the screen door for me.

Having somebody walk into the house at midnight would startle most, but Maizee didn't flinch, or even turn her head. She jes kept pacing and patting Rain, the way a momma would a colicky child. Only Rain wasn't the least bit fussy. He never cried. Maizee never give 'im a chance.

I knowed better than to try and approach her too quickly. That'd be like trying to corner a scared cat. They're either going to tear you up or tear up your house. It's much better if they come to you for comfort.

So I sat down on the edge of the davenport. Zeb shut the door and leaned easy up against it. Maizee turned on her bare feet and walked into their bedroom. I looked at Zeb. He shrugged his shoulders as if to say, "See what I told ya?" The house smelled of turnip greens and cornbread, the leftovers of which were sitting out on the kitchen counter.

Maizee came straight back seconds later, patting Rain, muttering something. I tuned my ear to hear her. She was singing softly: "Sin stains are lost in its life-giving flows. There's wonderful power in the blood." Then, quick as a rabbit, she turned on her heels and strode back into the bedroom, repeating the chorus as she went.

"Mind if I heat up some water?" I asked Zeb. "I aim to make Maizee some tea." I rose from the davenport and headed for the kitchen.

"Give me a minute to git a fire going," Zeb said, grabbing a couple of kindling sticks from a box sitting next to the dinette table.

I feared Maizee would walk the pads off her feet before I managed to git her cure made. Zeb fussed with the fire, while I grated some of the root. When the water was hot, I poured it over the root and let it steep. Then I poured in a smidge of the monkey rum.

"You outta try and take Rain again," I told Zeb.

"Aw'right," he said. Zeb waited till Maizee was at the far end of the sitting room and then he stood right in her path. Maizee stopped walking and singing.

Zeb didn't say anything as he reached out and lifted Rain off Maizee's shoulder.

"Come over here and sit down, honey," I said, taking Maizee by the elbow and leading her to the table, where I'd set the cup of steaming tonic.

Maizee looked hard on me, anger popping like bacon grease behind her dark eyes. Jerking her elbow away, she hauled off and—WHAP!—slapped me. My left cheek smarted something fierce.

"*Maizee!*" Zeb shouted. "What the hell is wrong with you?"

"Don't yell at her, son," I said. Taking hold of Maizee's shoulders, I said calmly, "It's okay, honey. I know you're scared. Everything is aw'right."

"Burdy?" Maizee whispered, sounding as surprised as if she'd jes woken from an afternoon nap to find company come to visit and no supper ready. She clasped her hands together. Taking them, I folded mine over hers and said, "Come, sit down at the table. I made you some tea."

"That's so sweet. You're so good to me, Burdy," Maizee said. She walked over to the table, sat down, and started drinking her tea. "I'm so thankful to have you and Zeb watching after me. How'd I git so blessed?"

Maizee didn't appear to have any recollection of having slapped me only moments before. And she didn't seem the least bit bothered about entertaining company at such a late hour. She didn't appear to have any idea what day it was, much less the time. Zeb stood behind her, cradling Rain, and shaking his head from side to side in a disbelieving way.

"It ain't a hard job," I said. "You're a pleasing soul." I flashed Zeb a wry grin.

"Burdy's right," Zeb added. "Loving you is as easy as tending after this here baby. You're such a good momma, he's never give us a moment's trouble."

Seems downright clear, looking back on it now, but at the time didn't none of us know that the reason Maizee was such a restless soul was because she lived in fear of displeasing voices only she could hear.

19

Nothing about Rain's birth had give any of us cause for alarm. It'd been as routine as a Sunday morning church service. He was born on the first day in August, a day so hot the flies didn't bother moving. They sat contented on the porch railing, waiting for the evening cool, which is the blessing of living in the shadow of mountains.

Not long after dinner, I'd walked out the dirt drive to collect the mail from the box when I heared Maizee calling to me from her porch.

"Burdy! Hey, Burdy!" She was waving me over, her belly clinging to her scrawny frame like a hive on a sapling.

I gave her a half-wave to let her know I'd heard her. When I got inbetwixt her place and mine, she said, "My water's broke."

"You sure?"

"Yes, ma'am."

"You having any pains?"

"Some but they ain't the bad hurting sort."

"Well, that'll change soon enough. Go on inside and lie down. You cain't be standing around, leastwise the baby's cord could git all tangled up. I'll grab my doctoring tote and be up directly."

"Yes, ma'am," Maizee said, turning to go back into the house.

"Did you call over to Mosely's for Zeb?" I asked.

"Not yet. Think I ought to?"

"I'll see to it. Go on now. Lie down."

When I rung up to Ida's place, she said the tractor broke down and Shug and Zeb had taken off for Rogersville to pick up a part. I told her to send Zeb on home when he got back, and I asked her to send somebody over to fetch Doc and Leela.

By the time the Lawsons arrived, Maizee's pains were bearing down on her.

"How's she doin'?" Doc asked, poking his head around the bedroom door.

"Won't be long now I don't reckon," I said.

"Lemme know if you need any help."

"Aw'right."

Lifting her head from the pillow, Maizee gave her uncle a brief but reassuring smile.

"You're doing good work there, honey," he said. Then Doc shut the door and left us to it.

It was dusk when Zeb finally burst through the front door, hollering, "I'm sorry! I'm sorry!"

Leela walked out of the bedroom carrying the baby she'd jes warshed and dusted. "If you'd waited thirty more minutes, I mighta run off with this here boy," she said.

"A boy? I got me a boy?" Zeb ran a hand acrost his cheek. The reddish stubble made a sandpapery sound. His dark eyes were bright, like a burn barrel lit up.

"Yep. And, far as I can tell, he's got all the necessary equipment in working order," Doc said.

A glaze of bright, eye-squinting snow shellacked the mountains and the fields when the fever lit upon Rain. Zeb came for me early, told me Rain been squalling since daybreak.

Maizee fussed with him, but truth was she couldn't tolerate Rain bawling. She'd do near about anything to keep him from it. And if she couldn't stop 'im, she'd chime in. I'd never met a momma who cried as much as Maizee. She wept buckets after Rain's birth. We all thought she was suffering a bad case of the mulligrubs, and hoped, prayed, they'd ease right soon, but Rain passed the halfway mark on his first year and Maizee's blues hadn't eased up nary a bit.

Rain was sprawled between quilts and feather pillows on his papa's bed, red-cheeked and snotty-nosed. Despite the fire sizzling in the coal stove in the other room, shaves of ice coated the inside corners of the bedroom window. Maizee had pulled up a ladder-back chair next to the bed. She was rubbing Rain's belly with one hand, singing a hymn softly. Her dark hair tumbled willy-nilly over the pink chenille robe she was wearing.

With the other hand, she picked at her temple scab. The sore appeared the week after Rain was born, and Maizee picked at it so much, it had nearly doubled in size. All the hair there was worn clean off, leaving behind a bald spot as big as a half-dollar. Zeb called it her worry spot. I'd given her a tonic made from the leaves of Joe Pye weed, but it hadn't seemed to take effect. Elsewise she wasn't using it. She was skittish as a cornered cat.

I didn't want to alarm Zeb or Maizee, but I seen the rash on Rain's cheeks from acrost the room.

"When'd you last feed him?" I asked, glancing at Maizee.

"Last night."

"He drunk anything since?"

"No, ma'am."

Pulling the covers back from Rain, I felt his chubby arms and legs. They were hot as tater cakes, but there was no sign of the rash moving...yet.

"Put some vinegar in a pan of warm water and bring it to me. And bring me a warshcloth too," I told Zeb.

"Yes, ma'am."

The sharp stink of pickles and sauerkraut rose from the pot Zeb carried into the bedroom. Maizee picked up her chair and toted it to the sitting room. She had growed a dread of water since birthing Rain. If that child messed himself, Maizee would fuss over him till he was clean as a boiled egg, but he was the only reason she'd go near water. The potatoes and carrots she dug from the garden sat on the kitchen counter till Zeb got around to cleaning 'em. She give up bathing, too. Maizee wouldn't even take a whore bath.

An unnatural fear of dying snagged Maizee shortly after Rain was born. If she needed a drink, she wouldn't take more than a spoonful at a time. I ain't a'kidding about that. She'd take a spoon from the drawer and dip it into the water bucket, one swallow at a time, till she was quenched. It might take her a half hour on a hot day. I didn't see how she had the patience for such foolishness.

But the one time I drummed up enough gumption to ask her how come she didn't drink straight from the dipper like everybody else, she give me a stare like I was barking at the moon in broad daylight. Then she cut her eyes sidelong at me and said, "I know what you're up to, Burdy Luttrell, and I ain't the crazy one."

I wanted to tell her she sure was putting on a good show of it if she weren't, but I didn't say nothing. I could see she was agitated enough. There's no point pissing in the wind.

Maizee wasn't drinking enough to keep her own self sobby, much less feed a growing baby. When Rain was first born, milk oozed from Maizee's ripe breasts, soaking through the rags we folded and placed between her nipples and her bra. But not long afterwards, her milk clabbered, and her nipples shrunk and wrinkled like dried muscadines. Rain was bottle-fed from then on.

Rain whimpered as I warshed his forehead, neck, arms, chest, and legs. His diaper was dry as a bone. A sure sign he was in a bad way.

"You got more water on the stove?" I asked Zeb.

"I believe there's some left in the kettle, but it ain't hot," he said. "I can git it hotter if you're needing it."

"Come over here and hold this warshcloth over Rain's chest," I said. "I'm gonna fix him a bottle."

I poured the barely warm water into a glass and added some shavings from Life Everlasting flower and a dollop of molasses. When it turned the color of weak tea, I poured it into a bottle.

I scooped up Rain and sat on the edge of the bed.

"Hey darlin'," I said. Rain's milky eyes were open but they weren't focused.

I put the nipple up to his mouth, but he turned away.

Shifting him in my arms, I held his head so he couldn't turn it so easily. Then I tried again, but Rain wasn't having none of it. His tongue was puffy and red as a June berry. I put a finger to it. It was ember hot. Rain let out a painful holler. Bloody pus seeped from a rising in Rain's right ear.

Zeb stood in the doorway, one eye on his boy, the other on Maizee.

"Go outside and scoop me up a bowlful of snow," I said. "Don't git me any of that soiled snow. Git the whitest, freshest stuff you can find. The kind we use to make snow cream."

"Aw'right," Zeb said. "But I don't think he's gonna want any snow cream."

"Go on," I said. "And hurry up. I ain't got all day."

Zeb grabbed a pan and headed out the door.

The rash was tracing its way south, down Rain's neck, onto his chest. His legs and arms were showing signs of it. It wouldn't be long 'fore his whole body was ailing with the fever. His hair was clumped and wet. His heart thumped wildly, like a claw hammer in the hands of an angry man.

I pulled Rain's nightshirt up over his head, and tossed it in a corner. I seen the welts circling under his arms and the inside of his thighs.

Zeb come back in with the snow. I took a smidge of it and put it on Rain's tongue. It soothed him some. So I took another dip and give it to him.

From the other room, I could hear Maizee humming the same tune over and over: "'Tis so sweet to trust in Jesus. Jes to take him at his word. Jesus, Jesus, Precious Jesus, oh for grace to trust him more."

I didn't care what she hummed and prayed so long as she kept out of my way.

"Here, help me," I said, motioning for Zeb to saddle up next to the bed. I put Rain down in the middle of it.

"Take some and rub it over him like so," I said, gently easing the iced snow acrost Rain's left thigh.

"Like this?" Zeb asked, lightly rubbing snow acrost the other leg.

"Yep. Jes like that."

Zeb seen the welts, the rash spreading like richweed.

"It looks like something's burning my boy," he said.

"Yes, there is," I said. "Scarlet fever."

20

Rain's fever raged hot for three days before it eased off, leaving his heart strong, but we had the lasting thought that we were missing something.

After the dogwoods bloomed out, late like everything else that year, whatever was ailing Maizee cowered away some. She went back to drinking water from the dipper and taking regular baths. She kept her hair brushed, and she laughed again, loud as ever.

On Easter Sunday, the church was so full you'd have thunk God had put out a "last call for repentance" warning. I reckon most folks there didn't know Preacher Blount give out the same sort of message every Sunday.

Zeb, Maizee, and Rain squeezed in the seat next to me 'cause there wasn't room left in any of the other pews. Leela was up front, sitting in the alto section of the choir loft. Doc was standing at the back of the church with the rest of the deacons.

"What are all these sinners doing in church?" Maizee asked. She was wearing a pretty dotted swiss dress, pale pink. Leela made it for her.

"Beats me," I said.

"Well, I wish if they were going to show up on Easter they'd eat less at Christmas," Maizee whispered, scooching her hip up next to mine, and wiggling it some.

"Yeah, well, if bullfrogs had wings they wouldn't be bumping their asses on the ground all the time."

Maizee threw back her head and laughed so hard that Leela shot her the stink-eye from the choir loft and Zeb give it to me from the end of the pew. But I didn't care. I didn't feel the least bit guilty about using foul language, even in God's house. It was good to hear Maizee's throaty laughter again. It had been such a long, troubling winter.

On Rain's first birthday, Doc and Leela invited nearly everyone from Christian Bend up to their place for the afternoon. Shug and Ida Mosely brought Gentle Jo along, to give pony rides to all the kids. Doc, Zeb, and some other fellows were busy barbecuing one of them hogs Doc and Zeb butchered late last fall after a hoarfrost numbed the mountain. Leela shucked a crate of corn and made one of her four-layer coconut cakes. Embry Mae showed up with a bowl of potato salad and a sack full of birthday hats fashioned from newspapers and string. She tied one on everybody's head, including Preacher Blount and Sheriff Duncan.

Rain was running around, chasing after Leela's hens and the Blount children. But when he run up next to the pit where Zeb and Doc were barbecuing, Leela screamed, "RAIN! GIT AWAY FROM THERE!" Everybody but Rain stopped right where they was and what they was doing. Everyone but Rain, who continued running headlong toward the open pit.

We all held our breath as Zeb bent over, grabbed his boy, and hoisted him away from the flames. Rain wiggled out of his daddy's arms and took off running in the other direction, toward the apple orchard.

"Lawd o' mercy!" Ida said. She left Gentle Jo with Shug and walked over to help Leela, who was setting out dishes on a board that served as the picnic table.

"That boy acted like he hadn't heard a word you said," Ida said. Her tone was punishing, and her advice was meant to be too. "Maizee better figure out how to make that young'un listen to his elders, or she's gonna have hell to pay one day."

Leela was reeling so much from the thought of Rain running into that pit that she didn't know how to answer Ida.

Besides, Leela would never offend a guest by challenging them; she was much too mannerly for that.

Not me, though. I could think of plenty of things to say to Ida Mosely in that moment, such as "You're one to talk, given those two hellions of yourn." But, out of respect for Leela, I held my tongue and reached for a large spoon. Then I picked up one of Leela's coffee cups and headed out for the orchard.

"I'll be back."

"Burdy, what are you up to now?" Embry Mae asked, walking in step beside me.

"Not sure jes yet."

"Burdy Luttrell, you are up to something," Embry said. "And I am not going to stand by and let you hex Ida Mosely over that loose mouth of hers."

"Aw shit, Embry. Don't tell me you believe in all that witchfoolery talk about me."

"I certainly do. I know good and well anybody can cure folks the way you do can make 'em sickly, too."

We walked past the pit where the menfolk were standing about. All except Shug, who was leading one young'un after the other on Gentle Jo up and down the dirt drive to River Road. The smoky, sweet smell of pig roasting settled over our hair and clothing.

"Parfume of the Israelites," Embry said.

"Nah," I said. "God's a lamb man. He don't eat pig."

"You reckon he's a Yankee?"

"Might as well be."

We found Rain sitting in the orchard, gnawing on a green apple, a banty hen pecking the ground around his feet.

He looked up and gave us one of his eight-tooth grins. Any boy as pretty as Rain should've been a girl. His dark eyelashes were so long they touched the arc in his brows. Maizee couldn't bring herself to cut his hair, so it fell in soft curls over his ears. His cheeks were full and pink as the petals of wild azaleas.

Kneeling beside him, I took the spoon and rattled it around inside the cup next to his left ear, soft at first, then hard. Rain went right back to gnawing on his apple. He didn't try to reach up and grab the spoon or the cup. I moved around to his right side and did it again. The racket didn't seem to bother him none. He didn't pay it any never mind at all.

I glanced up at Embry. She seen what I seen.

Leaning over, I whispered Embry's name into Rain's ear. Nothing. I said it louder. Then louder yet, till I was practically shouting it. But he didn't turn his head or nothing. Bless his heart, Rain had managed to notch his teeth into the hard fruit, but he'd barely broke the apple's green skin.

"He's going cross-eyed trying to eat that dern thang," I said.

"I see that," Embry said. "You think he's deaf?"

"Sure looks that way. Go over by that tree and call out his name."

Embry paced off five or six feet, turned and called, "RAIN! RAIN!"

He studied her as she walked off, but soon as Embry started yelling his name, Rain went right back to chomping on his apple.

"Should I yell louder?" she asked.

"Wouldn't do no good," I answered. "I don't think he can hear a lick."

"How's he been gitting by all this time?"

"Probably taking clues from his momma. She ain't hardly left him be since he had that fever. He's a hip baby. I'm surprised he can walk much as she carries him around."

"How you gonna tell her and Zeb their boy cain't hear?"

"I dunno," I said, rising to my feet, dusting grass and leaves from my knees and butt.

I started to reach down and pick up Rain, when something glistening up against the tree in the far corner caught my eye.

"Wait right there," I told Embry Mae.

"What for?"

"I gotta see 'bout somethin'."

The afternoon sun yawned away from the treetops, yanking black shadows acrost the cool dirt. Bright green fruit lugged tree branches downward, like bobbers trying to git a steady hold on the surface separating heaven from earth. Apple harvest was at least another four weeks away, but I caught me a scent of cinnamon and butter crust baking.

I eyed a sheet of silver webbing stretched out acrost the grass about a foot wide. I knew it to be the work of a bowl-and-doily spider. Their hammocks are common in the fields where goldenrods grow thick and pines grow thin.

Auntie Tay was the first to show me how the spider threads its silk into bowls big enough to hold a melon after Hota and me come upon several silver webs down by the barn late one summer when we was kids.

"Look there," Auntie Tay had said, pointing at a crocheted web. "See that?"

"What is it?" I asked.

"A bowl-and-doily spider," Tay said. "She's weaved herself a bowl and a lace doily to set it on."

Sure enough, directly under each glimmering web was a woven silk hanky.

"Come closer," Auntie Tay said. She was standing directly over top the black lady's hideout.

"Where's the spider? Where is she?" Hota asked. He was practically standing on his momma's feet.

"Be careful, you don't want to bump her home."

I snuggled up next to Auntie Tay's hip. I wanted to see, but I didn't want to git too close. I weren't sure if this spider was the friendly sort or not. I didn't know how it'd take to people poking around in its home.

"She's waiting for something to git stuck there," Tay said. "See?"

"She's upside down," Hota said.

"That's so she can git at her food quicker."

"What's she eat?" Hota asked.

"A gnat, maybe a fly," Tay answered. "She'll kill it and eat it or wrap it up for supper later."

The spider was so small my young eyes had a hard time sighting it.

Now, stooped next to the large hammock in Leela's orchard and relying on aged eyes, it felt like I was trying to find a black-eyed pea in a bin of sugar.

A wick of sharp pain flared up my neck and exploded in my head. A bright light flashed milky blue then white. I shut my eyes, rattled my head. The pain stopped. I looked blinkingly at the web again.

That's when I seen it—the message in the spider's under-belly—"MC." The revelation didn't come to me right then. It came upon me slowly, after much pondering of the matter. But when it finally did, the understanding of it all was the same as when chosen folks decipher the praying tongues of others—the truth of it was clear. Still, I couldn't do pea squat about it or Rain's deafness, neither.

Most of the time, the gift of knowing can be about as useful as skunk scent—it gives off a powerful warning, but that's it. Folks got to figure out for themselves if they're going to heed the warning or not.

I started praying right then and there for wisdom for the dark days ahead. It turned out Maizee was in need of more prayers than I could muster.

21

Maizee

I never knew for sure if it was Hitty that chased 'em off or the pleading I done with God, but that following spring, when the wild dogwoods bloomed pink and white, the voices stopped all their ugly chattering, and life returned to the way it had been before they came. I was thankful for it.

Zeb never made mention of my odd ways, never made me shamed for not bathing, for talking out of my head. But I think we both worried in silence about what would happen if I got pregnant again. Would it git worse next time?

Spring had long been one of my favorite times of year, even after Momma dropped dead under the lilacs. It's an eager time. Wobbly-legged calves chasing after heavy udders. Golden daffodils marching one by one under the morning sun. Everybody seems to be anticipating something—company coming or Gabriel's trumpet.

Me and Zeb were jes eager to see an end to the long winter. Rain had been so sickly. A bad fever had come upon him and he liked to have died, but Burdy saved him with some of her roots and her healing powers.

By Easter, Rain was crawling, and by the first day of summer he was walking on his own, with legs steady as a mountain goat's. He was a climber. He'd climb up the back of the davenport, or the kitchen chairs. One time after Sunday services, Rain climbed up the altar, then into Preacher's chair, and stood there pointing and jabbering like he was giving a sermon.

Me and Zeb thought he hung the moon, 'course, but it seemed to us that nearly everyone in Christian Bend felt the same way 'bout Rain. Folks were all the time offering to keep him, although the only ones we ever left him with was Leela-Ma, Doc, or Burdy.

Once Rain got able enough to run, he'd chase after Zeb whenever he went. Rain did not like seeing his daddy go off. Zeb had quit working for Shug and was working upriver at the sawmill. I know Zeb didn't like seeing the timber cut from the woods he'd loved so well, but he said he had a family to care for now and the mill was paying a buck-fifty a day.

Zeb would come home bone-weary, but he'd muster up the energy to take Rain fishing up at Haw Lake, or hiking up to the meadow. Oftentimes after supper, Zeb would spread a blanket out on the lawn and sit with Rain, rolling a ball back and forth between them while I cleaned the dishes. I'd watch 'em from the window over the sink. As soon as I was done, I'd go out and join 'em. Zeb was all the time talking and wishing, wishing and talking. He wanted in the worst way to build his own home.

"I've always wanted a house made from river stone," he said one evening as we were sitting watching Rain run barefoot through the clover. "Would you like that?"

"Could I have a room for sewing and reading?"

"Sure."

"And a window that stretches from the floor to the ceiling in our bedroom?"

"Well, I don't know about that. I don't want all the neighbors looking in on us," Zeb said, giving me one of his pie-eating grins. He was laying with his head in my lap, chewing on a blade of grass.

"Okay," I said, running the back of my hand over the rough stubble on his cheek. "How about the living room? Can we have a big window there and a stone fireplace?"

"Whoa, Nellie," Zeb said. "Where'd you come up with that champagne taste of yours? Remember we're on a beer allowance."

Shortly after that evening, Zeb talked Shug into promising us five acres of land over near Haw Lake. The deal was we wouldn't build nothing on it till it was all paid for. By December, Zeb had managed to give Shug a down payment.

We didn't git much news on the mountain, except what somebody else brung in. Few folks had radios. Burdy owned one of the only ones in Christian Bend. After she heared about the Japs dropping them bombs on Pearl Harbor, she run over to the house and told me and Zeb.

The next day everybody on the mountain was talking about it. On Thursday the news came that Sheriff Duncan's boy Matt, the one that married Charma Morris, had been onboard the *USS West Virginia* when bombs hit it. Matt was alive but badly burned, and in need of a lot of prayers, and maybe a miracle or two.

When we got the news about Matt Duncan, I believe that's when Zeb decided he was going to join up. I knew there was no use in arguing with him about it. Leela-Ma always said a man's got to do what a man's got to do. Besides, Zeb didn't tell us what he'd done till after he'd gone and done it. I was thankful at least that he wouldn't be leaving me and Rain till after Christmas.

Money had always been scarce on the mountain. Most everything we had we grew, made ourselves, or traded somebody else for it. Burdy hated canning, so I'd traded her twelve quarts of beans for Tibbis's bone-handled pocketknife. I felt awful, her giving away something so personal like that, but Burdy insisted. She said it weren't of any use to Tibbis no more, and that it had been more for decoration than for use anyhow. She had her a good knife, and she pulled it from her apron pocket to show me. "Got it from my daddy," Burdy said. "It's not as purty as the one Tibbis carried, but you can see for yourself it's been well-abused." I figured if I hadn't given the knife to Zeb, Burdy would've.

I kept it hidden in a sock in my dresser till Christmas morn. Rising up before light to fix breakfast, I tossed a couple of sticks of wood in the stove and let it heat up while I made biscuits. As I worked, I could hear the steady swell of Zeb and Rain's breathing. If it hadn't been for Rain's breath being more shallow than his daddy's, it would've sounded like one fellow sleeping instead of two. Most nights Rain slept curled up between me and Zeb. Sometimes, after he fell asleep, we'd move him to the davenport so we could have the bed to ourselves.

While the biscuits cooked, I set the table with the Blue Willow dishes and some red napkins. I sprinkled a pinch or two of flour over a bowl of pinecones and put it in the center of the table. They looked like I'd carried them in from a snow. I took the knife, still wrapped in the sock, and put it on Zeb's plate. Then I scrambled up the eggs Leela-Ma had given me and made some milk gravy.

Soon as I got everything nearly ready, I stood in the doorway to our bedroom and sang out, "Merry Christmas sleepy heads! Wake up!" Zeb rubbed his eyes and smiled at me, but Rain didn't stir at all. The fever that nearly robbed him of his life had left him hard of hearing. Shortly after Rain's first birthday, Burdy said she feared he couldn't hear a thing, but I didn't believe it. Jes because Rain didn't talk didn't mean he couldn't hear. He seemed to understand me fine, long as I was speaking directly at him.

I didn't know then that others can see things about our children that our brains refuse to consider. Things too awful to mention in daylight, because even if children fall deaf, demons never do. They are always lurking around, waiting for us to speak the wrong thing, to give them permission to pounce. I wasn't about to be the one to give some demon the word.

Zeb left Rain sleeping, yanked on his breeches and pulled on a shirt. I was gitting a jar of jam from the cupboard when Zeb wrapped his arms around my waist and snuggled up to me from behind. Burrowing his head up against mine, he said, "Merry Christmas, Maizee Delight, Child of Light."

I turned around and hugged him tight. "Morning, Mr. Hurd." Zeb pressed his lips to mine and kissed me warmly. Zeb had soft, full lips and searching hands that could make my belly flop.

"It looks like the angels have been kissing you already this morning," he said, running one hand down the curve of my spine and wiping a smidge of flour from my cheek with the other.

"You want your present now or later?" I asked.

"Depends on what it is," Zeb said, giving my backside a quick squeeze.

"Go on, sit down, 'fore this food grows cold."

Zeb picked up the sock before he pulled out his chair.

"Is this my sock full of coal?"

"Might be."

Reaching into the sock, Zeb pulled out the bone-handled pocketknife. He turned it over in his palm, flicked open one of three silver blades as his jaw went slack. "Gawd, Maizee. This is a dandy knife."

"Do you like it?" I knew he'd love it, but I longed to hear him say it again.

"I think it's the finest knife I've ever held," he said. "Where did you find it?"

"Burdy," I said. "It used to belong to Tibbis. I traded her some beans for it."

Zeb held the knife up to his face and studied his reflection in the blade. He run his thumb over the sharp edge.

"She said Tibbis didn't use it much. She weren't sure where he come acrost it. But I think if I hadn't give it to you, she would've give it to you herself. Burdy said you'd be needing this when you go off to Georgia."

Soon as I mentioned his leaving, I wished I hadn't. A hardness came over Zeb's brown eyes. Last week word come to the mountain that Matt Duncan was doing poorly. He was battling some infection. We didn't speak any more of Zeb's leaving that day, but the knowing of it weighed on us like guilt on a saint.

Zeb left for basic training in Fort Benning, Georgia, the second day of January 1942, a Friday. On the third day of the new year, it snowed on the mountain. I got up, put another couple of pieces of wood in the stove, and checked the thermometer. It was twenty-eight degrees outside. I crawled back under the covers and snuggled up next to Rain.

I had not cried a drop when Zeb said good-bye.

Silence is the only way I knowed to handle hard things. Me and Zeb spent our last night together, sitting on the davenport, listening to the wood crackle in the stove, not saying nothing. I cain't say what Zeb was thinking, but I kept pondering on that day when Mr. Drennan, the ferry master, took me away from my daddy and brung me to Christian Bend. I never did return to the house where Momma raised me, and I only saw my daddy once after that.

Daddy showed up at Doc and Leela-Ma's one afternoon in late June, the second summer I lived at Christian Bend. I was in the garden, hoeing weeds, when I heard the crunching of boots on dry dirt and rocks. We hadn't had a rain since May. Soon as I

126

seen him, I knowed it was Daddy. I dropped the hoe between the tomatoes and case beans, and run into the house. Leela-Ma leaned over the table, cutting fabric. Startled by the door slamming behind me, she looked up.

"What's wrong with you?" she asked. "You look as though you've seen last-day locust swarming."

"I have. Daddy's coming up the road." I broke into a nervous sweat all up underneath my arms and on the bottoms of my feet.

"Mercy sakes," Leela-Ma said, putting her pinking shears aside. "That ain't nothing to git all worked up over."

I would never talk back, but it was clear Leela-Ma didn't understand. My momma wasn't cold in the ground before Daddy decided to git rid of me. I hadn't seen hide nor hair of him for over a year, and now he comes trodding up the road pretty-as-you-please. I had plenty to git worked up over. What if he was coming to carry me back to town?

I should've known better. Daddy didn't want me to come back home, which was fine with me, since I had no intentions of leaving Christian Bend even if he did. He come by to tell us he was leaving, and to bring me some of Momma's things.

"I thought Maizee might like to have these," he said, passing a poke to Leela-Ma. "I ain't got no use for them."

I was standing inside the door, no more than a screen separating us.

"Maizee, ain't you gonna come outside and speak to your daddy?" Leela-Ma asked.

"Aw, she don't have to if she don't want," Daddy said.

Opening the screen, I sidled up next to Leela-Ma. Daddy studied me.

"I believe you've grown a foot," he said.

"Yes, sir."

"You've not give your aunt and uncle any trouble, have you?"

I shook my head.

"She's been a big help to me," Leela-Ma said. "He'ps me in the garden and the kitchen. Does whatever she's asked, and is always so polite. Nan would be proud."

When Leela-Ma mentioned Momma's name, Daddy bit down hard. I seen his jaw flinch.

"Well," he said. "That's good to hear. I'm glad she ain't been no trouble." Daddy spoke around me, as if I wasn't his own blood kin standing directly in front of him. He lowered his eyes, fiddled with his hat.

"I come to tell you I'm moving," he said. "I got my things packed and heading out in the morning."

Leela-Ma tipped on the back of her heels like she knocked a thigh and hurt it. "Where you headed?"

"Crossville. I've got me a job with the county." Then, looking straight at me, Daddy asked, "You been reading that Bible of your momma's I give you?"

"Yes, sir. Every day."

"Well," he said. "Good. Your momma would be proud."

I wanted to ask Daddy what could I do that would make him proud. What should I have done to keep him from sending me away? What could I do to keep him from leaving me altogether? But I didn't. Sadness clung to Daddy like dust from River Road. There wasn't no point in asking him why. I already knew the answer—nothing. There was nothing I could've done to keep him from sending me away, to keep him from leaving me now.

It was the same with Zeb. Nothing I did or said would've kept him home. Leela-Ma was right—a man's got to do what a man's got to do. And so does a woman.

That's why I didn't cry when Daddy patted my head and told me, "So long, Maizee. Be a good girl."

And it's why I didn't weep when Zeb hugged me and whispered, "Promise you'll meet me 'neath the chestnut come summer."

"I promise," I said, and kissed him good-bye.

But lying in the bed next to my silent child on that cold January morning, I cried and cried and cried.

I feel asleep to the sound of distant voices, calling, "Maizee! Maizee!"

22

Zebulon

When Maizee and I got hitched at the Hawkins County Courthouse on June 3, 1940, it jes so happened to be the very same day that Germans routed British forces at Dunkirk, France, forcing the Brits to hightail it back acrost the English Channel in dinghies before the Germans took captive those left behind. Not that I was aware of any of that then. Fact is, back then I had more pressing matters on my mind than what the Germans were doing.

But now my every waking thought and much of my restless nights concerned their next move.

Maizee and I celebrated our first anniversary with Doc and Leela-Ma at Haw Lake. Leela-Ma packed us a dinner of ham, potato salad, biscuits, and cake. Doc and I packed the fishing poles. Rain was crawling but not yet walking. We waited until the noonday sun passed and Rain woke from his nap before we headed out. The lake was on Shug Mosely's property, but he gave us permission to fish it anytime we wanted. We didn't want to take advantage of Shug's hospitality so we only went up there on special occasions.

My momma considered fishing more of a necessity, a means to put food on the table, than a treat. But not Maizee. She loved to fish. And she wasn't the least bit squeamish about any of it. She'd wade right out in thigh-high water to find a good hole. She brought home the longest string of catfish that night, and I had to put up with her bragging about it every day for the next six months.

To avoid gitting showed up again, I took Maizee on a trip through the Smokies for our second anniversary, which we were forced to celebrate early since I was shipping out. I made arrangements for Doc and Leela-Ma to watch after Rain for the weekend, but Maizee couldn't stand being away from him for that long so we only spent one night in Gatlinburg instead of the two I'd planned on. I haven't been home to share birthdays, anniversaries, nor Christmases since.

23

Memorial Day came and went at Cottesmore Airdome in relative quiet, except for the occasional shoving matches erupting at the poker and craps cots. Brawling sprung up sporadically in the barracks, like choke weed through cracked concrete. I kept my distance from it.

"Hey Hemingway, whatcha writing?" Sergeant Harootunian asked. He was standing at the foot of my cot.

"A letter to my wife," I replied. "Our anniversary was yesterday."

"Yeah. Which one?"

"Number four, Sarge."

"I didn't mean which anniversary, Hurd. I was asking which wife," Harootunian said. He leaned his head back and let go a rafter-trembling laugh.

"I ain't got but one, Sarge."

"Hell's bells, Romeo! Your honeymoon sheets had to have been still warm when you left."

"Yes, sir. I guess they were."

"Hey, Hurd, why don't you join me in the mess hall for a cup of coffee as soon as you finish that letter?"

"All right, Sarge, if you can give me another five minutes."

"I'll meet you there."

Harootunian and I met at Fort Bragg, where we were both part of the 82nd Airborne Division. A tough cuss, Sarge had a straight-up spine, the thick forearms of a long-haul driver, and a face of cut rock. I knew he left behind a wife and two boys back in Norman, Oklahoma, but that was all I knew of his personal affairs.

Our unit, the 505th, arrived at Cottesmore not long ago. The last stop before a combat jump. The place looked like any other barracks—cots, cots, and more cots.

Harootunian was pouring a cup of coffee when I arrived in the mess hall.

"Black?" he asked.

"Yes, Sarge," I answered. He handed me a cup and nodded toward a table.

"When's the last time you were home?" he asked.

"January of '42."

"You got any kids, Hurd?"

"A son."

"I got two boys myself." Harootunian reached into his back pocket and pulled out his wallet. He opened it up to snapshots of two boys in striped shirts, with high foreheads and square jaws. Spittin' images of their daddy.

"Those are two fine-looking boys, Sarge," I said.

"How old is yours?" he asked.

"Nearly four."

"Mine are eight and ten. Sawyer, the oldest, is a natural-born athlete." Harootunian pointed to the picture of the bigger boy. "Sawyer says he wants to play for the Sooners when he grows up."

"Sounds like he might have what it takes," I replied.

"Nothing would make me prouder. What about your boy, Hurd? He any good at sports?"

"Too early to tell yet," I replied. I took a swallow of joe. I didn't like explaining Rain's problems to folks. Their immediate reaction was always a sympathetic one, and while they meant well, I didn't want anyone feeling sorry for Rain. Hell, for all I knew Rain's silent world was a better one. If Hitler had been born mute, I wouldn't be sitting at this table worrying about tomorrow's combat jump.

Harootunian continued to rattle on in that nervous way folks do when they are worrying about something they fear mentioning. He talked about his boys, his wife, the best fishing holes in Oklahoma, and the spot where he hoped to build a home one day.

"You ever seen a home made of them big river rocks, Hurd? That's the kind of house I'm gonna build."

"Yes, sir. I hope to build one myself someday. I grew up in a house sided with labels."

"Labels? What kind of labels?"

"We got us a Card and Label factory back home. They make the labels for soup and bean cans. Folks in the factory carry home the misprints and use 'em to side their homes or paper their walls."

"Shit, Hurd. Where the hell is it you come from again?"

"East Tennessee."

"Y'all got electricity yet?" Harootunian asked.

"Those who can afford it got it."

"You know any hog farmers in East Tennessee?" Harootunian asked.

"Well, jes about everybody I know raises hogs," I replied.

"Back when I was a boy growing up in Oklahoma, my daddy took me with him to visit Mr. Paul Johnson," Sarge continued. "He was a farmer who lived on the far north end of Lawton. Had to, on account of the smell from all those hogs of his.

"Mr. Johnson had him a big outfit, with dozens and dozens of hogs. Daddy parked his Chevy truck up next to the pen. The hogs was standing around, staring at us, like they was disappointed we hadn't brung them a picnic dinner.

"I looked over at Mr. Johnson and asked, 'How come them hogs are standing around that way? Why ain't they wallering?'

"Mr. Johnson looked at Daddy and asked me, 'What did you say, son? I ain't sure I heard you correctly.'

"So I repeated myself. 'How come them hogs of yours ain't wallering?'

"Well, son," Mr. Johnson replied, "it ain't wallering season."

Laughing at the memory of his boyhood self, Harootunian said, "I was jes a kid. I took Mr. Johnson at his word. I didn't know until later, when I asked Daddy on the drive home when wallering season is, that I learned Mr. Johnson had been pulling my leg. The idea of hogs waiting around for a wallering season."

"Damn, Sarge," I said, laughing.

"Yeah, well, I figure by the time we get this next jump out of the way, we're going to feel like we've been waiting on wallering season," he said. The laughter between us give out.

"What's your wife think of your career choice?" Harootunian asked. He took a drag from a cigarette and rested the smoke on the edge of his empty coffee cup. He offered me one but I declined. I quit smoking when Maizee was carrying Rain. The smell of tobacco upset her stomach, and she had hard enough time keeping food down. I figured giving up my smokes wasn't nearly as great a burden as toting around a baby for nine months.

"She don't like it much," I answered. "We never figured on living apart when we married, but then we didn't figure on Pearl Harbor either. I joined up right away. Might as well, they would have drafted my ass anyway. Got a letter from Maizee yesterday. She said one of the town boys had been locked up for desertion and that the Army intended to execute him and probably would've, except the governor intervened and put a stop to that.

"The boy's mother was all torn up over it. Said the Army Police drove all the way over from Fort Campbell searching for the fellow after he went AWOL. They went through his momma's house, tearing up closets, turning over dresser drawers, ransacking the chicken coop, before they finally found the boy hiding out in the cellar. He didn't cooperate with them even after all that. He said that he didn't start this war and that he'd rather fight for the Germans than for the Americans."

"Hell, Hurd, I always thought folks from the Deep South were our best patriots."

"That's true mostly, but our mountain people are an independent lot. A passel of 'em sided with the Yankees on the issue of slavery. During the Civil War, some of my kinfolk even posted signs on their front doors saying they believed freedom was the right of all men."

Harootunian lit another smoke with the tip of the one he was finishing. Both our coffee cups were empty. I looked out the open door. The afternoon sky was full of droopy grey clouds. I could smell the rain coming.

Harootunian followed my gaze.

"There's a chance tonight's jump will be postponed. Depending upon the weather," he said, with a nod toward the door.

"I'd jes soon git it over with myself, sir."

"I know how you feel," Harootunian said.

24

We were scheduled to board the planes at 2000 hours the night of June 4. Shortly before the hour, I slipped on my main chute and strapped a reserve chute acrost my chest. In addition to my landing gear, I carried an M1 rifle, pieced in three parts; a belt loaded with 30-caliber ammo; two frag grenades; one smoke grenade; twenty feet of rope; a first-aid pack; a canteen filled with water; several K-rations; a trench knife; and the pocket-sized New Testament that Leela-Ma gave me. I even had a wad of French currency that had been issued to us earlier that day, although I had no idea what I was supposed to do with it.

After everything was snapped, tugged, and tightened into place, I glanced around the barracks. It was full of soldiers in various states of preparation. Some were lacing up boots. Others were cinching up chutes. All the poker chips were cleared away. All the bravado bullshit stopped. A strained silence followed. Combat jumps were a gamble of a different sort. The stakes higher. We'd been told repeatedly throughout the week that many of us would not make it back.

As I stood there counting the almost dead among us, the call came for us to assemble outside *without our gear*. The invasion was postponed twenty-four hours due to bad weather over the English Channel. The stick of paratroopers, already agitated by a case of nerves, groaned.

"Dadgum sum'a bitch," muttered one soldier as he yanked off his chute and tossed it on the cot.

Maizee came to me in my sleep that night. She was sitting in the crook of a tree. Her blue eyes swollen, rimmed in redness and wildness, as if she'd a bad reaction to poison oak. Her black hair was disheveled. Her hands were unsteady, trembling, the way they'd been when she undressed in front of me for the first time.

"Maizee, what's the matter?" I asked, reaching up for her.

Jumping down, she turned away, acted as if she hadn't heard me, or didn't recognize me.

Maybe she didn't.

She'd been sitting in the crook of a trail tree. Cherokees fashioned trail trees by tying two saplings together. They would fork one sapling like a slingshot and pull the trunk of the other sapling through its prongs. Then, using rope, the Indians would stake the branch end of the saplings so that the tree's trunk grew slaunchwise to the ground. Over time the trunks of those oak or hickory saplings thickened, creating a forest of wooden pews.

Sometimes Cherokees scarred the ends of the trees where the trunks stopped and the branches bent skywards. They'd carve marks into the elbow ends. It was their way of pointing others to nearby game, creeks, shelter, or dangers. Sometimes they would nick out holes in the knobby ends. Then they would hide messages for fellow tribal members in the holes behind a drape of thick moss. Maizee always called these crooked trees Indian Day Stars.

Pushing her hair back off her face, Maizee turned to study me for a minute, then she took off running through a forest of Indian Day Stars.

I gave chase.

"Maizee! Wait! WAIT!!!"

But she kept on running from bent branch to bent branch, stopping now and then to stick something in the hollowed-out ends. I was torn on whether to stop and check for her messages, or to continue to give chase.

I kept running. The forest was thick with tripping doghobble, stinging pine needles, squaw root caked in mud, and brambles of berry bushes coiled like razor wire. Maizee ran over it barefoot with the ease of a hoof-footed deer. The jump boots I was wearing slowed my gait. I couldn't keep up.

"Maizee! MAIZEE!" I cried, reaching for her. My arms ached with the want of her. "Wait!"

Whenever she stopped to shove something in the end of the Day Star, she'd turn and wave, motioning for me to follow. There was something troubling about her. Her face was blank as a moonless night, full of shadows. She didn't smile. Her eyes didn't light up. There was no sign that she was elated to see me.

Did she want me to follow because I was her husband? Or was she motioning to me simply because I was the only other being in the forest? If only I could take her in my arms for a minute, grasp her tight the way I done when we said our goodbyes. I wanted to feel her breath again. But the more I give chase, the quicker Maizee ran. The more I hollered, the less she looked back.

She finally stopped at the far end of the woods. She hopped up on the sideling trunk of a trail tree, leaned her head against its angled branch, and studied me as I ran, ducking around the elbows of oaks and clomping over bramble spirals. She held out both arms and called to me: "Run, Zeb! Hurry! I'm waiting! Please hurry!"

Rounding the last clump of trail trees, I fell to my knees at Maizee's feet.

"Oh, Zeb!" she cried. A glimmer of knowing eased the wildness in her eyes. She flashed a smile my way. I reached out for her, but before we could embrace Maizee disappeared. She was gone, quick as morning fog. I was left clutching the gnarled branch of a Day Star.

"MAIZEE!" Bending over the tree's altar, I wept. Then, remembering her messages, I ran back over the path, searching frantically through knobby ends of the trees. I checked five trees before I found one with a hollowed end.

Pulling back the moss, I peered inside and yanked out an envelope. I ripped it open, dumping the contents onto the ground. I leaned over and picked up a cutout image of Maizee, holding up the string of bass she'd caught at Haw Lake on our first anniversary. In the original photo, I'd been standing next to her, one arm wrapped around her waist, the other arm holding Rain. I studied Maizee's image in my hand. The only evidence that I'd been standing next to her were my four fingers still circling her waist.

Shoving it back into the envelope, I ran to the next tree. Nothing. And the next. Nothing. Back and forth I ran, from Day Star to Day Star. There was no pattern to Maizee's messages. I run around in a half-blind stagger, yanking out another envelope, then another from a carved elbow.

I run all day from tree to tree, elbow to elbow. I didn't stop until I had gathered a dozen envelopes. Each one contained an image of Maizee. There was her grade-school picture from the year her momma died. A snapshot of her standing in the Holston River in her baptismal gown. There was even a picture of Maizee sitting on the davenport at Leela-Ma's house, cradling Rain when he was an infant. Only Rain wasn't there. He'd been cut out of her arms. Maizee was left cradling a black hole.

The last image I pulled from a tree was taken on May Day, 1938. The date was written on the back of the cutout. In the photo Maizee was standing in front of the maypole kissing Kade Mashburn. They were snipped out together, two bodies joined as one.

I woke with a start. My heart pounding. My groin throbbing. A chilling sweat drenching me. My chest splotched red, a telltale sign of the searing jealousy I harbored toward Kade.

Sergeant Harootunian stood over my cot.

"You okay, Hurd?"

I swung my legs around and sat up. I felt dazed.

"Sarge?"

"I heard you hollering over here. Thought I'd better see what was the matter. You were yelling something about rain."

I held my forehead with both hands. Wiped the sweat off my brow. Took a breath and tried to calm my pounding heart.

"Rain's my boy. I'm sorry to have disturbed you."

Harootunian squatted down so he was eye level with me.

"It's not a problem, Hurd." He placed a hand on my shoulder. "Times like these are bound to disturb a man's sleep."

"It was a bad dream. That's all, Sarge. Sorry."

"I understand, Hurd. No need to apologize. You want to get some fresh air?"

"What time is it?"

"Oh-dark-thirty."

Harootunian wore a tee shirt, khakis, and his boots. Some of the men in the barracks were awake, reading by flashlight or writing letters home. Others were dressing quietly, trying not to disturb those still sleeping.

Standing up, I jerked on my pants, shirt, and boots. I had this powerful hankering to take off running. If I could run fast enough and far enough, I'd find me a place where dreams and combat cain't haunt a man.

The fresh sweat of morning bubbled atop the hoods and windshields of trucks, jeeps, and planes. Harootunian shook a pack of smokes and offered me one. This time I took it. Snapping open his lighter, Harootunian covered the flames for me. I inhaled deeply, allowing the smoke to settle in my lungs.

"Something troubling you?" Harootunian asked.

"No more than the usual pre-jump jitters," I replied.

"You sure?" Harootunian asked. He bent his head down and cast me a dubious glance. He didn't believe me. And I was too rattled to try and persuade him otherwise.

"It's my boy Rain. I'm worried about him."

"Any particular reason why?" Harootunian took a long drag from his cigarette, then flicked the amber ashes onto the asphalt.

"Rain's got problems. I'm not sure his momma can handle him if something were to happen to me."

Harootunian continued walking and smoking in silence, leaving it up to me to fill the space between dark and dawn. A few minutes passed before I answered him.

"My boy's mute, Sarge. He cain't speak or hear. Maizee manages him as good as anyone, but I worry about her. She ain't been herself since Rain was born."

"I'm damn sorry about your boy," Harootunian said, flicking his smoke and crushing it with the heel of his boot. We were standing next to an aircraft's wing. Row after row of C-47s stretched out beyond us. The cigarette curled up in my palm was mostly ash.

"When Maizee were about seven months along, she started having trouble sleeping."

"Hell, Hurd. That's pretty common for pregnant women. My wife didn't sleep well with either one of our boys. Kept having to get up three or four times a night to go pee."

"Yes, but Maizee's restlessness were more than that. She talked outta her head, like an addled person. She accused me and others of trying to starve her to death, but she wouldn't eat nothing we fixed her. She only gained fifteen pounds with the baby, and Rain weighed nearly nine pounds when he was born.

"After his birth, she got her appetite back, but she never could rest easy again. Don't get me wrong; she's a real good momma. That's why we didn't know Rain was deaf for so long. Maizee wouldn't let him cry, not for nothing. If he so much as opened his mouth to yawn, she was right there, making sure he was dry, powdered, and fed. The two of them are thicker than ticks on a hound. There were times when they didn't seem to need me at all."

A lieutenant walked past, and we saluted as he went. He returned the salute. The sun, pale as cat piss, began its slow but steady rise. Harootunian coughed, then spit a torpedo that landed near the cockpit door.

"I think most men feel ignored some when they become a father the first time, Hurd. It's the nature of things. Shit, I wouldn't worry about it if I were you."

I saw no reason to keep talking. There was nothing Harootunian could do, and there was no way to tell things in a way he could understand. Not even those closest to Maizee seemed to see how touched she got after Rain was born, and I ain't talking about that sentimental way most mommas git. Maizee got touched in a scary-some fashion.

"Sarge?"

"Yes?"

"If something were to happen, the worst, I mean, would you mind checking in on my wife and son from time to time? Our folks are gitting up there in years, and I'd rest easier knowing you were looking after her and Rain."

"First of all, Hurd, ain't nothing going to happen. Got that? This jump is routine stuff. It'll be like a night in Nashville. We're going to go in there, do a lot of hell-raising, make a lot of noise, and generally tear up the town. Nothing hard about that, right?"

"Right."

"Don't worry about your wife and boy, Hurd. You're going to be fine. But, if need be, I'll look after them myself. You have my word."

"Thank you, Sarge, I appreciate that."

I stuck out my right hand, and Harootunian shook it.

25

The mess hall was packed by 0700 on the morning of June 5. There's something about the routine of breakfast that eases a nervous man. If he shuts his eyes and breathes in the smells of bacon sizzling, coffee percolating, and eggs scrambling, he can almost persuade himself he's back at home reading about the war in the Sunday paper, instead of being smack-dab in the midst of it. That's if a fellow can git beyond the noise. Mess halls are thunderously loud, what with the clanging of spoons, shoveling slop, the thud of trays on tabletops, and the roar of a brigade all yammering at once. It wasn't at all peaceful like the home me and Maizee rented from Burdy Luttrell.

I ate the last of my bacon, cleaned my mess kit and fork in the drum of boiling water sitting outside, then headed back to the barracks. I wanted to take another look at the letter I'd gotten from Burdy yesterday. I didn't have much time. The last of the briefings for the delayed jump would start at 0900.

I felt unsettled over last night's dream. I hoped Burdy's letter, which I'd jes read quickly the day before, might give me some peace about Maizee and Rain. Burdy wasn't much one for writing, but the few letters I'd got from her were worth the wait.

Leela-Ma was dubious about the Widow Luttrell. She'd tried to talk me out of renting a place from Burdy. Leela-Ma wouldn't come out and say it directly, but I knowed she feared Burdy would hex me or Maizee. Truth be told, Burdy Luttrell is an oddity. She's got the hair of an Indian, the skin of a black, and the greenish-blue eyes of, well, like no human being. There's nothing those eyes of hers miss.

I was sitting on the front stoop with her one morning when she looked off toward Shug Mosely's place and seen a cougar sneaking into Shug's barn. I could barely make out the barn's open door, and even then I had to squint.

I would've never believed Burdy—cougar sightings were like ghosts on the mountain, more tall tales than real life—if Shug hadn't come around later that evening with a disturbing story of how his dog, Jackson, was eaten alive by a cougar. When I asked Burdy how it was that she could see something from that afar off, she shrugged her shoulders and quoted a verse from Scriptures: "Then I saw a Lamb, looking as if it had been slain, standing in the center of the throne, encircled by the four living creatures and the elders. He had seven horns and seven eyes, which are the seven spirits of God sent out into all the earth."

From then on, I didn't doubt that Burdy Luttrell could see a cougar tearing flesh off its prey from ten miles away. As far as I were concerned, the Widow Luttrell could see things with her eyes shut that most people couldn't see in broad daylight with a pair of high-powered binoculars. I was convinced she could very well be one of the seven spirits of God.

Opening up my footlocker, I retrieved Burdy's letter and stuffed it in my back pocket. I needed someplace quiet to study on it, and the barracks was about as rowdy as a Saturday night chicken wobble. Everyone was standing about, talking over the latest news, wrapping up poker games, making half-assed predictions about the weather and the Germans' combat strategy.

I walked to the far end of the runway and sat under a C-47. Leaning up against the wheel of the troop carrier, I opened Burdy's letter.

May 15, 1944

Dear Zeb:

It's so hot here I might have to crawl under the house to find me some shade. I could borrow Rain and pretend me and him was searching for crawlers.

Me and Rain have been spending a good deal of time together lately. Yesterday, we went for a trek in the woods behind the house. We hiked all the way up to Horseshoe Falls. Rain stayed two steps ahead of me the entire time. You ain't going to recognize your own boy when you git home. He's shooting up like a river cane.

Me and Rain was both sweating like angry boars after that climb. We cooled ourselves down under the mountain showers. I cain't remember the last time I stood under those falls and let them warsh me thataway. Ma always said mountain water comes straight from Heaven's spigot. Rain couldn't git enough of it. He flapped around in that water while I sat on a rock, drying myself like an old crane.

I 'bout nearly fell asleep and might would've if Rain hadn't been with me. I was rising to my feet when I seen a pink flower growing near the rock I was sitting on. The last time I'd seen such a plant was when Ma took me and my sisters swimming in Georgia's Tallulah River. We was there visiting some of Ma's kin. I was 12 or 13, still a girl but jes barely.

The slopes angling down into the Tallulah were covered in white and pink antler flowers. They're the most fragile looking things. Tissue-thin spikes poked out in three directions, east, west, and south. It looked like some sort of forest creature. I told Ma that if that flower had legs, it would be running in herds. She laughed at me. Before we left the river that afternoon I picked me one of those antler flowers. I felt bad, like I'd jes murdered one of Creator's cherished pets. So I pressed it in my Bible and it's been there ever since. That's how come I knowed what it was I seen under the rock.

Don't worry. I didn't pick that one. Far as I know it's still blooming 'neath the rock at Horseshoe Falls. When you git back we'll hike up there so you can see it for your own self. The proper name for the flower is persistent trillium. It's a kin to the lily, which Ma always called the Resurrection Flower. It kinda makes sense to call a rare flower persistent, don't it? I mean if it weren't, it might not be around at all.

That Kade Mashburn fellow came calling last week. You remember him? He brought his fiddle and we all sat around the porch listening, and even though Rain couldn't hear it, he acted like he could feel the music. He danced all over my porch, arms flying every whichaway, and feet stomping. Course Rain kept going even after the music stopped. It was the funniest thing. We all had a good laugh over it.

I tell you, that Kade fellow's got a good ear. He might be a pleasant enough if it weren't for those eyes of his. They stray too much for my liking.

Come home soon as you can, Zeb. Maizee needs you. Rain misses you. I do, too.

Until then, be safe,
Burdy

Burdy was right—if it weren't for Kade's wandering ways, he'd be an okay fellow. There'd been a time when Kade and me were pretty good buds. It was the year before I got hitched. Kade and me worked topping and suckering tobacco for Mr. Bunch, who lived upriver at Stony Point.

Kade was younger than me by a couple of years, but he wouldn't shy from hard work. On the hottest of days, he'd volunteer to climb the rafters in the barn and hoist up the bundles of leaves. I respect any man with that kind of work ethic.

I knew he'd been sweet on Maizee, but that year he started seeing a girl from over at Starr Mountain. Maggie Harlan. She had a reputation for being a fine girl, with a singing voice so good she'd been invited to sing at some tent shows in Knoxville. Kade went after her like a martin to a gourd.

One puthery morning, as we were in the rows topping, Kade called out, "Hey Hurd, do you believe in predestination?"

"Depends," I said.

"On what?"

I was a row over to Kade's left. I stopped working in order to give my back a stretch and answered, "Well, what kind of predestination? Do you mean the religious sort or the fate sort?"

147

"What's the difference?" Kade asked, turning to look at me. He'd rolled up the sleeves on his shirt.

"As best I understand it, there's them that believes God predestined us. Some to do evil, like Judas did, and some to do good, like Joseph. If you buy that, then there's really no reason to worry about fate—it's pretty settled. But I never bought into predestination thataway."

Kade slapped at a deer fly on his cheek. "Then you don't believe in predestination?"

"I didn't say that. What I mean is I believe when it comes to doing evil or doing good, the choice is ours. But I think some are more prone to doing good than others. God didn't make Judas betray Jesus. Judas did it for the money. There's them that like money better'n others. Judas was one of 'em."

Powdery soil covered my boots. I bent over another plant and chopped off a flowering stalk.

Kade was doing more standing than bending. "But didn't somebody have to be the Judas?" he asked. "I mean, how would the Jesus story play out without a Judas?"

"Maybe. But without his betrayal, God could've come up with a different way," I replied. "But Judas weren't forced into it. He could've refused. He made the wrong choice. I don't think he was predestined to make that choice, any more than he was predestined to make the right choice."

"What about the fate?" Kade asked. He was working his row pretty quickly now, kicking up the dust in the furrows.

"What about it?"

"Do you believe God's appointed you a time to die and one girl that you're meant to marry?"

"What are you doing, Kade, writing a damn book? I didn't know you were such a studied soul."

"I'm working on it," he said, giving me one of his slow grins.

"Well," I answered, "if you believe what the Bible says, it says our days are numbered, and that God knows that date. But I don't think that means I should run off this afternoon and lie down in front of a roaring train to test God or fate. If God checks his calendar, and he finds out I'm dying on the wrong date, will he throw the brake on the train to save my ass? I don't think that's how this predestination thing works. Maybe you're right. Maybe I don't believe in predestination, after all."

"What about the girl thing? You think God created jes one girl for you? Or do you think there are plenty of girls you could choose from and be jes as happy as with the next?"

"I'm pretty sure there's jes one gal for me," I said. "What about you?"

"I don't know, Hurd," he replied. "I cain't see myself tied to one girl, but if I was the kind of fellow who believed in fate, or predestination, I'm pretty sure Maggie Harlan's that girl."

The sharp whistle of a white-crowned sparrow interrupted our conversation. Looking up, I eyed one sitting on the wire fence around Mrs. Bunch's garden.

"What makes you so sure about her?"

"I dunno," Kade said, shrugging his shoulders. "We got a lot in common with her singing and my fiddling. She's a kind person but she don't act like she's too good for others. She makes me wish I'd made better choices. Sometimes, though, it seems like I'm destined to make bad ones."

I wanted to tell Kade I thought his view was pure bullshit. People can choose to do right and Kade could, too, if that's what he really wanted. But I figured he knew that and didn't need me acting like his nursemaid.

As the morning heated up, the only sounds were Kade and me thudding through the yellowing rows, and the slow-drawl *hush, hush, hush* of the Holston River easing on by.

Later that same year, I was in Sloane's Hardware picking up a new damper for the stove when Joe Greer came in. He was red-cheeked, gnawing on a plug of baccy, and eager to tell any who'd listen that the police had taken Kade Mashburn in for questioning on account of Maggie Harlan's drowning up at Bullit Creek.

Nothing ever came of all that, far as I knew, but Kade changed afterward. He took up with a rough crowd and spent his evenings at the juke joints between Kingsport and Knoxville, playing his fiddle in exchange for free drinks and pocket change.

The last time I saw Kade was the day Maizee and Rain seen me off. We'd stopped at a diner in town to grab a bite to eat, when we passed right by Kade, sitting in a booth. I didn't hardly recognize him. His red hair was hanging all down in his eyes, and he was slumped over his coffee, like it was the last bit of warmth from a burn barrel. Maizee nudged me and said she thought that was Kade. I stared hard and seen she was right about that. Sliding into the seat acrost from his, I asked, "Hey buddy, do you believe in predestination?"

Kade looked up, give me one of his slow grins, and answered, "Depends."

"On what?" I asked.

"Depends on who's asking."

"I'm asking."

"Well, it seems," Kade said, looking up at Maizee holding Rain, "from the looks of things you've found your destiny."

"And what about you?"

"I'm still searching for mine," Kade said. He dipped a forefinger into the bottom of his cup and picked up some grounds. "Think these can tell me anything?"

"Yeah," I said. "Your future is looking dark."

"You're full of shit, Hurd, you know that?" Kade said.

We laughed, and he wished me well and told Maizee to call him if he could be of any help. When we walked away, I told Maizee that Kade Mashburn better be the last person she called if she needed anything. That was the last I'd seen or heard of Kade till Burdy's letter.

The troops were gathering at the far end of the runway for one last briefing. I folded Burdy's letter and stuck it my shirt pocket.

26

A dozen or so guys from the squadron, along with Sarge, were standing around a table. Spread out acrost it was a clever map, with roads, towns, rivers, hillsides, beaches, and other landmarks. For weeks, we'd chewed the bark off that map, studying and committing to memory names of places foreign to us: *Merderet River, Chef du Pont, Ste. Mere Eglise.* Even though we were safe in England at Cottesmore, it weren't hard to grasp the dangers awaiting us. We'd been warned: *No paratroopers will be returned to England unless they are disabled or dead. Any paratrooper who refuses to jump will be court-martialed.* This weren't the time for acting feather-legged.

The straight of things was we meant to cut the Germans off from the beach. The plan would put us in charge of the shoreline and the road running north and south. But we'd be flying in a total blackout. Hundreds and hundreds of planes flying without radio or lights. Instruments only. Over the Channel. Our pilots would be dropping us half a mile north of town, slowing down that beastly plane to a hover over the ground at about the same height as the grandfather chestnut on Horseshoe Ridge.

Harootunian tried to reassure us. He told us we'd all be fine, as long as we didn't git our asses blown off on the way down. Sarge had a liar's knack for comforting the scared shitless. The jump itself didn't bother me. I'd jumped off of plenty of barn roofs and tree limbs as a boy, but nobody never shot at me from close range while I was doing it. That worried me some. Mostly, I fretted about what would happen if the jump went catty-wampus. I'd be in a right smart mess if I got out there in the middle of some damn French town and couldn't find nobody I knew. I told Harootunian my worry.

"English is my second language," I said, "hillbilly being my first, though I've nearly forgotten how to speak country since I hooked up with this stick. I don't speak French or German so I'm pretty darn sure I ain't gonna stop and ask somebody for directions."

"Shit, Hurd. I thought the only map you Appalachian boys needed is the stars."

"Yeah, but I ain't never read the stars in French," I said.

Harootunian laughed. He pointed once again at the map, directly at the Drop Zone (DZ) for our stick, and started to say something, but a blood-curdling scream interrupted him.

"What the hell?"

Harootunian took off running. I was right on his heels.

A crowd had gathered outside the hut's door. Pitiful moans rose up from somewhere directly beyond. Pushing his way through, Harootunian yelled, "Outta my way. What's going on here?"

"Corporal Robertson shot himself, Sarge," said a pointy-nose fellow.

"Damnit!" Harootunian said, spinning the fellow around by his shoulders. "What do you mean Robertson shot himself?"

"He's yellow-bellied, Sarge. He's been yapping for days now about how he didn't want to make this jump. Kept saying he might as well shoot himself as let the Germans do it. Me and Flegal got tired of hearing him carrying on like that. We told him to either do it or shut up about it already. We didn't really think he had the balls to do it."

Sure enough, Robertson had done shot himself. Picked up his sidearm and blew his left foot nearly clean off, boot and all. Harootunian ripped the sleeve off his shirt and tied up a tourniquet to ebb the blood that was spewing like horse piss all over the place.

153

I'd never liked Roberston. Never trusted him. He couldn't keep his yap shut. He talked more than any man I ever come acrost, or child for that matter. He was jittery, doped up on joe, which he drank by the buckets. He knew everything about anything—baseball, guns, politicians, irrigation. He wasn't married, and I could see why. I didn't know any woman who'd put up with a man yip-yapping like that all day long. Maizee probably would've cut his tongue outta his head, thinking that would be a more practical way of fixing his problems—and hers—if she was married to someone like him.

Still, I'd never considered Robertson for a lowdown yellow-belly. To hear him tell it, he was the stud of every herd. He claimed he rode bulls bareback at his daddy's ranch in Yakima, Washington. And that he was a champion swimmer who once swam from Washington to Oregon, acrost the Columbia River. I'd never seen the mighty Columbia River myself, but what I'd heard tell of it made me doubtful.

Roberston was sitting on the floor in a puddle of piss—his own—and blood, also his own. His eyes were green and wild as a trash-fed cat. His hands clutched his knee as Harootunian and a medic worked over his hamburgered-up foot.

"You are one sorry dumb shit, you know that, Robertson?" Harootunian asked.

"It was an accident, Sarge," Roberston said. "I was cleaning my gun."

"The hell it was," Harootunian said, as he and the medic moved Robertson to a gurney somebody had carried in. "But if it's as you say, an accident, that makes you the resident idiot, you know that, right?"

"Yes, Sarge," Robertson replied. He wasn't being sheepish or remorseful in his reply. He was smirking the entire time. Robertson figured he'd managed to outsmart all the rest of us. Likely the only injury he'd sustain in this war was a self-inflicted one. He decided his own fate rather than letting the Germans gamble with God for it.

All that foolishness with Roberston put everyone on edge. Nothing a shot or two of Jack Daniels couldn't have settled, but damn it all to hell, we didn't dare. We had orders to be in full battle gear by 2100 hours.

Several weeks earlier, a practice run had gone badly. The Brass were pretty tight-lipped about it. All they would say is that it was under investigation. But the talk around Cottesmore was that the pilots got discombobulated on the return flight and started crashing into one another. I didn't know the ones that died, but I knew of 'em. And, if the truth be known, those deaths were on my mind when the order come that it was time.

Half an hour after we got the orders, some two hundred jumpers boarded seventy-something birds. Even though it was dark out, it weren't hard to find which plane was ours. Somebody had marked numbers to the side of the bird's door so we wouldn't end up on the wrong mission.

Cinching up the straps on my chute and my helmet, I climbed the steps of the C-47 and took a seat on the cold aluminum bench. When the pilot revved up the engine, my backside shook with the fervor of a Pentecostal's tambourine.

I was in fourth position to jump, right behind Barrett, Worstell, and Flegal. I'd never knowed Flegal to be so quiet. He was acting like a deacon at a prayer meeting, leaning forward from where we all sittin'. Flegal's head was down, his hands clasped between his knees. Barrett nudged me and nodded toward Flegal. His way of asking if he was okay or not. Weren't much I could do about it. I shrugged. Barrett had given me a shove from behind when we come up the aircraft's steps, since my pack was heavy and the plane's steps narrow. I wondered should I repay him the favor and give him a push out the door when we reached the DZ.

The plane rumbled into position for takeoff. No turning back now. I thought of Robertson—that low-count—tightly tucked into a warm bed in the medical unit, no doubt snoring with the aid of a sleeping pill. I hoped he suffercated in his sleep. If Burdy were around, she'd probably hold the pillow over his head. Burdy didn't tolerate slack-twisted men like Roberston. None of us did.

Planes lined up like magpies on the runway, each bird waiting to take flight. Closing my eyes, I leaned back and readied for the lift as the pilot set the throttle. My bowels were in an uproar in a good way. When you're raised in a place where electricity and indoor plumbing are uncommon, you cain't hardly imagine driving a car, much less flying.

Sure, the job had its cautions. Nothing makes a gunner more glad-eyed than a paratrooper floating through the sky with his apron wide open. Jumpers could be easy pickins, even for the most nearsighted fellow.

Given the flying conditions—hundreds of planes jes like ours flying blind at midnight—I should have been as restless as a pig in a poke, but I wasn't. I was settled with an unnatural calm. I'd come from a long line of free men, and I intended to make sure Rain remained as free as a boy trapped in a silent world could be. My stomach only seized at the thought of any harm coming to my boy. I must've nodded off because I liked to have come outta my boots when Captain Coale, our jumpmaster, hollered, "Twenty minutes!"

Over two hours had passed since we left Cottesmore. Had to be the hand of Almighty God that we had made it this far without incident. We'd passed over checkpoints and the Channel with no crashes, no gunfire. But as soon as our pilots turned the plane toward the town of St. Mere Eglise, we immediately recognized the Aacckkk! Aacckkk! Aacckkk! of anti-aircraft shells erupting around us. The plane pitched like a boat on rough waters. I couldn't see nothing and had no idey what the pilots might be dealing with. Somebody yelled "fog bank," and all of sudden we were nose up. A fireball exploded jes beyond the open doors. Then we were nose down, but, mercifully, not in that crash way. We were headed to the DZ.

Captain Coale rose to his feet, near the doors.

"Ten minutes!" he said. "Get ready!"

My gut juices flowed as I flashbacked to the days when the Mosely brothers and I would climb on the roof of their daddy's barn and pretend we were gunners shooting down enemy planes. Back then our rifles were fashioned from hickory sticks and the enemy planes were squawking crows. There was never any real bloodshed, and the only danger was the whupping we'd catch if one of us were to fall off the roof, causing the others to confess to climbing up there to begin with. When we were young, the sound of anti-aircraft was something to envy. Poke Mosely was a great mimic. He had a guttural Aacckkk! that sounded exactly like a machine gun firing.

But this was different.

The gunners below were drilling us like they had when we jumped into Sicily a year ago. Fireworks flashed acrost the pre-dawn sky.

"Outboard personnel stand up!"

We were all on our feet when the plane lurched and shivered as a round burst nearby. The pilots fought to steady the craft. The light flashed red and Captain Coale shouted, "Hook up!"

All twenty-seven of us snapped into the line.

"Check equipment!" Coale ordered.

Harootunian, who was behind me, checked my chute, making sure nothing had come undone. Barrett was standing in front of me, so I checked his. It smelt like a couple of guys must've crapped their pants. I didn't blame them. Patting the pocket Bible that Leela-Ma had given me, I uttered a psalm that I'd learned as a young boy: *"He shall cover you with his feathers, and under His wings you shall take refuge. You shall not be afraid of the terror by night,nor of the arrow that flies by day."*

Three minutes. A blast of air about knocked our knees out from under us. My mind raced. Keep your feet and knees together. Gotta git down in one piece. Sweet Jesus. Gotta git loose of the chute. Gotta find my gun and be ready.

"One minute!" Coale shouted and gave a hand signal, in case we couldn't hear.

The first man in line, Worstell, rotated and faced the door.

The red light flashed green. Coale motioned with his right hand and hollered, "GREEN LIGHT! GO!"

Worstell jumped, then Flegal, Barrett, me, and Harootunian. The jumping part was rote, but what followed wasn't.

The harness tightened around my groin as my chute unraveled overhead. I heard the rounds that struck Flegal. Down and to my right, through the dark, through the yellow haze of gunfire, Flegal crumpled. He was dead.

Twisting, I looked to my right and then to my left, searching for tracers to dodge. That unnatural calm I'd felt earlier was gone. I had an urge to shit. My breath came in short spurts. Would I be shot on the way down or as soon as I landed? Would I have time to assemble my rifle? To kill a Kraut or two? God, I hoped so.

27

The early morning sky was dark as a fresh bruise. A light drizzle fell. I could make out the silhouette of a farmhouse over the rise, and the dark trunks of trees to the right of that, but very little else. Blood—mine—seeped out around me like the whites of an egg, cracked and frying.

Harootunian yelled as fiery shards of shells flew all around us. I had landed on my belly, arms and legs outstretched, left hand grasping a clump of grass, right hand white-knuckling my M1.

The earth was hard as I laid there, my left ear pressed against a grassy mound. My helmet pushed down over my eyes, temporarily blinding me. Pushing it back, I could see the hedgerow that Harootunian and I had plunged through jes moments before.

"I'm hit! I'm hit!" I cried out. I'd survived the jump, even managed to git my chute released and my rifle assembled before being struck as I attempted to take cover.

It was not the face of God that flashed before my eyes in that moment. It was Maizee's face. I seen hers, and then Rain's.

Pressing up on his elbows, Harootunian shouted, "Can you move?"

I tried but my right leg wouldn't budge. I let out a scream. Harootunian crawled over beside me, grabbed a knife from his boot, and sliced open my pant leg so he could inspect the wound better.

"Holy Mother of God!"

I wasn't sure if Harootunian was praying or cursing, but either way I took it as a bad sign. Grabbing me by the shoulders, he yanked me back under the hedgerow. The shells continued pounding. Whatever was left of our company was either hunkered down behind the hedgerow or looking for cover in the fields and barns scattered around Ste. Mere Eglise.

Harootunian took off his belt and fashioned a tourniquet that he tied over my thigh. Pain, hot as a branding iron, afflicted me. I let out a holler like a pig marked.

"Get me a medic! I need a medic now!" Harootunian yelled.

It felt as though my entire leg was in flames, from the hip socket down. I hoped someone could hear Harootunian over all the racket of shells exploding.

He tore open a first aid kit and gave me a shot of morphine.

"This'll help until Doc gets here," he said.

My body began to shake uncontrollably.

"You're going to be fine, Hurd. Don't worry," Harootunian said. He applied sulfa powder and bandages to my hip, my leg. Then, yanking the rosary beads from around his neck, Harootunian began reciting a prayer. I don't know if it was the morphine or the prayer, but the fire in my leg eased some. The shaking subsided. My lids were heavy. I wanted to sleep.

Harootunian popped backwards, arms flailing upward. He groaned loudly as he was pelted with bullets from behind. Then, he fell forward, directly acrost my chest, still clutching that rosary.

"Harootunian! Harootunian!" I screamed, cradling his head. Blood soaked his back, his head, my hands. He gurgled, then exhaled like a balloon deflated.

Somebody reached down and yanked him off my chest. I could make out the forms of two soldiers. I wasn't sure if they were with the 82nd Airborne or not, until one of them stood over me and hollered something I couldn't make out.

"Damn you, Kraut!" I answered, hoping my tone was understandable even if my words weren't.

"Shoot him."

28

Maizee

Zeb had been gone over a year when somebody brung me the Kingsport paper. I cain't remember who now. It weren't Burdy, and it weren't Leela-Ma. Neither of them would've done such a thing. They was all the time trying to keep things from me 'cause they figured me to be weak-minded and they feared bad news might render me altogether addled. Ida Mosely brung it, maybe.

Whoever it was clearly wasn't considering how it felt for me to spend my days and nights waiting: waiting beside the mailbox for a letter, waiting beside the radio for war news, waiting for the day when Zeb could come home and we could start living as a family again.

I probably shouldn't have done it, but I cut the photo out of the newspaper and stuck it in my momma's Bible, the one Daddy give to me. I suspect whoever brung me the paper hadn't even bothered to open it up to the picture on page five. I don't know how a person could miss something like that. I couldn't git it out of my mind if somebody was paying me to.

The little dark-haired girl was sitting barefoot in rubble, leaning up against a concrete wall, blowing her nose on a stretch of toilet paper, and grasping hold of her baby brother. His mouth a squalling circle, tiny hands clutched in front of him, like those of a dying man praying. "Bomb Killed Their Mother." That's what the headline over the photo said. The story underneath said that the little Italian girl had found her momma dead in a bomb-shattered home. It also said the little girl was confused and frightened, but anybody who looked at that picture could see that for themselves.

I mentioned it to Kade when he come up to the house one Friday evening. I asked had he seen it. He said no, he didn't like reading the newspaper much on account of all the generally unedifying reports. That's what he said, and I didn't argue with him over it; I jes pulled the picture out of the Bible and showed it to him.

"It's been bothering me ever since I first seen it. I cain't git it out of my head."

"I can see why," Kade said, studying on the pitiful girl and her wailing brother. He folded the picture and handed it back to me. "You really shouldn't dwell on all this war news, Maizee."

"That's easy enough for you," I snapped. "You ain't got no reason to worry about it." It was a hateful thing for me to say, but keeping all my ugly thoughts to myself was poisoning me.

Kade dropped his head. My sharpness stung 'im bad. He'd tried to enlist but was turned away because doctors said he had a weak heart.

Kade's weak heart was caused by all that mess with Maggie Harlan. People said Kade was at fault for Maggie's drowning. Some even said he'd held her head under, but that was pure nonsense. Her drowning carved a big knothole in Kade's heart that he tried to fill with drinking and juking.

Before Zeb left, he told me to stay clear of Kade, but that was school-boy jealousy speaking. Zeb and Kade had been good friends once. Kade was not a threat; matter of fact, he'd been a big help to me and Rain. He give us the milk he got from the ration coupons, saying he didn't drink the stuff and that Rain was a growing boy and needed it more. Kade even carried the cans of waste fats me, Burdy, and Leela-Ma collected to the meat store uptown and brung us the money back. The fats were used for the glycerin in the shots given to the soldiers.

Sometimes Kade would bring his fiddle over and play for us. Rain liked to have danced a hole in Burdy's porch. He loved that music of Kade's, even though he couldn't hear a lick of it. I hated admitting it, but Burdy had been right about Rain's hearing. When he was only a year old, I could manage to fool myself into thinking he could hear, but when he turned two and still hadn't even said the words "Ma" or "Pa," there was no denying it—Rain was deaf.

I wrote Zeb and asked what he thought I should do about our boy. Zeb said we ought to treat Rain the same as before. So that's what I'd done. Or tried to do. I would talk to Rain same as before, but once I knew for sure he couldn't hear me, I got down right in front of 'im and would talk straight at 'im so he could see me speaking.

I'd put his fingers over my lips and repeat a word over and over. That's how he learned the words "berry" and "no." I'd taken him over to visit with Doc and Leela-Ma. Rain climbed up on the fence rail and grabbed a handful of berries off a vine of poke salat. Purple juice squirted between his balled-up fingers. Doc grabbed him from behind, while I held his hands. Leela-Ma ran and got some water and we warshed him good.

Once we were sure all the poison juice was off Rain, I sat down with him in the grass by the poke salat vine and plucked off a stalk. Pointing to a clump of berries, I repeated the word "berry" over and over and over again, holding Rain's fingers to my lips each time. Then, when I was sure he knew what I meant, I added the word "no" and shook my head over and over. Rain shook his head the same as me. I gave him the stink eye and repeated the word. I put a berry in my palm, said the word "no," and tossed the berry away. Then I give Rain a berry, and he did the same. That's when I knew he understood me, even if he couldn't hear me.

I seen the way people looked on Rain and I knowed they felt pity for 'im, living in a silent world. But I envied 'im that. I had so many voices in my head for so long, I believe Rain was better off than most, certainly better off than me. If a child starts out never hearing their momma's voice, maybe they don't miss it so much when it's gone, the way I did with mine.

I mentioned to Kade once that I thought Rain was better off not hearing and he give me a quare look, like any mother who confessed to such a thing ain't fit to be a mother. Kade leaned against the door of his pickup. Black paint was scratched off in the dent over the rear wheel, from where he had backed into another car after gitting into a fight at some bar up in Knoxville.

"What exactly do you mean by that?" he asked me.

"I mean that I might be better off if I was deaf like Rain."

"Why's that?"

"'Cause I wouldn't have to put up with all these voices in my head."

The truck wasn't the only thing roughed up from that fight. Kade bore a crescent-shaped scar under his right cheek from a knife wound he got. Somebody sliced open his cheek like they was quartering an apple. Kade referred to that fight as his Damascus moment. "The night I seen the light," he said. He swore off drinking and juking, but by then Kade had built a reputation for being a low-count. Nobody around these parts believed he could or would change, except me and Rain, I guess. Rain had spent more time with Kade than he had his own daddy, and for all I knew Rain mistook Kade to be his daddy.

Kade's coming about bothered folks on the mountain, especially Burdy, but I didn't care. Them people didn't know how lonely it could git for a girl to live by herself with a deaf child. Whatever notions people ascribed to Kade didn't make no never mind to me. He was a friend I could count on. But I didn't mention his regular visits to Zeb. Zeb already had enough things on his mind; he didn't need to be worrying about me cheating on him. The friendship me and Kade shared was born out of brokenness, nothing else.

Kade took a drag of his cigarette and offered it to me. I took it. Rain was in the back of the pickup rubbing Kade's hound dog,

Butterbean.

"What voices?" Kade asked.

"Ah, that was jes talk," I said.

"For the longest time after Maggie died, I'd hear her," Kade said. "Did I ever tell you that?"

I shook my head and handed Kade's smoke back to 'im. "You ain't never mentioned Maggie or her death at all that I recall."

"Haven't I? Well, that's odd, considering it's about the only thing on my mind." Kade cupped his hand to his face and took a slow drag from the cigarette. He held the smoke in his lungs for the longest time, then let it seep out the corners of his mouth. "Sometimes I wake to her singing 'The False Young Man.' Ever heard it?" Kade sang me a verse: "When your heart was mine, my old true love and you lay your head on my breast, you could make me believe with the falling of your arm that the sun rose in the West."

"Cain't say that I have."

"Well. It's beautiful and never more so than when Maggie sang it." A shadow crossed over Kade's face. It was a familiar shadow but troubling all the same.

"You really loved her, didn't you?"

"I suppose as much as a man like me can love one woman." For a few minutes neither of us said a word. Kade flicked the cigarette into the gravel and put it out with his shoe. Then he turned and walked to the back end of the truck. "C'mon Butterbean," he said. "C'mon boy." Rain and Butterbean jumped out of the truck bed and took off running alongside Burdy's house.

"About those voices, Maizee."

"Yes?"

"Don't you worry. They'll quit pestering you soon as Zeb returns."

29

Kade might have been right about them voices disappearing once Zeb returned, but according to the telegrams them government men sent me, Zeb wasn't ever coming home again.

A clerk from the telegraph office in Kingsport paid me a visit on Thursday, July 6, 1944. I was behind in my chores on account of I spent most of the day Tuesday celebrating Independence Day along with most everybody else from Christian Bend at the catfish fry at Haw Lake.

Kade had cut a fishing pole special for Rain. My sides hurt from laughing after Rain about jumped in the lake trying to git ahold of the five-inch trout tugging his line. I wrote Zeb a letter all about it and was over at Burdy's borrowing a stamp when one of them government cars pulled up and a man got out.

Burdy turned to me and said, "Wait here, Maizee." That's the last clear thing I recall. All my other recollections from that day and the others that followed come to me in quick images, like a skittish hare—staring at me one minute, gone in the brambles the next.

The clerk asking Burdy if she knew how to reach Mrs. Zebulon Hurd. Me asking the man, you have a message for me? Burdy asking the man, when, when did Corporal Hurd go missing? Me asking Burdy, what does that mean, missing-in-action? Burdy asking the man, where, where was Corporal Hurd last seen? Me asking the man, who's looking for my husband? The Army? Is the Army looking for him? Are the Germans? Burdy asking the man, you sure Corporal Hurd isn't a prisoner of war; how can you be so sure? The man asking me, is there anything else I can do for you, ma'am?

"Yes," I said. "Send them government men a message. Tell 'em to find my husband."

Preacher Blount called a prayer meeting. People all over Christian Bend stopped by the house to tell me they was praying for Zeb's safe return. Sheriff and Mrs. Duncan came by and recounted the story of how their son Matt was expected to die after he was burned so badly at Pearl Harbor but how, through the miracle of prayer, he'd been spared. They didn't make mention about how Matt and Charma had split up after he come home on account of him staying drunk all the time. Or how behind his back, people were all the time saying how sad it was that the war ruin't Matt.

Leela-Ma came and stayed at the house with me that first week or so. She looked after Rain, greeted company, and seen to the chores. Doc was going back and forth uptown nearly everyday. He was trying his best to find out as much information as he could about what happened to Zeb. Kade come by the house, too, but he didn't stay long, didn't say much, other than how sorry he was and to tell me not to worry about the garden, that he'd see to it for me.

I stayed in bed, mostly. That's where I was when Doc come in one afternoon.

"I've brung you the paper," he said. "There's a story on Zeb."

"Lemme see it," I said, reaching for the *Rogersville Review*. There, underneath a headline that read "Hawkins Men Wounded and Listed as Missing" was Zeb's Army photograph. The one in his military uniform. It didn't seem much like the Zeb I knew on account of that stern look on his face.

Doc put a pillow behind my back and I sat up to read the story. "Several Hawkins county men were reported wounded this week and one is missing in action in France. Mrs. Maizee Hurd of Christian Bend has received word that her husband, Corporal Zebulon L. Hurd, has been 'missing following action in the line of duty' in France since the 6th of June. Corporal Hurd has been in the service over two years and has been overseas eight months. The couple have one child, a son, Rain L. Hurd."

Seeing Zeb's photo there in the paper thataway made the nightmare all the more real. I'd thought I was all cried out but a new fountain bubbled up from within. Doc held me as I sobbed. When I fell back onto the pillow, plumb give out, he said, "Maizee, I spoke to Senator McKellar's staff today. He said they would do everything they could to make sure Zeb gits home safely."

Doc looked as though he'd sat up for three nights straight. The folds in his jaws and chin were covered in grey stubble. I wondered when had he got so old. I pulled my knees up to my chest and jes lay there, trying to shut out the voices screaming inside my head. Voices that kept telling me Zeb was dead.

Six weeks later, on Friday, August 25th, a military man in a government car brung me a Western Union telegram and Zeb's dog tags:

MRS. ZEBULON L. HURD
ROUTE 2
CHRISTIAN BEND TENNESSEE
THE SECRETARY OF WAR DESIRES ME TO EXPRESS
HIS DEEPEST REGRET THAT YOUR HUSBAND CPL.
ZEBULON L. HURD WAS KILLED IN ACTION IN
FRANCE 6 JUNE 44.
E. A. COPE THE ADJUTANT GENERAL
1944

I sware my very first thought wasn't about Zeb but about what an awful job this young fellow had, going from home to home telling folks their husbands and sons were dead.

I was home alone with Rain when the military man showed up. He asked if there was anybody he could call to be with me. I shook my head no. I didn't need anybody. I didn't allow for any crying or wailing or gnashing of teeth. He asked me again. I told him no and he asked if I was sure. I was. What good would it have done? I knew how to swallow sorrow. I could be stubborn that way.

Burdy came over early the morning after I got word of Zeb's death and hung sheets over the mirrors, to keep the spirits at bay. Burdy was all the time doing crazy things like that. She give me some hot tonic that she said would be good for my nerves, though I didn't see why I needed any.

Preacher Blount called on us, inquiring as to when I'd be wanting to hold a memorial service for Zeb. I told him it didn't matter to me. I didn't tell Preacher, but I had no intentions of attending any memorial service for my husband without a body to bury. The government man said they couldn't find no sign of Zeb.

Preacher Blount held the services the following Tuesday. Me and Rain stayed away. Doc and Leela-Ma come by later to check on us and to tell us what a nice service it had been. Doc said he'd ordered Zeb a headstone, which I thought odd. Why would anyone put a headstone over an empty grave? Was it proper to even call it a grave? My head hurt from all the details.

Dear Lord, I'll never git rid of the voices. They'd yapped all day and night since Zeb went missing. I couldn't sleep, couldn't eat. Once the voices heard Zeb wouldn't be coming back, they moved right in with me and got good and comfortable, and loud, loud, loud.

I didn't tell nobody about the nuthatches, or the creeping cockroaches I seen trailing after me and Rain. A brigade of roaches, some nearly three inches long, would line up around the bed in the morning, soon as my feet or Rain's touched the floor. They'd march behind us all day long, from sitting room to kitchen, from kitchen to bedroom. They even followed us acrost the yard from our front door to Burdy's back one.

I asked Burdy if she could see 'em, but she shook her head side to side and give me one of them stares people do Rain when they think he cain't understand nothing, jes because he cain't hear. But Rain seen 'em, I know he did, 'cause when I took out the fly swatter and started killing 'em, Rain grabbed a shoe and started smacking 'em with it.

I'd slap. He'd stomp. I'd slap. He'd stomp. I didn't have the heart to tell Rain that all that stomping and swatting wasn't working. But he wasn't blind, he could see for himself the way every time we killed one roach, two more came in its place. Finally, I got out the sugar and poured a line from the bedroom to the back door. I'd got it in my head that roaches will follow a sugar trail, like ants, but these didn't. Burdy didn't make mention of the sugar trail, but she got the broom and swept it all up the next day.

Two nights later, I was lying in the bed next to Rain, with all the lamps shut off, when I heard a tap, tap, tapping sound. It grew louder and louder. The voices told me nuthatches were poking holes in my walls. Sure enough, when I throwed back the covers and got up to look, I seen half a dozen of 'em flitting down the walls, upside down.

I opened the front door and tried to shoo 'em out. I couldn't imagine how they'd managed to git into the house in the first place, but there they were, creeping along my sitting room walls, pretty as you please. But whenever I tried to herd them out the door, they'd disappear like ghost birds, if there is such a thing.

Now, that troubled me. Seeing them birds evaporate thataway. Something else was pestering me, too. Them chattering voices in my head told me to take the butcher knife from the kitchen drawer and cut myself. They claimed the only way to make sure that Zeb and I would be together in the afterlife was if I was willing to suffer as much as he had. It was kind of crazy, since truth was I didn't even know for sure how Zeb died, or if he suffered at all.

I waited till the seventh day after I got word of Zeb's death. Preacher Blount once said that seven is one of God's holy numbers. I didn't believe God to be some sort of gambling man the way Preacher Blount did, but damn it all to hell, if Preacher said seven was one of God's numbers, who was I to argue?

I waited till Rain was asleep, then I darkened all the lanterns in the house, save for a very dim one I used in the bedroom. Then I sat down on the floor in the kitchen next to the stove and began to cut the fleshy part of my thighs. Blood trickled down my legs like oil. I jes sat there on the cold wood floor and watched it pool and dry.

The Bible says blood has power, and I believed it after that. The chattering hushed. I could hear Rain's soft snore floating around me. The burn inside my head cooled. I wouldn't call it peace really, but something akin to it calmed me. I fell asleep there on the floor.

That's where Burdy found me the next morning, lying in a small puddle of caked blood.

"My lands, Maizee!" she said, kneeling down beside me. "Have you completely lost your mind?"

"If I haven't, I hope I do soon," I answered. "If it'll help stop this hurting."

"Well, keep this up and you'll manage to weave yourself into something you'll never git free of, MC," Burdy said. She took a closer look at the cuts on my thighs and seen they wasn't that deep. She grabbed a dish rag, wet it, and began cleaning off the dried blood on my arms and legs. Rain was still asleep.

"Come again? Did you jes call me MC?"

"I did."

"How come you to call me that?"

Burdy held my thigh in her palm and gently warshed around the cuts.

"I had a vision come to me several years ago, Maizee. We was over at Leela-Ma's place. It was Rain's first birthday. Remember when he almost fell in the pit fire?"

I nodded.

"Embry Mae and I were in the apple orchard with Rain. I come acrost a spider. A bowl-and-doily spider. Ever seen one of those?"

"Yes, ma'am."

"This one had woven herself a fine, fancy web, big as any I've ever seen. She was hanging in it upside down on the bottom of the bowl, between it and the doily. But it appeared she had woven such a complicated web that she'd trapped herself in all that spinning. I seen a sign that day on the spider's underbelly. It was a tattoo."

"What sort of tattoo, Burdy?"

"It looked like MC."

"What does it stand for?"

All of a sudden, Rain was standing in the doorway between the bedroom and sitting room, watching Burdy clean me up. His hair was ratted in back, where he'd slept on it.

"Well, what come to me that day was this here—you cutting yourself thisaway. MC might stand for Maizee Cutter, or Maizee Crazy. It's six of one, half a dozen of the other, as far as I can tell. Don't seem to really matter, considering." Burdy waved a hand out over the floor, like she was God splitting the Red Sea. She was always one for speaking plainly. "I fear what's happening to you, Maizee, is you're like that spider, weaving a web you cain't git free from."

"How do I make sure I don't git trapped?"

"That's the thing I don't know for sure."

"Burdy?"

"Yes?"

"I know I ain't thinking clearly."

"Well."

"Whatever happens, don't let me hurt my baby."

"You don't have a baby, Maizee."

"I mean Rain."

30

Zebulon

I dreamt of Rain, of Maizee, of home. Maizee was toting Rain around on her hip, his chubby legs and arms clinging tightly to his momma as she went about the house gathering up stuff. My stuff. Socks. Work boots. Coveralls. The locket I'd given her the day I'd left her standing at the station in Knoxville.

She shifted Rain from hip to hip as she shoved my belongings into a sack from Sentry's Market. Then, grabbing a box of matches on her way out, Maizee carted all that stuff and Rain to the burn barrel out back. She put Rain down on the ground and put the sack in the barrel, then dropped in a match. When the flames started leaping, Maizee bent over, picked up Rain, and dropped him in the barrel. He thrashed against the fire. His chubby legs and arms flaying, reaching for his momma. Tears streamed down his face as the fire caught hold of his hair. He screamed and screamed but no sound came.

"No! Noooo! MAIZEE!" I cried. "NOOOO!!"

I tried to run to her, to save Rain, to stop Maizee, but in my haste I fell from the roof of the house, where I was repairing a gutter. My legs crumbled like clods of dry dirt. I couldn't move.

"Nooo!" I cried. "DON'T, MAIZEE!"

31

Maizee

Days passed. People keep coming in and out the house. I didn't git up to greet 'em. If Burdy or Leela-Ma weren't around to handle 'em, I ignored the callers. Sometimes, even when Leela-Ma and Burdy were around, I still refused company.

When Kade come by the house I didn't want to visit, but he told Burdy he'd only stay for a minute or two. I sat up on the bed, atop the sage and pink quilt Leela-Ma and the church women give to me and Zeb when we was first married. Kade stayed a whole half-hour, sitting on the edge of my bed, drinking coffee. He didn't say much, jes sat with me, real quiet like and still as a newborn.

Rain run into the room and jumped up on the bed. He didn't have any idea what was afoot. I hadn't tried to tell him anything about his daddy. Shoot, Zeb been away so long, I wasn't sure Rain understood what a daddy was. Kade's coffee spilt out over the quilt when Rain bumped him. The coffee was warm, not hot, so nobody got burned, but it soaked right through Kade and the quilt.

I didn't care. Shit, I didn't care about breathing. If I could hold my breath long enough, I'd float to heaven and join Zeb there. And Momma. She had been waiting for me for so long. Wonder what would her eyes be like in heaven? Jesus' hands and side still bore the mark of the crucifixcion. Would Momma's eyes be empty sockets?

Kade folded up the quilt. Said he was going to take it to his sister's.

"I'm sorry, Maizee. I know how much this quilt means to you. Winfreda's good with stains. She'll git it out."

I didn't say nothing. I was thinking about Momma. Surely, she had eyes by now. What's the good of being in heaven if you ain't got eyes to see it with?

Kade said he'd bring the quilt back in a week or two. Before he left, he handed me an envelope.

"Here," he said.

"What's this?" I asked.

"Ah, jes some ramblings. You ain't got to read it now. Save it for later."

I folded it in half and put it in my skirt pocket.

Kade said something else, but the chattering in my head had growed so loud I couldn't barely understand 'im, something about being back to check on me. It seemed life was coming apart at the seams.

After Kade left, I unfolded the note he'd written with an unsteady hand:

It saddens me today
The news is out
Little Rain has discovered his worst of fears
His daddy has disappeared.
Zebulon Hurd was a good man
Of that, there is no doubt
And all of heaven is crying tears
For this fine man from Christian Bend
We all knew his life could end
But why did it have to be?
Rain will miss his daddy
Will his weeping ever cease?
I pray Zeb did not suffer
But if he did, I hope angels attended him

From Christian Bend to Jordan's River
A fallen soldier's final welcome home

I know he meant well, but Kade's note tore me up. I wished I hadn't read it. Afterwards I pulled out a box of family photos from under the bed, and sat by the stove, cutting myself out of each photo. I couldn't say why exactly. Some voice told me that was what I ought to do, so I did it. But that cutting didn't stop the voices the way the other cutting had.

After I got word of Zeb, them voices started telling me that I ought to set Rain a'fire. At first, I wasn't sure I heard them right, so I listened closer. But it was true. They was telling me that Rain would be better off dead than without a daddy. They told me that I wasn't fit to raise Rain on my own. I was evil and that's why Momma died the way she done, so she couldn't see all the evil in me, her only child.

"Listen here," the voices said. "The only way you're ever going to live together as a family is for you and Rain to join Zeb."

I started having visions, visions of me, Rain, and Zeb together. I seen Zeb standing in the yard, leaning against the hickory. He was wearing his soldier's uniform and motioning for me to c'mon. When I opened the screen door, he disappeared like the ghost birds had the other night. I called for him to come back, but then I seen Burdy standing on her back porch, staring at me, so I went back inside and shut the door.

Rain was sitting on the couch, turning the pages on a book Doc had given him. I sat down next to him and pulled him onto my lap. He looked up at me. Everyone said Rain looked like me, but there was something about him, the cut of his jaw, maybe, the fullness of his lips, that was all Zeb. I ran my hand through Rain's dark hair. He'd only had a couple of haircuts in his four years, but I couldn't bring myself to shave his head.

"Cleanse his blood."

"Keep 'im pure."

"Set 'im afire."

"Cut his throat."

"Hold his head under the water."

"Warsh the evil away."

"Sanctify 'im."

"Purify 'im."

My head hurt from the noise of it all. I couldn't turn the voices down. They were growing meaner, louder. I put my hands over my ears. Rocked back and forth. Stomped my feet. I went into the kitchen and took out all the pots and pans, hoping the clamor would drown out the sound of them. But nothing did. Not even talking over them helped. It only made my head hurt worse. It felt like it was swelling from the inside out.

I held Rain close and sang softly: "Would you over evil a victory win? There's power, power, wonder working power in the blood, in the precious blood of the Lamb."

Rain put his fingers to my lips as I sang, and smiled.

It was Zeb's smile.

I looked away.

"Sanctify 'im."

"Purify 'im."

The voices were chanting now.

I kept right on singing and humming, clutching Rain. I prayed as I sang. I prayed for the noise in my head to stop, stop, STOP! In Jesus' Holy Name. Amen.

But it didn't stop. It got louder and louder. I heard the bombs dropping. The screams of that little girl and her brother as they come acrost their momma's charred body. I heard the screams of thousands of children, all of them fatherless or motherless, like Rain, like the girl and her brother in the photo.

I prayed, begging God, "Stop the voices, please, please, please."

The pain in my head was making me sick at my stomach. My hands were sweaty. The backs of my legs were sweaty. Sweat was dripping down my lip, a river of salt running into the corners of my lip. My stomach cramped up like it'd done the day Rain was born.

I pushed Rain from my lap. He scooted to the far end of the couch, thinking he'd done something wrong. I'd hadn't meant to, but I'd shoved him too rough. I was an evil mother. I smiled.

"Wanna go for a walk, honey?"

Rain always wanted to go, anywhere. I grabbed a couple of things and stuck 'em in my pocketbook.

I intended to leave the voices behind, but they followed us down the drive, past the church, and beyond the grandfather oak rooted in the center of the graveyard, its reaching arms sheltering the dead. I had a vision of Rain hanging from a rope in that tree. His body swaying gently in the morning breeze.

"Sanctify 'im."

"Purify 'im."

The chant continued.

I held Rain's hand tight and hurried him along, past the cemetery, past a clump of cedars and a plot of yellowing tobacco, till we come to Leela-Ma's place.

32

Leela-Ma

I knowed something was bad wrong long before the afternoon clouds crowded together on the other side of the ridge and began spitting at the earth. My bones were hurting, a fierce burning, like somebody piled 'em in a kindling heap and struck a match to 'em. It was all I could do to sit upright on the porch and keep an eye on Maizee's son, Rain. She'd dropped him off at the house early this morning. Said she had to go into town to tend after some business.

"Mercy sakes, Maizee! I'm telling you what, that boy has grown a foot this summer," I said as they walked up the dirt drive.

"That's the gospel truth, Leela-Ma. He's already grown out of his baby fat." She let go of Rain's hand and he run over to me. I grabbed him up in a hug and lifted his tee shirt so I could see he was wearing the belt me and Doc give him for his fourth birthday. I ran my fingers over the shiny buckle with the bucking bronco and up his tummy. He giggled in silence and swiped my hand away.

"I don't 'spect I'll be back until after supper, Leela-Ma," she said. "So don't you go worrying after me."

I didn't like the idea of Maizee going off to town on her own. She'd been having more dark spells since them men come to town with news of Zeb. I'd tried to git Maizee to come live with us after Zeb left, but she wouldn't consider it. Not even when she come down with the croup that first winter Zeb was gone and I went over to her place during the day to tend to her. I would have stayed there every night, but Burdy insisted on caring for Maizee. It bothered me some that I didn't have Burdy's healing powers, but I didn't put up a fuss. I wanted Maizee better, and whatever it was Burdy done seemed to have worked. Maizee was outta the bed and her old self again.

"You meeting somebody?" I asked. I didn't want to pry into Maizee's business, but I knew that Kade Mashburn fellow had been around to her house several times, and I didn't care one bit for him. He was a mucckly low-down. Always had been. Always would be, if you're asking me, which Maizee wasn't. She answered me with a question.

"You got any errands you need me to run while I'm in town?"

"Come to think of it, there are a coupla of things. Wait right 'chere."

The screen door slammed behind me. I walked over to the sewing machine standing in the corner of the sitting room, pulled out a spool of thread and my scissors from the drawer, stuck 'em in a poke, and carried it back out to Maizee.

"I need some more of this yella thread," I said, handing her the poke. "Gimme one of the big spools if they got 'em, or if not, git me two little 'uns. And see if you can git Mister Sloane over at the hardware store to sharpen my scissors. They've dulled up on me."

I pulled my change purse from my apron pocket and took two dollars out. I handed them to Maizee. She pushed my outstretched hand away. Her eyes and lips narrowed into thin slits.

"Your money ain't no good with me," she said. "Keep it."

If it weren't for Burdy Luttrell, I didn't see how Maizee could manage. Doc told me Burdy wouldn't take no rent money, no matter how much Maizee squawked about needing to pay it.

I feared that part of the reason that Mashburn low-count kept coming around had to do with money. As little as Maizee had, it was more money than he made playing his fiddle at the juke joints. A'course the other reason was plain to see—Mashburn was a man of earthy ways, if you know what I'm a'saying. He wasn't a family man like Zeb or Doc. But poor Maizee, she couldn't see it. Doc said maybe it's because she seen in Kade Mashburn something familiar—a soul adrift.

"For pity's sake, girl, you don't got to be so high and mighty with me," I said. My tone was cross. "You're doin' me the favor. The least I can do is pay for it."

The pinch between Maizee's brows eased some. Her shoulders fell. Grabbing me by the waist, she pulled me into a heart-to-heart hug. "I'm sorry, Leela-Ma. I don't mean to be so hateful."

"Nobody's saying you're hateful, honey." I reached up and took Maizee's face into my hands so I could look straightways at her. "I know you ain't been yourself lately. It's understandable, given all you been through. I don't mean to be cross."

Healing waters dribbled out the corners of Maizee's blue eyes. "You're a good momma to me, Leela-Ma. I love you big as God's morning sky."

Maizee was quoting to me from a verse I used to recite to her when she first come to live with me and Doc:

Handing her back the money, I said, "And I love you big as the mountains of Christian Bend."

"That's big enough for me," Maizee replied. She stuck the money between her breasts and puckered up. I kissed her wet salty lips, then each of her eyes and her forehead. She laughed in her rumbling way.

Taking Rain's hands into hers, Maizee got on her knees and told him face to face, "I love you," but the onliest sound I heared was that of leaves flapping in the breeze and a tractor engine puttering.

Maizee hugged her boy and took off down the drive. I held Rain's hand and we waved goodbye. When she got to the bend at River Road, she stopped and waved back.

"I love you BIG!" she shouted and blew us a kiss.

Rain spent the better part of his day building a fort in the front yard with sticks we'd gathered from under the apple trees out back. He had a couple of plastic brown horses that he kept riding into and out of the space that was the fort's gate. He pushed along on his knees as he galloped the horses with his hands.

"Giddy up! Giddy up!" I yelled. "Faster. Faster. Thataway! The robbers are headed over yonder." I pointed toward a bed of clover. Rain looked at me and ran the horses uphill. It didn't matter that he couldn't hear me, Rain was good at understanding me.

For some reason that I've never been able to decipher, Maizee was convinced that her son's ailment was all her fault. But the truth is a fever lit upon him during one winter when he was a baby and left him deaf as a snake. "I think even God regrets the day I was born," Maizee said one afternoon as we was in the kitchen warshing and peeling plums for jam.

"Mercy sakes, girl! What in the world would cause you to say such a thing?"

Rain was asleep on the sofa, his diapered rump rounded upwards like a camel's hump. Nodding her head toward him, Maizee said, "Seems obvious that God's put out with me over something or another, that's all."

"Jes because that baby has an ailment doesn't mean God's mad at you, sweetie." I never could speculate why whenever things go bad, people always pin the fault on God. Doc claims it's because God is so big he makes for an easy target.

That was the first I knowed for sure that Maizee felt a curse upon her life. I suppose she'd felt that way ever since the day my sister Nan keelt over in her own backyard near the lilac hedge.

It was well-nigh past suppertime. Rain sat at the kitchen table making a log cabin from a box of toothpicks I'd given him. The kitchen was as comfortable a spot as any in the house. The wood stove sat off in one corner, the sink in the other. The icebox was pushed up against the wall, between the sink and back door. Doc's grandfather had made the table. The chairs were a mix-and-match brand picked up here and there over the years. Since the table sat in the middle of the kitchen, the front and back doors could be seen from any one of those chairs. We'd been sitting there for a while, waiting on Doc to git home.

"Wonder what's waylaid Doc this time?" I put my face right in front of Rain's so he could see my words, even if he couldn't hear 'em or answer me. Rain shrugged his shoulders and shook his head sideways so fast I thought it might spin on around. I reached over and put my hand, palm down, on top his head.

Rain favored his momma so much it seemed a shame to waste all that prettiness on a boy. He had her hair, wavy thick and black as fountain ink. His bottom lip was full even when he was smiling, something Rain did most of the time. Laughter was Rain's way of communicating. His laughter wasn't throaty or high-pitched. It was more of a halted groaning, which sometimes startled folks not used to a mute child's ways.

"Is that thunder or is your belly rumbling?" I placed my hand on Rain's tummy. "You hongree?"

Nodding his head yes, Rain put four fingers in his mouth in mock gobbling fashion. Pulling a gold chain from my pocket, I checked Doc's timepiece. I'd saved up two years of S&H Green Stamps to buy Doc a watch, but he never carried it with him unless he was headed to church. He only pulled it out then to time Preacher Blount's sermons.

"Well, I reckon so. You ought to be starving by now. It's nearly six-thirty." I looked out the window. The storm was moving in on us. Doc would have to walk through a frog-drowner if he didn't hurry on home soon.

I ladled out some soup beans I'd put on that afternoon onto a plate, taking care to drain off the soup but leave a chunk of fatback, and cut a piece of the cornbread warming on top the wood stove.

Thunder crackled so loud the jars in the cupboard rattled together. Where was Doc? The sky opened up and water pellets pounded the tin roof like a barrage of gunfire. Mercy sakes. What was taking Maizee so long?

Rain grunted. I turned to see him pointing at the honey jar sitting in the open cupboard. If his momma would allow it, Rain would eat honey all day long. Clasping his dimpled hands and leaning up on his elbows, Rain smacked his lips as I drizzled a spoonful of the nectar over the cornbread. Doc yanked open the back screen.

"Leela."

He called my name out careful, like he'd seen a dark spirit hovering over me and didn't want to disturb it, but urgent, like he wanted me to move and fast. I'd knowed something was bad wrong, had knowed it from the way my bones ached all day.

I put the plate in front of Rain and slowly turned to the door, fearing what I must see. Reaching behind me, I untied my apron and then placed it on the counter.

"What?"

Doc walked over, grabbed my shoulders, and pulled me to him. I could see he'd been crying. His moist lids were clumped. His hollowed-out cheeks shone red, like they jes had a scrubbing with fresh lye. Doc's arms, made strong by the lifting of wood, water and slop, felt drawed up, like Samson's after Deliah chopped off all his hair.

"Oh, Leela." Doc said, resting his head in the crook of my neck. He begun to moan like I ain't never heard from a man growed up, 'cept in church overcome by the Holy Ghost. My stomach clawed up bad. I didn't say nothing. Couldn't think of nothing to say. I clutched Doc like he was the last branch before a hard fall.

Rain got down out of his chair and came over and wrapped his arms around Doc's knee and my thigh. He buried his face betwixt us. Pulling away, Doc bent over and lifted the child up. Rain pressed his forehead against Doc's.

That's when I caught the first glimpse of a ghost in my husband's tired eyes.

33

Maizee

For the first time ever, I lied to Leela-Ma. I told her I had to go into town to take care of some business. I left Rain there with her. I had to. I didn't trust myself with him.

I felt bad about the lying, and the leaving, but I had to git out of Christian Bend, away from the voices. I had a bad feeling that went beyond plain grief. Grief was familiar to me. It had been my most steadfast companion for a long time now.

I couldn't tell Leela-Ma about the voices. I feared she'd think me addled. She might try to take Rain from me. She'd always wanted a child of her own. Reckon she'd do that?

I dropped Leela-Ma's scissors off at Sloane's Hardware before noon and asked Cal to sharpen them for her, like she asked me to. Cal said they'd be ready at one o'clock. I thanked him and said I'd be back before two o'clock to pick 'em up.

Then I lit out for Winfreda Mashburn's place. She had my quilt. I needed it. Winfreda lived at the north end of Depot Street, right smack-dab up against the tracks. Her three boys—one redheaded, the others tow-headed—were running slanchwise up the hill beside the house.

"Your momma home?" I yelled out, as the tallest of the three boys ran down the hill shouting, "Kill the Krauts!"

"Yes, ma'am," he replied. "Go on in."

Tomatoes, some ripe, some ripening yet, lined up acrost the porch railing. I stepped around a poke full of Shellie beans sitting on the steps. A rusty horseshoe hung over the door, upside down.

I knocked on the screen door, waited, knocked again. Still no one answered. The front door was open, so I stepped inside and looked around. It was so dark, all I could see were purple and red spots. I thought about calling out for somebody, but I decided not to. I didn't want to talk to nobody if I could help it. I'd only come for my quilt.

The room was hot and smelt of salty piss. A chamber pot full to the rim sat at the foot of a bed pushed up under the far window. The bed was unmade. Magazines, newspapers, a stray sock, and several pair of shoes, all different sizes, were scattered about. Gray and white mounds erupted and flowed out of the ashtray, onto a bedside table and the wood floor. A picture of a blonde-haired angel guiding two children acrost a footbridge hung cockeyed above the only chair in the room. My quilt was folded up neatly and sitting on the arm of the couch.

I overheard two people arguing in another room. I recognized the man's voice as Kade's. I took the other to be his sister. Grabbing up what I come for, I hurried out the door and was halfway up the street when Kade grabbed me from behind.

"You gonna jes leave without saying hello?"

He startled me. I studied on him for a bit then answered, "What's the worth of a child?"

"Come again?"

"That's the theme for the Sunday School program for this fall. What's the worth of a child? Do you like it?" I turned from Kade and spit on the ground. And followed that spit with another.

"Maizee, are you alright?"

"I'm fine," I said, spitting again. "My mouth is dry. That's all."

Kade took a step back. Either to avoid my spit fits or the better to study me. Thick knotted brows shielded his eyes. He looped his thumbs through his belt hoops. He was barefoot, not having taken time to put on his boots to chase after me.

"I see you found your quilt," he said, nodding toward the blanket in my arms.

"Mm-hm."

"I told you I'd bring it up to you. Winfreda got the stain all out."

"I seen she did. Thank her for me. I bet she knows the worth of a child."

Kade turned his head sidelong and cut his eyes at me. "Maizee, you're not making any sense. Why don't you come back inside and let me git you a glass of water or an iced tea?" He reached out for my elbow.

"No!" I shouted, backing away from him. "DON'T TOUCH ME!"

A neighbor woman watering her flowers turned and looked our way. Kade put both hands in the air and took another step back. "Calm down," he whispered. "I ain't hurting you."

"I have to go," I said, and spat on the ground right in front of his feet.

"Why are you in such an all-fired hurry?"

"I got to pick up some things for Leela-Ma at Sloane's."

The neighbor lady turned her back to us.

"Lemme git my shoes on and I'll walk you over there."

"No," I said. My head was hurting again. I looked hard at Kade, but all I could see was Rain swaying in the breeze, hanging from a branch on the graveyard oak. The voices were urging me: "Purify 'im, sanctify 'im, give 'im eternal life. Santify 'im, purify 'im, give 'im eternal life. Eternal life. Eternal life. A pure heart. A pure heart. A pure heart. Give 'im a pure heart."

I could read Kade's lips—he was calling my name—but I couldn't answer. I felt like I did when Wheedin used to hold my head underwater when as girls we played up at Horseshoe Falls. Wheedin had a mean streak. She'd laugh as she pushed me under. I couldn't yell or beg for mercy, for fear of drowning. I'd flap my arms, kick my feet, and struggle against her, but I couldn't break free from her grip on my head until Wheedin was ready to free me. I'd shoot out of that water, gasping for air, cussing at Wheedin, which only made her laugh more.

"I'm sorry, Kade."

"Sorry for what?"

"Can I ask you something?"

Kade was looking at me the same as Burdy did when she found the sugar trail in the house. He run a hand through his thick red hair and said, "Sure. What?"

"Do you think there's power in the blood like the hymn says?"

Kade shook his head back and forth, and rubbed at his chin. "Maizee, I really wished you'd come in the house and git out of the sun for a minute."

"I done told you I got to git going. I jes wanted to know what you thought but I know. I see it in your eyes. You're wrong. Zeb's not the one suffering. He's with Jesus. We're the ones damned to suffer! We don't know the worth of a child!" Little bubbles of spit ran out the corners of my mouth.

Two of Winfreda's boys run up to Kade and yanked on his arms. "C'mere, Uncle Kade. Come see our fort."

"In a minute," he answered them, then turned back to me. "Where's Rain?"

"I left 'im with Leela-Ma."

"C'mon, Uncle Kade!" The tallest boy with yellow hair pulled on Kade's belt.

"You go on," I said. "I'm fine."

"You sure?"

"Yes," I said. I turned and walked away, humming the song I sung to Rain earlier: "Would you over evil a victory win? There's power, power, wonder working power in the blood." The promises of that song stayed with me as I picked up Leela-Ma's newly sharpened scissors, and later as I walked alongside the Holston.

I took a deep breath. The river looked calm, still as Haw Lake. Tiny bubbles near the mudbanks were the only evidence of the life below. This was the trick of boiling waters. Making people think everything was calm when really the current was so strong it could pull a child under like the hand of Satan reaching up from earth's navel.

Taking another deep breath, I held it for a moment, listening, hearing the soft rhythm of my own heart and the sigh of wind as it moved past me. I leaned my head back so that God could read my lips: "Thank you," I whispered. "Thank you."

The voices had stopped. Finally. I whispered for fear of rousing them again.

There wasn't much of a riverbank along these parts of the Holston. Next to nearly every home was a square garden plot, like the one at Burdy's place. Up a piece from the trailing vines of pumpkins and squash was a bigger plot heaped with yellowing tobacco, piled in neat rows like matchstick teepees. A distance beyond that, the earth broke off jagged into the river. Some of the cedars and hickories stood ankle-deep in the water. So I knew when I seen a stretch of bank from the road what to do.

I followed a rough trail past the clumps of elderberry growing wild and over the stomped-down wiregrass and cattails. When I got to the bank and spread out my quilt, a ladybug landed in the corner where the church women had stitched in mine and Zeb's wedding date: June 3, 1940.

I smiled, remembering the first Sunday I came to Christian Bend. I'd been standing next to Doc, his hand draped over my shoulder. I was eager to git home and have a slice of the caramel cake Leela-Ma had made as a welcome for me.

Preacher Blount's sermon had gone over by twenty minutes. It was dinnertime and my stomach was growling. But Doc was talking to some fella about how to doctor an ingrown toenail turned sour. Leela-Ma knelt down in front of me and opened her hand. There on her palm was a bright ladybug, wings spreading.

"Whenever you see a ladybug it's a sign that you're where you're supposed to be," Leela-Ma said. Then, she cupped her hand around the ladybug and placed it into mine. "Welcome to Christian Bend, Maizee. This is the place you're supposed to be."

I cupped my hand to the corner of the blanket and waited for the ladybug to come to me. She did. I knew she would. I sat, ankles crossed, studying the delicate bug in my palm, envying the ease at which she took to life and new surroundings. The ladybug took off. Free to fly. Free to stay. Everywhere a ladybug goes, it belongs. I envied her that, too.

I never felt like I belonged anywhere except in Zeb's arms. My chest ached with the want of feeling his embrace again. I hoped he wouldn't be angry with me. I hoped he'd understand. I hoped Rain would, too. I loved Rain more than life itself. I loved him with the certainty described in the verse Leela-Ma used to recite to me:

I love you big as the bright yellow sun.
I love you big as the river that runs wild.
I love you big as the katydids cry.
I love you big as God's morning sky.
I love you big as the mountains of Christian Bend.
I love you big with a love that will never, ever end.

I took the scissors out from my purse and said a prayer of thanks for the mountains and the people that had embraced me all these years. I didn't cry, though. I'd promised myself I wouldn't, not even in that moment.

Smiling at my stubborn ways, I laid back and drove the sharp end of those scissors hard and deep into my throat. It didn't hurt. Not much, anyhow, and surely not as much as the vision of Rain swaying from that tree. A blood halo seeped out all around me as I stared at the mountains of Christian Bend and above them to God's big sky. I hummed, "There's power, power, wonder-working power in the precious blood of the Lamb."

It weren't long before I fell into the arms of Jesus. He put a crown of shiny pearls on my head and then carried me ever so tenderly acrost the rushing river.

Leela-Ma

There's not much bank along the stretch of the Holston River where Doc found Maizee that day. Face up, like a sunbather soaking in the late afternoon sun. Her hands clasped acrost her stomach. Her mouth slightly ajar. Her long black hair mopped out over the quilt that had been hers and Zeb's wedding gift.

Doc told me how he knelt down over Maizee and fought back an urge to lift her up into his lap like he'd done when she was a young girl and he read to her from the Good Book before bedtime each night. He didn't touch her. Didn't try to rouse her. With one single touch, Jesus had stirred the life within Lazarus and caused him to rise up again, but Doc knew the life had left Maizee long before she was found on that riverbank, and no amount of human affection would be able to restore it. Not even the adoring, forgiving love of a young son.

Or of an aging man and woman.

Doc recalled how the wetness of the river soaked up through that wedding quilt, creating a mud halo around Maizee's head, shoulders, elbows, hips, and heels. A turtle rested, undisturbed, on a thick snag near the bank. Cottonwood fluff floated over the river like lint from heaven. A farm truck rattled on the road behind them.

He said he knew before he knelt down beside her that Maizee had at last found a way to exhale. He saw it in the blueness that colored her lips and fingertips.

Doubling over till his forehead rested on hers, Doc let his brokenness spill out over the quilt. "Oh, my precious Maizee. Why?"

Rain slept in the big bed, between Doc and me. He was still resting when Preacher Blount paid a call first thing the next morning. Doc had took off for town as soon as morning light turned the mountain lavender. He was going to meet with the sheriff. I was sitting at the kitchen table near the stove, searching my Bible, praying, when I heared heavy footsteps climbing up the stairs.

Cinching up the belt on my worn housecoat, I opened the door before the first knock.

"I'm sorry to bother you this early, Mrs. Leela, but I heard about Maizee and thought you might need some company." Preacher Blount twisted the brim of his gray felt hat like he was pinching up the edge of a pie.

Stepping out on the porch, I shut the door behind me. The morning air was thick with dew and the sweet stink of hogs. Them hogs was all huddled together near the south side of the pen, near the corner where Christain and River roads hook. They was squealing something awful. Doc had neglected to feed them on his way out. I'd have to do that right soon.

"Mercy sakes, Preacher, you didn't have to come out so early."

"I came soon as I heard about your girl, Leela."

"I appreciate that."

"How's Rain?"

"He don't know yet. Doc and I ain't sure how to tell 'im. He knowed something weren't right when his momma didn't show up last night and when he saw Doc crying." I got a catch in my throat and couldn't say no more.

Preacher Blount looked away, allowing me some privacy.

"If there's any way I can be of help."

"I suspect Doc will be wanting to speak with you later this afternoon," I said. "But right now he's gone to town to meet with Sheriff Duncan."

"Mrs. Duncan's the one that called and told me."

The brass knob on the front door clicked. Rain was up, trying to twist open the shut door. I turned and opened it for him. His hair was poking out the sides of his head, quills on a porcupine. Smiling, I bent over and picked him up. He was cozy warm. He wrapped one arm around me, snuggled his head in the crook in my neck, and gave Preacher a shy wave with his free hand.

Preacher returned the wave, then patted him on the back.

"I don't mean to pry, Leela, but do y'all know…"

I didn't allow him to finish.

"Not yet. Doc's figuring to hear more in town."

"I see. Reckon when y'all might be wanting to have the services?"

"Soon."

Yesterday was Wednesday. Maizee would need burying no later than Saturday, in keeping with the third-day rising.

"You want I should call Embry and send her out to he'p you?"

"I don't mean to trouble you."

"It's no trouble, Leela. I got to be heading back to the church, but let's have a word of prayer first, okay?"

I bowed, shut my eyes, and took in a deep breath, inhaling the perfume of the confederate jasmine trailing up the side of the house and onto the tin roof. It was a fresh smell—the scent of angels and newborns, Nan always said. Rain wiggled in my arms. He was almost too big to pick up anymore, and age at four too old to be sucking on those three fingers the way he done. Preacher Blount prayed in a deliberate way, asking God for mercy, strength, understanding, and most of all peace. He prayed for our dead Maizee, that her soul would find the rest it needed, and for that joyous reunion that Maizee longed for—with her momma and with Zeb.

The notion of joyous reunion didn't seem fitting to me, given the circumstances. Still, I was glad Preacher prayed Maizee would find rest, because it was certain I wouldn't be finding none anytime soon, unless I, too, turned up dead on a riverbank somewhere.

"Did Doc say what time he'd be back?" Preacher asked after he'd finished his "In Jesus' Name, Amen."

"Didn't say."

The hogs was growing more discontent by the minute.

"Why don't I slop those hogs for you before I head out?"

"I cain't let you do that. You got your good shoes on." We both looked down at his feet. Preacher Blount had on his black Sunday shoes, not the scuffed work boots he usually wore.

"Won't take me no time a'tall to run home and change," he offered again.

"That's good of you, Preacher, but as soon as I'm dressed, me and Rain will see to 'em."

"Alrighty then." Preacher put his hat on. The sun had baked the dew clean off the grass, even though it weren't yet ten o'clock. It was already in the high seventies for sure.

Soon as Preacher walked to the end of the drive, I took Rain inside and fried him some eggs, hard whites with runny yellows. Rain liked to poke at the middle with a toothpick until the yolk oozed out. I poured myself a cup of coffee from the kettle on the back of the stove. It was still warm, although when I checked the stove there wasn't nothing but chunks of red embers turning to hot ash. No sense keeping the fire going as much as it was heating up outside.

I left Rain to his eggs and quickly changed, stepping into a slip and housedress. I pulled my graying hair back off my face with a couple of combs Maizee bought me on a trip through the Smokies she and Zeb made right before he shipped out.

"They're tortoise shell," Maizee had said, proudly displaying the gift she'd picked out at a store in Gatlinburg. I'd never been further south or west than town, and I didn't have any intentions of going north, unless it was to the hospital in Kingsport.

"Tortoise shell?"I kept turning them over and over again, wondering how is it a person makes a comb from a turtle's back. Seemed a mite shame to me, and the naked turtle, too, I reckoned.

"They ain't really made from a turtle, Leela-Ma," Maizee said. Leela-Ma was the name she took to calling me after her momma had been dead a year. She always knowed when something was bugging me, and she'd laughed when she saw relief ease over my face. The combs were awful pretty, but I wouldn't want a turtle to be without its home for my sake.

"Mercy sakes, they sho' are fancy things."

"I seen a movie star wearing some like 'em in a picture show called *Woman of the Year*. Zeb took me to see it."

"Reckon it'll make me a woman of the year?" I asked.

Standing before the looking glass hanging from a nail in the bedroom, I had pushed the combs through my hair. Maizee walked up behind me and fiddled with 'em.

"Them starlets ain't got nothing over you, Leela-Ma. You're the prettiest woman in all of Tennessee. Much prettier than them trashy-looking city women with their red lipstick and too snug dresses. I hope I'm half as pretty as you when I turn forty."

My gut seized up at the memory of Maizee's words.

Sitting down on the edge of my bed, I tried to catch my breath. Tears, strong and fierce, pressed and pushed against me, like a dogwood slapped by spring floods. Maizee wasn't going to see forty. She was only twenty-one.

Rain appeared at my side, stroking my hair. Taking a handkerchief outta my pocket, I blew my nose, dried my eyes, forced a smile. I felt limp, wrung out, like a cloth doll rescued from the bottom of the water tub.

"Leela-Ma's okay, Rain. Don't you worry, child. I'm okay."

I held his chin in my hand as I spoke the words slowly. Splotches of yolk colored his chin and cheeks. Rain couldn't yet read lips all that well, but he and his momma had been working on it some.

"Is that war paint you're wearing, Rain, or you planning on running off and join the circus as a clown?"

Rain squinched his eyes and nose as I took the wet hanky and scrubbed his face. Then he held out his hands, palms up. They was sticky yellow. I drew a heart in the messiest hand and an arrow on the other hand. I guided Rain back to the kitchen and warshed him up from a pail of clean water. Doc had drawn the well water early, before daybreak. It'd been cold when Doc first brung it in, but it had warmed up to room temperature.

"We got to git you dressed so we can go feed the hogs. You want to slop the hogs, Rain?"

A grin crept up his face. He ran for the slop pail on the back porch. Rain didn't have as much trouble understanding as some of the hearing do.

"Hold on jes one minute, Lightning! We got to git your shoes on," I said, following him and prying his fingers off the pail's handle. It was too heavy for Rain to lift or he'd likely been halfway down the road and him barefoot before I got out the door.

I hoped as long as I kept him busy with the chores, maybe Rain wouldn't worry about his momma, or when she was coming to git him. I didn't have any idea how we was going to go about telling him his momma was dead. Doc and I hadn't talked about Rain last night.

We spoke only of Maizee, and how he found her.

Doc told me how he was walking north along River Road. It's more dirt trail than road, winding downriver of Christian Bend, and fit for only one farm truck at a time. He was headed upriver when he eyed someone stretched out on the riverbank. Not many folks sunbathe along the Holston—too many snakes, skeeters, and not much beach, mostly mud and rock banks. Besides, the sun is too hot around these parts.

As Doc got closer he could tell it was a woman, fully dressed, like she was headed to town. Her pocketbook was sat down beside her, open. That's what alarmed Doc at first. That open pocketbook, tempting some no-good to come along and steal it. He ventured off the road, careful to step around the temples built by the fire ants, and past the blackberry brambles poking, and was jes two steps beyond the switchgrass when he caught sight of a quilt. He recognized it right away.

There was something else Doc eyed right away. My black-handled sewing scissors. The very ones I'd used to cut the squares of green and pink sewn into the blanket's interlocking rings. The ones I'd handed over to Maizee that morning, before she rounded the corner and walked off under the shadow of the mountain of big love.

"That's enough dwelling. I cain't do this no more," I said, willing myself out of misery for the moment.

Rain yanked his boots on by himself and took off out the backdoor again. This time he didn't try to lift the slop pail. He left it for me to carry.

36

Embry Mae came walking up Goshen Road carrying a cake plate in one hand and a platter in the other. Rain hopped down off the fence rail and ran at her. I was pushing my way through the hogs to the trough, boots sloshing in the sod soaked with pig pee. I yelled after Rain, for all the good it did me. "Wait!"

"Oh, he's all right," Embry Mae yelled back.

"If you ain't careful he'll knock you over," I warned.

Embry tightened her grip on the goods and steadied herself for Rain's clumsy embrace. He grabbed her around her knees. Embry's tall, nearly six feet, and as strong as any man around. Life in these hills demands women to be stout. Weak women don't thrive in these parts.

I shook my head. My mind was fading this morning. Maybe it was the sun. Maybe it was the sorrow. Maybe it was the stench of the hogs, but I felt out of sorts.

Scooching down till she was eye-level with him, Embry held out the platter for Rain.

"You want to carry the fried chicken?" she asked. He nodded and reached for the plate. "Two hands. You got to use two hands." Embry held onto it until Rain grasped both ends. "Not too heavy? That's good."

Rain clutched the platter up against his chest and held it with all his might, determined not to drop it.

Embry was our nearest neighbor. She lived a mile or so away, uphill, and had walked over from her place, a good piece aways on foot, since that's the only kinds of roads there are back in these parts.

The happiest day in my life, not counting my salvation day, was when Maizee came to stay, but the joy was marred by the sorrow of losing Nan. Those conflicting emotions warshed over me again as I watched Rain walk alongside Embry, trying to match her one stride with two of his own. Rain would be ours to raise now, a gift from God in the autumn years of life, Doc fifty-one and me forty-four.

But the gift came at a price much too high, one I didn't want to pay.

My heart crumbled, like a cornerstone too weak for the weight it had to bear. I doubled over in pain. Embry sat the cake down in the middle of the road and rushed to me. Wrapping her arms around my waist, she held me up. Rain stood back, protecting the cake and grasping the platter of chicken. His lower lip trembling. His blue eyes purpled up in fear.

"Oh, Lord Jesus, give us strength," Embry prayed. It was all she knowed to do. "Hold on, Leela. You're gonna be fine. I'm here. I'm here." Embry tightened her grip and practically carried me to the front porch. She sat me down in the rocker and dipped a tin of water from the pail.

"Drink this," she said. Embry took a handkerchief from her pocket and wiped my forehead. "Lord, you're sweating like a fevered soul, but your skin is clammy cold."

As soon as the words were outta her mouth, a chill swept over me. My teeth started chattering. My legs and arms a'shaking. Embry looked out at Rain, who still hadn't left his spot in the middle of the drive. He was planted, a sapling taken root. If he had been a hearing child, Embry might have ordered him to run, run quickly and git her a blanket. But since he wasn't, Embry got up, ran inside the house, and yanked the bedspread off the big bed herself. She wrapped it real tight around me and held the tin up so I could sip from it.

"Dear Jesus, please, please, heal Leela from this fever that's beset her," Embry continued to pray. She knelt down beside me, rubbed my thighs, my arms, my neck. "Take a deep breath. That's right. Slowly."

It weren't long and the pain in my chest eased, along with the sweats and chills. My breathing came regular again. Leaning my head back, I closed my eyes and rocked gently, trying to calm the soreness that beset me. Embry continued to stroke my shoulder.

"God has not forsaken you," she said. "He's got Maizee in his arms. She's safe with him. Don't you fret. He's not gonna let any more harm come to her, or you, or Rain."

Embry's words were strangely comforting, even though I didn't believe a word of them right then. I wanted to. I wanted to believe that we'd done enough suffering for a lifetime, for three lifetimes, and that surely a merciful God would spare us any more. I wanted to believe that in the worst way, so as Embry spoke it, I let her reassurances soak deep inside my pores. If a person could put a curse on another with words, then maybe the right words could fix a person. Embry's words sure felt full of healing.

Bitter water seeped out. My shoulders shook. Bending over my lap, I let the tears and snot crawl in the corners of my mouth.

"Oh, God, why?" I cried. "WHY?"

Embry stood beside me, rubbing my back, not saying a word. After a few minutes, when the heaving stopped, my chest felt empty as a June bug's shell.

"Leela, you stay right here. I'm gonna go git Rain," Embry said.

I nodded.

She gathered Rain lickety-split. I rose from the chair to follow them, the blanket still wrapped around my shoulders.

"Don't git up. I'll come back for you in a minute."

"Mercy sakes, don't treat me like I'm feeble, Embry Mae. I jes got fuzzy-headed. I needed to catch my breath, that's all."

I held the screen door open and followed Embry into the kitchen, where she proceeded to cut us all a slice of pound cake. I poured Rain a glass of milk from the pitcher in the icebox.

"You ought to sit down and rest. I can do that," Embry scolded.

Ignoring her, I asked, "You want some milk? Or tea?"

"I'd like a glass of tea, if you got some made."

I folded the blanket and set it aside on the ladder-back chair. Then I grabbed a couple of jelly jars from the cupboard and poured us both some tea. I could feel the heat in my flushed cheeks. If it weren't for everything else happening, I would've sworn all this fluctuation in body temperature was a woman problem.

I knew Embry wanted to ask after Maizee, to say something to console me, knew she wanted to know what had happened. Did Maizee jes lay down and die there on that riverbank? Had someone come along and suffocated her while she lay sleeping? Did a cross-eyed hunter mistake her for a deer and shoot her accidentally?

Embry didn't know about Maizee's pecuilarness. She didn't know about Kade Mashburn lolling about. She didn't know about the scissors Doc found.

Embry's hazel eyes were afire with questions, but I knew as sure as I was sitting there that Embry would never ask me nary one of 'em. Not with Rain in the room. He couldn't have heard us any better than the table we was sitting at could, but Rain could do something that table couldn't; he could feel things. Things in the air. Unspoken things, even. We wouldn't speak of the dead, not with Rain present. Not yet.

"When's Doc due back?"

"Not real sure. Maybe not till supper." I glanced at the battery clock hanging over the Hamblen & Sons Feed calendar. "Gracious, it is 12:30 already? The morning's done got away from me." Everything about the day seemed otherworldly, even the time.

"I brought you some chicken for supper. I'd brought you a salad too, if I had more hands to he'p me carry it."

"I appreciate your kindness. But you really ought not have fussed over us so."

"Weren't no fuss. A person's got to eat."

"I ain't got much appetite." I hadn't touched the cake Embry cut. Rain finished his and was starting in on mine.

"Rain's sprouting up like tobacco," she said.

I looked over at him. Two pieces of cake wasn't a fitting dinner for such a growing boy, but it was the best I could manage today.

"I reckon he is."

I found myself wondering had Doc thought to pray over Maizee as soon as he found her? Was her head all droopy? Had the life ebbed out of her and left her limp, or had she been there long enough to grow hard as a beach shell?

Rain done drank all his milk and was climbing outta his chair. He came around to me and motioned toward the back door where the chickens were congregating. Those chickens were Rain's pets, or so he figured. He got plenty of encouragement from us for thinking like that.

Naturally, his favorite was the smallest of the banty hens, a spitfire called Henny. She never did git along with the other girls. I think it's because Henny was a bit of a run-around. She'd shun the perfectly decent coop Doc constructed and hop up on the fence railing at dusk each evening with Rock Rooster. From that perch the two of them could hop-fly to the roof's gutter. Then they would sidle down the gutter till they reached the limbs of the hickory tree. From there, they'd skip-fly over to a branch and roost there each night.

Rock Rooster was kind of a puny thing, with a high-pitched tenor crow. Doc thought Rock Rooster switched his tail feathers a little too much. "Rock acts like he wants to be one of the girls," Doc chided.

Henny liked to be carried and Rain liked to carry her. On the days in July and August when it was too hot for a person or a chicken to move, Rain would lay on the cool sod 'neath an apple tree and Henny would snuggle up right next to 'im. They'd spend an entire afternoon that way, dozing and daydreaming.

Grabbing my hand, Rain motioned for me to take him outside.

"I'll take him," Embry said. "You sit here and rest some more."

"There's feed for them in that bowl over by the sink," I said.

"I see it." Embry walked over and picked up the bowl of feed. "Git! Git!" she said to Martha as she pushed open the screen door.

Martha jumped down off the porch, but she didn't go quietly. A bossy creature, Martha didn't like others telling her what to do. I stood at the back door and watched as Embry bent over and let Rain scoop up a handful of corn. He tossed it at the chickens, and the girls scattered acrost the yard, clucking and chirping, warning each other to stay away from their grub.

I heared someone climbing the stairs out front. Embry heared it too. She looked up.

"It's Doc," I said. When you live with a man as long as I've lived with Doc, you come to recognize every stomp, step, or shuffle they take. I left Embry to see after Rain and walked to the front room.

37

Doc was carrying a poke in one arm and his jacket in the other. His bloodshot eyes sank into heavy pockets. His shoulders slumped under an unfamiliar weight. I'd never realized till then how much Doc looked like his daddy. A strain creased his forehead and pulled his mouth back in a way that reminded me ever so much of Papaw Lawson at first glimpse. His skin was stretched thin, like a worn sock over old heels. The resemblance sent goose pimples down my arms.

Handing me the poke, he turned to hang up his jacket in the cedar closet he'd built for our first anniversary.

"Sheriff Duncan's wife picked some squash and tomaters from her garden. Told Sheriff to give 'em to us," Doc said.

Not bothering to open the poke, I searched Doc's face for clues, any sign of knowing.

"So?"

"There's not much to tell, Leela. Sheriff said they'd be done with the autopsy later today. He'll release her body to Preston's this afternoon. Doc sat on the edge of the sofa, stared acrost the room, wouldn't look at me.

I was trying to remember back. I was pretty sure Maizee hadn't brung the quilt with her that morning when she dropped Rain off. Nope. She had on her go-to-meeting clothes. A navy cotton skirt with pockets trimmed in navy-and-white checks, and a white blouse to match. Her dark hair was warshed so clean it sparkled like a spanking new halo.

"Is he bringing that Mashburn no-count in for questioning?" I asked.

"Already did," Doc answered.

"And?"

"Kade told Sheriff he'd seen Maizee sometime before lunch, when she dropped by Winfreda's place."

"What business did Maizee have with trash like that?" I asked. Kade's sister, Winfreda Mashburn, was the town tramp, the mother of three children, every single one of 'em fathered by a different daddy. Not that it bothered her. She didn't have no shame. Winfreda thought being wanted by men was cause enough for a girl to brag.

Doc yanked his tucked-in shirt out of his pants. "It's warm in here," he said, tossing the plaid shirt acrost the back of the davenport. Sweat circled the underarms of his tee shirt.

"I hadn't noticed," I replied, figuring it wasn't only the temperature causing Doc discomfort. "I'm listening. What was Maizee doing over at Winfreda's?"

"Kade claimed she was there to pick up that quilt you all made for her and Zeb."

Well, you coulda knocked me over with a feather.

"Mercy sake! Why in the world would that quilt be over at Winfreda Mashburn's house?" I asked, my voice pulled tight as a rocking-stitch.

"According to Kade, he carried the quilt over to Winfreda's so she could launder it. He told Sheriff he'd spilt some coffee on it one morning whilst visiting Maizee. He claimed Winfreda was gitting the soil out." Doc's right cheek twitched backwards, a sure sign that he was disbelieving the story Kade tole Sheriff. "Maizee stopped by to pick up her quilt. Kade said that was the last he seen of her."

"Damnation, Doc! That don't make any sense a'tall!" I hollered. The anger in me swoll up like yeast in dough. I crossed my arms, clenched my jaw, fought furiously to keep from cussing more. Doc looked stunned. In all our years of hardship and heartbreak, I'd never cursed him. Or him me. We might git pissy with each other, but we wouldn't say much. A sour tongue can blacken a heart faster than tobacco tar.

He rose up from the sofa, walked past me and straight out the door. For a second, I thought about jerking him by his shoulder as he marched past, but I thought better of it. He was hurting jes as much as me, maybe more, since he was the one that found Maizee. There was no point of creating more problems than we was already dealing with.

I followed him. Speaking through the screen door separating us, I said "I'm sorry. I shouldn't have spoken so cross."

Doc started to say something but his voice cracked. He wouldn't, or couldn't, look at me. He stood with his back to me, staring out towards the barn, or into nothing, or maybe gazing back in his mind to the river.

"I wish I could tell you why Maizee's gone but I cain't. There are some things in this life we won't never figure out. All I know for sure is that Maizee is gone and she won't be coming back. Not now, not never. And we've got to figure out a way to explain it all to Rain."

Doc was right. How was we supposed to tell a deaf child that his momma wasn't never coming home? Maizee hadn't even got around to explaining to him about Zeb yet.

Rain stepped around the corner of the house, Henny perched on his right shoulder and Embry tagging along behind them. Doc sat on the stoop. Rain swiped at Henny. She squawked and shimmed down off his shoulder. Rain rushed over, running up between Doc's long legs, and plopped down on one of 'em. He wrapped his arms around Doc's neck.

Those two were thicker than bees on a melon. Sometimes it scared me to see how much Doc loved Rain. That kind of capturing love doesn't go unnoticed by Satan. I knowed if the Devil could have his way, he'd find some means to destroy their love and the both of them. Right then and there, I prayed this deal with Maizee wouldn't be Satan's tool. I pushed open the screen and walked out on the porch.

"I was thinking maybe I'd take Rain on up to the house with me," Embry offered. "Give you and Doc time to git some things settled. He could bring along a change of clothes and spend the night. If that's suitable with y'all?"

"I got a hunch this place is going to git swarming with folks once word spreads 'round the valley," Doc said. "It might be a good thing for Rain to be up at Embry's. Lestways till we can figure out how best to tell the child about his..." Doc didn't finish. I knowed he feared bringing Maizee up in front of the child, feared Rain would sense somehow that something was wrong with his momma.

The last thing I wanted to do was send Rain off. I wanted to hang on to that child with all my might, to never let him outta my sight, to draw him close at night, hear and feel his soft breath upon my cheek, to study the rising and falling of his chest. It don't make any sense, but when gravity ceases and the world falls off its axis, holding a child like Rain can right things gone wrong. But I knowed there was much to tend to before Maizee could be buried. Rain would be better off up at Embry's place for now.

"You sure it ain't a burden for you?" I asked Embry.

"It's no trouble at all, ma'am."

"Well, then, wait right here. I'll pack a bag for him."

Maizee had brung a pair of extra jeans and a clean shirt for Rain when she dropped him off Friday morning. He hadn't soiled himself in over a year, and even that was an accident at naptime. Rain insisted on using the chamber pot and outhouse from the time he turned three. Maizee was glad for it.

People who don't know any better will treat a mute child like he's retarded. And if a person never takes the time to teach a mute child anything, they might turn out feeble. Maizee was a good mother. She always treated Rain as if he was able.

I found Rain's jeans and striped shirt sitting right where Maizee had left them, in the bottom of the chifforobe. If he was going to his momma's funeral, he'd need a button-down shirt. I'd have to go over to Maizee's place later and look through Rain's clothes and see if there was anything suitable.

I put the clothes in a poke, along with the blankie he slept with each night. It was one I'd made him from scraps, all red, white, and blue. Big enough to cover a toddler, but small enough that sometimes Rain used it as a cloak. Maizee would clip it around him with a clothespin and Rain would jump from the porch steps, pretending his magical cape could help him fly.

Right now I wished I had wings, or a cape, something to help me fly. I'd wing my way to heaven and ask God what on earth He had in mind when He decided to open wide the gates of hell and turn loose of Satan. I'd ask God what was so loving about rendering a child deaf and then leaving him orphaned in a hearing world. If God was so all-knowing, then surely He ought to have better sense than to take a young boy's mother and father from him in the same year. Especially a boy as innocent of wrongdoing as Rain.

Pushing open the screen door, I walked out on the porch. Embry stood up. I handed her the poke, then sat down beside Doc and took Rain's chin into my hand.

"Miss Embry's going to take you over to her place. I want you to mind her good, okay?"

38

Preacher Blount showed up at the house again shortly after Embry took Rain off up to her place. His wife Dorcas came along. They carried canned peaches, a pot of stew, and a freshly made blackberry cobbler.

"That stew will keep in the icebox for a day or two," Dorcas said as she eyed the plate of fried chicken Embry brung. I'd uncovered it while fixing some lunch for Doc.

"I wished you hadn't troubled yourself," I said. Covering the chicken and the stew, I put them in the icebox, but I left the cobbler out in case Doc wanted some. He'd had a long day already, and it was only early afternoon.

"It's the least I could do," Dorcas said.

Doc and Preacher Blount were out back in the shade. I'd fixed 'em both a glass of tea. They were talking, whispering really. Preacher Blount was collecting ideas from Doc about Maizee's service. I was leaving all the details to Doc, and that's exactly what I told him when he sat down to eat his lunch. Thinking about burying Maizee made me sick to my stomach.

"Where's Rain?" Dorcas asked.

"Embry Mae came by earlier and took him back up to her place. She's going to keep him tonight."

"That's sweet of her. How's he doing with all this?"

"He's all right, I reckon. I think he knowed something's amiss. He's got to. Why else wouldn't his momma come git him? But he hasn't cried for her, not even when I put him to bed last night. 'Course he's used to me, and he loves Doc better than any boy ever loved a man. So he don't mind staying with us."

"Does he know his momma's dead?"

"No. Maizee hadn't even figured out a way to tell him his daddy's gone. I don't know how we're going to explain any of this. You got any suggestions?"

Dorcas adjusted the headscarf that was holding her blond hair back off her face. The fire in the stove had grown cold, leaving a musty smell and a light layer of ash on the stove and the kitchen table. I was glad for the breeze blowing through the house, bringing with it the scent of pumpkins ripening.

"I don't know much about how to explain things to a mute child, Leela. You probably already know more about that than I do."

"Sometimes," I said, "I think Rain understands me when I talk, like he's reading my lips or mind or something."

"Can he hear anything at all?"

"We don't know for sure, but since he makes no effort to speak, other than a few moans or grunts, we figure he cain't hear a'tall."

"Mrs. McFeeter said she thinks Rain understands the Sunday School lessons she teaches."

"Maybe it's because she uses those felt storyboards. Rain likes looking at picture books. But what am I supposed to do, sketch out a picture of his daddy and momma in coffins? Or with the stone rolled away? Or maybe with angel wings?"

Dorca's green eyes flinched with sadness. I knew she wanted to help.

"Mercy, I'm sorry," I said, as I twisted my braid up off my neck and stuffed it into a hairnet I'd pulled from my front pocket. "I don't mean to speak so harsh, especially when you and Preacher have been so kind."

"There's no need to apologize, Leela. You're asking some important questions. I wish I could tell you what to do. I don't know what the best way to handle all this with Rain would be. What does Doc say?"

"He says Rain's too young to understand, even if he could hear us explain it. I don't even understand it myself. Doc thinks we ought not take Rain to the service."

"Won't Rain wonder what happened to his momma? Why she never came back for him?"

"I'm sure."

"I don't know which would be harder on a child his age, never seeing his momma again or seeing her dead."

"The worry of that is eating me from the inside out."

"How did Maizee handle Rain when his daddy left?"

"Well, Rain weren't but two years old then, but Zeb insisted on taking him to the induction and farewell service uptown. The last time Rain seen his daddy, he was waving goodbye from a bus window. Who knows what Rain thinks? Who knows if Rain even remembers the last time he seen his daddy? Maybe he thinks Maizee's gone off to catch a bus herself."

"I don't mean to pry, Leela, but any word yet from the sheriff?" Dorcas wiped a layer of ash off the table onto the floor, crossed her arms, and leaned toward me. She asked her question in a quiet voice, so as to not disturb the dead or their spirits, I reckoned.

"Doc went to town this morning to meet with Sheriff," I answered. I could feel my pulse drumming faster, harder. There was a throbbing in the back of neck. "He jes got back a little while ago. The autopsy will be finished soon. Sheriff's supposed to release Maizee's body to Preston's."

Dorcas sat back, exhaled long and slow.

"I cain't help but feel like this is my fault," I said.

"Whyever would you think that?" Dorcas asked.

"Yesterday when Maizee come by the house, I asked her if she was meeting anybody in town, but she didn't answer me directly. She asked if I had any errands for her to run. I give her my scissors and asked her to take them by Mr. Sloane's

Hardware and git 'em sharpened for me. Doc found them scissors there, alongside Maizee."

Dorcas reached over and took my hand into hers. "This is not your fault, Leela! It has nothing to do with you."

"I should've made Maizee tell me where she was going, who she was seeing, what she was doing."

"She was a grown woman, Leela."

"Not to me she wasn't. Not to me. She was my girl. I should've done more," I cried.

Dorcas ran out of comforting words. She sat silent with me. I liked that. A warm breeze blew through the window over the sink, lifting the curtains I'd made when Doc's daddy moved out. They were the color of honeydew rind, a light green. I'd used the leftover scraps from the curtains to make Maizee's quilt.

"Doc said she was stretched out on that blanket we made for her wedding, looking for everything like she was taking a nap, or sunbathing," I explained. "Truth is, if Maizee's pocketbook hadn't been opened up and sitting down beside her, Doc might have walked right on by. But he said that pocketbook being opened like that disturbed him enough he climbed down from the road to the riverbank, and that's when he seen it was Maizee laying there."

"So were there bruises on her?" Dorcas asked.

I shivered. I hadn't asked Doc if he'd eyed any bruises or knots on Maizee. A part of me didn't want to know. It was bad enough knowing she was gone, without worrying about the struggle she might have put up in the process.

"That's how come Sheriff has ordered an autopsy and brung that Mashburn fellow in for questioning. Maizee went up to his sister's house yesterday after she left here."

"I didn't know Maizee and that Mashburn girl were friends."

"Yeah, well, it takes a mighty leap of faith to put the two of them together," I replied. "I don't know that they was friends. Kade Mashburn told Sheriff that Maizee went by his sister's place to pick up that quilt we'd made for her and Zeb. Supposedly, Kade had spilt some coffee on it and his sister was laundering it.

"Was Kade seeing Maizee?" Dorcas didn't wait for me to answer. She stood up, walked over the sink and asked, "Where do you keep the dish rag? I'll warsh up these dishes before I go."

It was a kind gesture, but I knew her real intent was to busy herself so that she didn't have to look at me while I pondered such a painful matter.

"Don't worry about them dishes," I said, while pointing to the rag hanging 'neath the sink. "Burdy told Doc that Kade started coming 'round the house not long after Zeb left. She weren't none too happy about it."

"No, I don' suspect so," Dorcas said, pouring water from the teakettle into the warsh bin. It wasn't hot, but it was clean. "You heard about that trouble he got into up at Starr Mountain, didn't you?"

"What trouble was that?" I asked as I took another cloth and started drying the dishes Dorcas warshed.

"He was sweet on a gal outta that Harlan clan that lived up there on Bullit Creek," Dorcas said. "She turned up dead one afternoon in the pool where all them rhododendrons grow wild. She'd drowned.

"I heard tell from the pastor's wife over at Tellico Plains that the Harlan girl and Kade went up the swimming hole with some of his juking buddies. They was drinking, carrying on, and what not. Kade claimed nobody saw her go under, and his buddies backed him on that. The sheriff ruled it an accident, but the Harlan clan never did believe a word of it. They figured

Kade caused the accident because their girl wasn't as sweet on Kade as he was on her."

"Mercy sakes, Dorcas, are you saying Kade Mashburn kilt the Harlan girl?"

"Well, I'm jes repeating what I was told. It's gossip, Leela. Don't pay no never mind to me. I don't know any of it for sure."

Dorcas wouldn't look me in the eye.

I might could've dismissed that conversation with Dorcas altogether if it hadn't been for Burdy Luttrell and her odd ways.

After Preacher and Dorcas left, Doc said we ought to go over to Maizee's place and find her something suitable for burying.

"I can carry it over to Preston's tomorrow," he said. "Preacher said he'd hold a viewing from ten to one on Saturday. The funeral will be at two o'clock. I've got to go over to Preston's anyways to pick out a casket. You want to go with me for that?"

"No," I answered, not giving a minute's pause to the question. "It's not right, Doc. Maizee wasn't supposed to die before us. She should be picking out my casket, not me hers."

Sitting down on the edge of the bed, I put my head in my lap and cried so hard the headboard knocked up against the wall from the force of it. Doc sat next to me, wrapped his long arms around my shoulders, and held me as tight as he ever had.

"You're right, Leela. It shouldn't be like this. It's not fair. It's not right." Crying right along with me, Doc let his hot tears fall against my neck. When the tears stopped, we leaned back against the mattress and held each other some more. It was comforting to feel Doc's heart pounding against my own.

Doc leaned up on one elbow and kissed my forehead, my eyes, and then, slowly, gently, he pressed his lips up against mine and said, "I love you, Leela." I opened my mouth and let Doc's words slip past my lips. Reaching up, I pulled him closer, savoring the taste of something familiar. Something I could find my way around, even in the darkest moments.

Kissing Doc in the midst of all that hurt calmed me the way a fresh snow does a scorched earth, covering all the blackened scars and burning spots with heaven's healing powders. I didn't want to do anything but lay in that bed with Doc for the rest of the day, maybe for the rest of the year, and forget all about burying Maizee or tending to an orphaned child. Doc ran the back of his hand across my cheek and said, "We'd best git going over to Maizee's place before the sun dips behind the mountain." With that, he rose up off the bed and held out his hand to help me up.

39

Burdy Luttrell

Doc found Maizee dead down by the river. It was Ida Mosely who brung me the news. It hadn't been long, maybe a few moons passed, since them military men came a'calling about Zeb. If Zeb worried about what would happen to Maizee if he failed to return from overseas, he never said so. Leastwise not to me. Maybe he said something to Doc, or Preacher Blount. I doubt it. Zeb seen going off to war as his duty. He hated leaving Rain, especially, and Maizee. I suspect it eased his mind some to know she was having one of her good spells. The man in Zeb was ready for an adventure, to explore the world beyond these hills.

It was an unclouded September day. Warm enough still to melt pine sap. I was hammering a catfish I'd jes caught to the sweetgum out back when Ida come up the gravel drive, hollering for me. I gave that nail one last pounding before turning to answer her.

"Back here!" I called. Taking out my pocketknife, I sliced a circle around the bottom of the cat's head. Then, with a pair of pliers, I began to strip away the fish's slick hide.

Ida come marching around the corner, wiping at her brow with one of Shug's snot rags.

"Did you hear yet?" she asked.

"Hear what?" I replied.

"Maizee's gone."

"Gone where?"

"She's passed, Burdy. Doc found her dead down on the Holston."

Ida's news sucked the wind right out of me. I leaned my hind end up against the tree, clinched my hands on my thighs, and tried to steady myself. I felt airyheaded.

"Baney call't over the house jes minutes ago," Ida continued. "Said she heard Mrs. Duncan talking to Preacher Blount about it. He's headed over to Doc and Leela's this very minute."

If Baney White told it, then it was the gospel truth. Baney was the party line operator, and privy to all Christian Bend's goings on.

"I'm sorry to be the bearer of bad news," Ida said, though we both knew she didn't mean a word of it. There was nothing Ida enjoyed more than giving other folks bad news.

"Where's Rain?" I asked, looking down at the black flesh hanging from the pliers.

"Baney said Maizee took him up to Leela's yesterday. He's still there."

"She say how Maizee die?"

"No. According to Baney the sheriff's got a case of lock-jaw when it comes to discussing that."

I suspected I knew why that was so.

Her tale done told, Ida excused herself. "Got to git back. Shug'll be wanting his dinner soon."

Flies, big as lima beans, were crawling around inside the cat's head. Its black and freckled hide was right where I'd dropped it at the sweetgum's feet. Picking up the hammer and aiming for the flies, I struck the fish. I pounded and pounded till the only thing left of that big ol' cat was its whiskered snake-like head and slimed bark.

I didn't know I was crying till I'd stopped.

I knowed it was wrong to dishonor that fish the way I done.

Before the sun rose up high over the ridge, I'd pressed through scratchy milkweed, praying Creator would gift me a fish for supper. I knew right where I was likely to find such a creature, too. I had gone straight up to the jigsaw portion of the river, the part where it looks like God broke off the earth the way a person does peanut brittle, all uneven, and I stretched out, head first, on my belly. Taking the bait I brung with me—dough balls soaked in vanilla—I pushed a couple of the balls over the hook.

Cats are drawn by smell. Shug used rancid hot dogs or viennas, or white bread slicked in souse meat. But me, I figured why use something so nasty smelling? Cats don't care if it smells nasty or good, and I'd jes as soon have vanilla scent myself.

I wrapped one end of the line securely around my palm and lowered the bait over the ragged ledge. Cutbacks make good holes for catfishing. As I leaned out over the warming water, I seen a faint shadow of my twinself staring back up at me. My face and hair were very nearly the same color as the river's muddy bottom. I'd weaved my hair into a willow twist last evening and wrapped a hanky around it this morning, but that didn't keep the graying hairs from springing like coils out the sides of my head.

The air smelt of fish exhaling, like they knowed I'd come for them and were preparing to give up the ghost. There was a pinch of pepper seasoning in the air, on account of the pawpaw trees growing yonder near the rise.

I weren't sprawled out like that more than five minutes, maybe six, when I felt a tug on the line. Looking down, I seen the cat's head. It was wide as my knee, and I knew better than to jerk the line. I held on good and tight and waited. Sure enough, the cat tried to swallow the whole bait and took the hook with it. Yanking up the line with my right hand, I grabbed for the fish's mouth with my left, taking care so as not to git finned. Tibbis had a buddy up in Kingsport who nearly lost his hand after a catfish finned him. The venom swoll his hand up till it was nearly as wide as a frying skillet. There are some cats I can catch one-handed, but this one was big. It weighed ten pounds or better.

On the way home, I'd stopped and picked a bunch of Black-eyed Susans from alongside the road. I had me a red vase that needed some cheering up. I'd thanked Creator for both the fish and the flowers, figuring this was goin' to be a fine September, all in all. Boy, was I wrong. Good thing I knew how to fish; I'd never been able to eat if I had to rely upon my gift of knowing for a living. I'd known Maizee was in a bad way, knew more troubling times were ahead for her and Rain, but nothing about my knowing prepared me for the news Ida brung.

I hated to do it, but I had to call Wheedin. Baney White put me on hold while she tended to some other calls.

"I need the long-distance operator," I said when she finally come on the line.

"Guess you heard the news about Maizee then," she said.

"Yes ma'am," I said, not offering Baney any more information than need be.

"We ain't had news like this since the Japs hit Pearl Harbor," she said. Her remark was followed by a long silence, like Baney was waiting on me to serve her gossip on a platter. Well, she could keep on waiting. I held my tongue, and finally, she said, "I'll connect you now."

"Thank you."

Wheedin took the news jes like I figured she might—she come apart like a two-dollar suitcase. She dropped the stack of books she had hold of. I heard 'em crash to the floor, then I heard Wheedin's scream as she let go the phone. I hung up and waited for her to call me back, which she did in short order. She wanted to know all the same things everybody else did: How did Maizee die? Who found her? Where'd they find her? What about Rain? Where is he now? Does he know about his momma?

Of course I didn't have many answers. I told Wheedin what I knew: I don't know how Maizee died. (I didn't see the sense in sharing my suspicions.) Doc found her down by the river yesterday. Leela had Rain. I don't know if he knows about his momma.

Through her sobs, Wheedin declared, "Well, I ain't coming home for the services, so don't even ask me."

She might well as not even wasted her breath. That's what I told her. I knew before I called her that Wheedin wouldn't come home for the services, even if they was Maizee's. I told her that, too.

Wheedin didn't have much else to say after that, and I didn't neither. There wasn't much use in paying good money for empty silence, so I told Wheedin goodbye. But before she hung up, Wheedin said something I hadn't expected.

"I love you, Mam."

I couldn't remember the last time Wheedin, if she ever had, spoke them words to me.

Wheedin won't say it outright, but she never intends to come back to Christian Bend. I suspect she won't even come home to bury me when my time comes. The only scriptures Wheedin faithfully adheres to is "let the dead bury the dead." If I'd lived a righteous life, I could walk on to be with Jesus, or maybe he'd send a chariot to swing down and pick me up the way he done for Elijah, but it was too late for that now. Impressing God, or anyone else, had never concerned me much.

Wheedin came by her devil-may-care attitude honestly. I couldn't blame it on nobody but myself. When you're widowed young, the way I was, you learn real quick. Everything. When to speak up and when not to. What matters and what don't. Mostly, you learn to keep to yourself. It's the only way to keep people from messing in your affairs.

Leela imagined something blooming between me and Doc, ever since Tibbis passed. She's never cautioned me or anything of that nature, but I seen the green shadow of jealousy cut cross her brow a time or two. I seen it the day after Maizee died, when her and Doc stopped by the house to git some of Rain's things.

I'd warned Doc about that low-count Kade Mashburn turning up soon as news of Zeb spread through Christian Bend. But Doc told me not to worry; he said Kade was an old friend of Zeb's and it was natural for him to show his condolences to Maizee. I tried to tell 'im how I'd seen the dark spirits gathering 'round Maizee. How I called upon her ancestors and mine to protect her, but none came. I don't know why they wouldn't tend to her. Ancestor spirits have minds and wills of their own. They don't take direction from the living. The best hope we have is that our pleas will invoke mercy from them.

I'd pleaded on Maizee's behalf since word of Zeb's passing came to the mountain. But no matter how many prayers I uttered, they wasn't enough to keep Maizee safe. It didn't take any special gift for a person to see her soul had departed from her body long before Doc found her on the river.

Later that evening, after I told Wheedin and after Doc and Leela come by to git some of Rain's things and had gone on home, I walked down to the Holston. I sat against a cedar and wished with all my might that what Ida Mosely told me was a lie. But it's like Auntie Tay always said—wishing stuff don't make it so.

It didn't seem right that the sun should rise and set in the same fashion, as if things at Christian Bend were the same as they had always been, when nothing was, nothing except the rising and falling of the sun, which at this very moment was blooding up the river with its red veins of light. That right there angered me. If ever there was a time when the earth, moon, and sun ought to cease their ritual dance, shouldn't it be when daughters die? Had the sun no respect for Maizee? For Doc, Leela, and Rain? For all of us who loved this family? These are the questions I shouted at the sun as it set over the Holston. But the sun answers to no one, don't make no difference how loud a person yells or how disturbed they might be. It jes goes on setting and rising, setting and rising. Maybe that is the sun's answer. Ma always claimed keeping to a familiar path is the best way to straighten out the twisted things of life.

40

Leela-Ma

When me and Doc got to Burdy's place, she was sitting on her front porch with a fly swatter in one hand and a spit jar in the other. Burdy had many habits I didn't much care for, but the worst offense of all, lestways in my mind, was that nasty snuff habit of hers. She kept a tin of snuff in her apron pocket, along with a hanky. And after every meal, and sometimes betwixt them, Burdy pinched up a hit of powdered tobacco and dipped it under her tongue or in the pocket of her bottom lip and sucked on it till her saliva turned the color and texture of cocoa syrup. Sometimes the stained juices oozed out the sides of her mouth when she talked. Often her conversations stopped so she could spit out the excess into a jar.

I never could quite figure out the habit. I mean, if snuff is so appealing, why not jes swallow the juice, how come folks spit it out? I asked Doc that once. He said it's because swallowing tobacco juice can give a person the runs or cause them to vomit. So why suck on the stuff in the first place? I asked. Doc shrugged his shoulders. He was one of the few men in this valley who didn't smoke or chew.

Burdy rose up outta of her rocker as soon as she eyed us walking up the road. She spit into that jar of hers and waved her hanky our way. Doc waved back.

Burdy walked out to the edge of her property and greeted us. She owned some of the best property in the valley. Acres and acres of it. But the only acre cleared out was the one her home stands on. It's not a mansion like some of those brick places up in Kingsport, but it's as nice a home as any around the valley, with a proper sitting room with fireplace, upholstered sofa, and a dulcimer that I've never heard played. Burdy's got a kitchen with two sinks and a big wood stove, a storage room for all the pantry goods, and two bedrooms, both with fireplaces of their own. Her home's also got a back porch that's all screened in, where a person can sit and look out over the house that Maizee and Zeb live in and into the surrounding forest.

"Doc, Leela," Burdy said, nodding our way.

"Good evening, Burdy," Doc answered. "Hope we aren't keeping you from your supper."

"Not at all. I have a pot of beans on. They'll keep. I'd ask what brings you out, but I already know. I've unlocked the front door to Maizee's place. Help yourself to anything you might be needing," Burdy said.

"So you know about Maizee, already?" I asked.

"Yes, Leela."

I wanted to ask who told her, and how many others she'd done told, but I didn't. I didn't have to. It was like Burdy could read my mind, and there's some says that's exactly what she was doing.

"I seen the darkness coming," Burdy said. "I saw it headed this way, like a cloud of starlings swooping in and perching on Maizee's roof."

I was confused. What in the world was Burdy talking about?

"I tried to stop it, Leela. Tried to warn Maizee, but she couldn't see it. Her vision was gone. I called upon her ancestors for protection but none came. They wouldn't come." Burdy dropped her head, shook it back and forth, then shot loose a long spittle that went clean acrost the drainage ditch. "I don't know why they wouldn't come."

When Burdy looked up, there were tears rolling down her face. Doc reached out and put his arm around her shoulders.

"Ain't your fault, Burdy. Ain't nobody's fault. We all done the best we could for her. Thank you for being good to our Maizee."

With that, Burdy turned her face away from us. I had no earthly idea what darkness Burdy was talking about. She often talked out of her head that way, carrying on about the Creator, which was her way of saying God, and her ancestors, and great spirits, and such. She was all the time telling the story of the day the townfolks hung the elephant up in Erwin. I think she liked that story best because she was a half-breed and there was some moral in it for all of us whites. Burdy's a dramatic woman when it comes to telling tall tales, part of her coloredness showing through, I reckon. I had half a mind to quote my granny to Burdy: "That's your tale, and I'm a-sitting on mine."

Truth is, I was more than a might perturbed that Doc reached out and put his arms around Burdy, especially with me standing right there. If anybody needed consoling it was me, not Burdy Luttrell. Mercy sakes! For all I knew she might've hexed Maizee. I was not the least bit moved by Burdy's tears. Without saying nary a word, I walked on past Doc and Burdy, to Maizee's place. They could stand there carrying on all day for all I cared.

I didn't tell Doc right away, but I was taken aback by the mess I found in Maizee's house. Growing up, she'd always been so particular about her things. She kept her socks on the right side of the dresser drawers, her undies on the left, folded so tight they looked like handkerchiefs instead of briefs. When she did her schoolwork, she had to have two writing utensils, a pen and a pencil, which she always placed at the top of her paper when she wasn't using them. And when she ate, Maizee kept her mashed potatoes on one side of her plate, her meat in the center and her beans on the other. She could not tolerate it if the food touched corners.

When she was a youngster, I fretted that Maizee's peculiar ways were a sign of a deeper trouble, but Doc laughed when I suggested it to him.

"There's nothing wrong with that girl, Leela. She's got her own way of doing things, that's all. Most women would be glad to have a child as orderly as her."

I knew Doc was right about that. I never had to chide Maizee to pick up after herself. It weren't uncommon for Maizee to pick up my dirty glass or dishes and carry them to the sink and warsh them up.

But looking around her place on that Saturday, it didn't appear like she'd cleaned her house since Zeb left. The bed was unmade. Clothes was strewn all over the floor in the living room and bedroom. There was a pillow and afghan on the sofa, like maybe she'd been sleeping there, or somebody had. Maybe that Mashburn fellow? Dishes were unwarshed and stacked along the counter, on the table and in the sink. Mercy sakes! I bet there wasn't a clean dish or cup in her house. Rotting trash soiled paper sacks and the kitchen floor where they sat. The sweet smell of spoilt food made my nose burn.

Next to the cold stove on the floor was a box of Maizee's pictures.

I bent over to pick them up. That's when I seen that several of them were mutilated. Somebody had cut on every picture. Maizee, I figured. It looked like she was cutting a paper doll out of her own self. There was a stack of Maizee images. From the time she was a young girl, to the day she married Zeb, to Rain's last birthday. Every single photo had a cutout where Maizee used to be. It was like she was trying to erase every memory of her own life. Good and bad. Shivers prickled me from head to toe.

"Lawd, girl! What in the world were you thinking?" I asked as I put the pictures and the stack of photo cutouts back into the box and covered it with the lid. That's when I seen it. A letter. It was dated Thursday, September 7, 1944. I glanced at it long enough to see who it was from and that it was addressed to Maizee. I stuffed it in my dress pocket.

While Doc stood outside carrying on with the Widow Luttrell, I went about gathering up all Rain's things. His clothes. His shoes. His picture books. His toys. When I got them packed, I set them on the porch and yelled over at Doc.

"I'm gonna need your he'p toting these things!"

During the walk back home, I never mentioned one word to Doc about the mess inside Maizee's place or the letter I found. I figured, given all her witching ways, Burdy Luttrell probably knew all about the letter in my pocket, and that Kade was the one who wrote it.

41

Maizee was put to rest on Saturday, September 16, 1944, in the church cemetery next to Zeb's plot, or the place where he'll be laid if his body's ever recovered. Right now it's jes an empty grave marked by a headstone.

The church hadn't been that full since Easter Sunday, 1942, the first Resurrection following the attack on Pearl Harbor. People were squished together in the pews as tight as hay bales on a truck bed. What ones couldn't fit stood in the aisles, spilt out the back door onto the church stairs, acrost the front lawn.

People came from as far away as Sevierville, Morristown, and Greeneville. I didn't have any idea how they heard about Maizee. The ferry run clean through till midnight, carrying people acrost the Holston so they could be at the service.

God give us a beautiful day. The sort of day that would lift anyone's spirits, even grieving folks. The sky was as clear as a newly warshed window, looked like if you stared at it long enough, a person might spot their own reflection. The sun was soft and warm, puffs of dandelions. Golden maple leaves were piled around many of the tombstones. Along the church's north wall, the burning bushes looked like a row of flaming campfires. Off in the field south of the church was Shug Mosely's barn, full of hay.

Maizee looked beautiful for her burial. I'd seen to that. There wasn't much question as to her burial clothes. Maizee didn't have a lot to choose from, but there was one outfit she had hardly worn. Doc and I'd bought it for her the second Christmas that Zeb was gone. It was a faint blue dress, the color of Maizee's eyes, decorated with a splash of purple-and-green forget-me-not flowers all over it. It had a scoop neck, belted waist, and short sleeves.

She'd rushed into our bedroom and tried the dress on as soon as we give it to her, then came floating into the living room, twirling around on her tiptoes, the skirt poofing like a hibiscus bloom. "I love it! I love it!" Maizee exclaimed. "I feel like I'm floating. Like I'm an angel."

"You are an angel," Doc said. "Our angel. You always have been, always will be."

"You're supposed to save that dress for when Zeb gits home," I said. "That's for your reunion day."

The thought of Maizee dancing around in that dress tore me up.

Around her neck was the necklace Zeb give her the day he left. Maizee almost always wore that locket, the one with the picture of Rain inside, but I'd found it in her jewelry box the day Doc and I went for Rain's things. I intended to put it on Maizee after the folks at the funeral home finished dressing her for burial, but Doc had insisted on doing it. Said it wasn't right for me to handle the dead.

Preacher Blount preached a powerful message from Psalms 91, one of my favorites and Maizee's, too: *If you make the Most High your dwelling, even the Lord, who is my refuge, then no harm will befall you, no disaster will come near your tent. For he will command his angels concerning you, to guard you in all your ways. They will lift you up in their hands….*

Once, when Maizee was thirteen or fourteen, she come to me one afternoon while I was scrubbing the laundry and said her momma had appeared to her as she was walking home from Wheedin's house: "Momma come to me from outta nowhere, jes like an angel, only without the wings."

I believed every word Maizee told me, and I didn't make no exception to it. If Maizee said her momma came to her, I didn't have any reason to doubt her. When you're raised up believing the Bible the way I was, there's no question that the dead shall rise, and sometimes return, usually with a message.

"Mercy sakes! Did Nan say how come she was there?" I asked, reaching into the tub of suds and rubbing together the knees of Doc's work jeans.

"She told me I needed to quit worrying so much about her," Maizee said. "She said God was taking good care of her, and she wasn't in any pain. And you know what, Leela-Ma?"

"No, what?"

"Momma looked like her ownself, only better. Her eyes were all healed up. You couldn't even tell where them chickens had pecked at them."

The old is gone and the new has come, that's what I said to Maizee right after she told me Nan's ghost paid her a visit. Of course, I was speaking of Nan's new body, the one she got on her resurrection morning. But now, looking at Maizee laying up there pretty as a bride as Preacher carried on, I thought how cattywampus everything's turned out, with me sitting here alive and Maizee dead. *The new is gone and the old remains.*

If Maizee could've heared my thoughts, she would've thunk 'em funny. She had a twisted way of looking at things. She told me one time, "It takes a sinner like me, Leela-Ma, to make a saint outta folks like you." She repeated that line for days on end to anyone who'd listen. Remembering it made me want to laugh out loud, and I might would have if it hadn't been Maizee laying up there in that casket.

We decided against bringing Rain to the funeral. The day before me, Doc, and Embry Mae sat with Rain in Mrs. McFeeter's Sunday School class. Mrs. McFeeter used the storyboard to help us tell Rain about his momma and daddy. Doc said as long as we was telling him about the one, we might as well tell him about the other.

Doc sat in one of the small wooden chairs and held Rain on his lap while Mrs. McFeeter took cutouts of Maizee and Zeb that I had given her and put them up on the black felt board beside one of a risen Jesus. You could tell Jesus was risen because of the halo around his head, which Mrs. McFeeter pointed to as she knelt in front of Rain.

Never turning away from Rain, Mrs. McFeeter spoke slowly, nearly whispering as she told Rain that Jesus had gone to heaven and taken his momma and daddy with him. She put a couple of clouds on the felt, one over Maizee's feet and one over Zeb's. Then, Mrs. McFeeter placed a halo over Zeb's head, then one over Maizee's.

Her pink-polished nails flit through the sky like hummingbird wings as she showed Rain how Jesus had swooped down and carried his momma and daddy off to live with him. Mrs. McFeeter took a picture of a stone mansion from her lap and put it on the felt board beside her. Then, she put Jesus, Zeb, and Maizee underneath its stone arch, in front of the wooden door.

I knew the minute Rain understood what she was telling him. He turned away from the storyboard and climbed up into Doc's lap. Pressing Doc's cheeks between his dimpled hands, Rain searched Doc's eyes, like he was begging him for another story. When Doc didn't offer him one, that's when Rain understood.

Jumping down off Doc's lap, Rain ran over to the storyboard, grabbed the cutout of Jesus and his mansion and ripped it in half. I started to reach for him, to stop him, but Embry held me back.

"Let him alone, Leela."

"But it's blasphemy," I said. "He doesn't know what he's doing."

"So then it isn't blasphemy," Embry said. "It's Rain's grief, and I think God is big enough to handle a young boy's hurt."

"She's right," Doc said. He leaned forward and clasped his hands together. Mrs. McFeeter let Rain be as he ran around the room, grunting and moaning like a dog does when it gits its hind paw caught in a trap. Rain pounded the storyboard till it fell over, sending the cutouts of his momma and daddy flying acrost the room. Maizee's landed at my feet. I bent over to pick it up, but Rain shoved me away. He grabbed up the picture of Maizee and the one of Zeb and ran back over to Doc.

Doc pulled Rain up onto his lap. The boy sobbed and clutched the pictures of his momma and daddy to his heart, and then pressed them against Doc's chest. There are times when the best thing a person can say is nothing at all. Rain taught us that.

Embry Mae offered to keep Rain at her place until after the funeral. I agreed, and was glad I did so when I seen how many people turned out to pay their respects. Being around all those adults, weeping and carrying on, would have surely been confusing for the boy.

I was glad when it came time to rise to our feet and sing the doxology. Doc gripped my right hand in the two of his and led me out the church, behind the pallbearers. I couldn't even tell who they was. Some menfolk that Doc rounded up, along with Poke Mosely and his brother, Tupper. Wheedin didn't show. That surprised me some, given that she was Maizee's best friend. But truth was Maizee had always been a better friend than Wheedin. That girl never did anything that wasn't in her own best interest.

On the way out the door, I seen Kade Mashburn out the corner of my eye. He was standing off to the right, near a bed of wild roses. His head was hanging heavy, like fruit on a bent branch. He looked tuckered out. I couldn't believe he'd dared show his face around these parts, and I said so to Doc as we walked behind Maizee's casket.

"Mercy sakes! The nerve of that fellow," I whispered, nodding my head toward Kade, so Doc could see who I was talking about. "Can you believe him? I have half a mind—"

"Let it go, Leela," Doc said, interrupting me. "We got more important matters to tend to."

I knew Doc was right, but even so, I noticed that Sheriff and Mrs. Duncan took care to stand between me and Kade Mashburn for the rest of the services, with good reason.

The other day when we had walked over to Burdy's place, Doc had asked if I wanted Maizee buried uptown, next to her momma and daddy. I didn't hesitate for one minute. "No, I surely do not," I said. "I want her right here where I can tend after her. Besides, Maizee would want to be here, next to Zeb, when he gits home."

"Okay, then," Doc said.

And so it was at two o'clock that afternoon, as the church bells clanged, our dear Maizee was laid to rest in one of the plots that Doc had bought some years ago for the two of us. Doc's momma was to Maizee's right and Zeb's plot on her left. As Preacher Blount offered up his final prayer, I studied Zeb's tombstone. The folks at Preston's put it up. The sparkling white granite had a cross on it. Beneath the cross was these words: "Zebulon Linton Hurd. Tennessee. Cpl. Co. H. 82nd Airborne. DOD: June 6, 1944."

There was nothing on it to testify to Zeb's life as a husband or a father. I didn't care for that. Nor was there any mention that his body had never been brung home.

When Doc asked me what I wanted on Maizee's tombstone, I told him, "Git some pink marble from that quarry place up in Rogersville and have them put a cross on it to match the one on Zeb's."

"Anything else?"

"Yes," I said, pulling out a chair at the kitchen table and writing it out exactly like I wanted for it to read: "Maizee Delight Daggett Lawson Hurd. 1923–1944. Mother of Rain. We miss you with a big love that will never, ever end."

When night came on, Embry Mae brought Rain home. I heard them walking up the road and met them on the front porch.

"I intended to keep him until morning, let you and Doc git some rest," Embry Mae said. "But Rain got to wimpering, and I knew it was you he wanted."

Rain held his momma's Hitty doll in the crook of one arm and reached out for me with the other. I'd taken the doll from Maizee's place when Doc and I went to git her burying clothes.

I heaved Rain up, and he buried his face into my neck. "Mercy sakes, you are growing into such a big boy."

The night air blew keen and strong from the other side of the pasture. Far, far off, I caught a faint sound, like someone crying out Maizee's name.

"Listen," I said. "Do you hear that?"

"Hear what?" Embry Mae asked.

We both leaned toward the darkness. The only sounds were that of the katydids sawing.

"Never you mind. I thought I heard someone crying down by the river," I answered.

"You're jes worn out," Embry Mae said. "Go on inside and git some rest."

"Lemme git Doc to walk you back home."

"No. I'll be fine. I got my flashlight. I'll check on you tomorrow."

"Okay," I said. "But be careful."

"I will." Embry Mae turned to go, waving me off.

Rain was sitting up straight in my arms now, holding Hitty up to his ear.

"Is that doll babe talking to you?" I asked.

He pressed Hitty's face up next to my own ear.

"She's telling you how much your momma loved you, ain't she?"

Rain might be deaf, but he sure knew the word "momma." His face lit up brighter than a July firefly, and the smile that crost his face, well, that was as good as any spoken word.

—The End—

Glossary

Acrost: across; on the opposite side; from one side to another.

Afeared/feared: afraid, fearful.

Ague-weed: gall flower; wildflower; used to treat a fever.

Apple butter: a bread spread made by spicing and sweetening stewed
apples.

Bacca, baccer, baccy, backy: tobacco.

Beautyberries: purple berries that last well into the winter and are an
important survival food for birds and other animals. Highly
astringent, beautyberries are made into wine and jelly. Also
used as an herbal preventive against mosquito bites.

Blasted: form of cursing; damned; confounded.

Bloodroot: red Indian paint; wild plant; stems "bleed" when broken; red
juice used to make a tea and a dye; laxative; expectorant.

Borry: to obtain from a neighbor or friend when one's own has gone out.

Cattywampus: twisted or careened to one side. Also out of line, out of
plumb.

Chestnut/American chestnut: once one of the most important trees in
the eastern United States, occupying about 25 percent of the
hardwood canopy. By the early 1950s, the tree was virtually
eliminated by chestnut blight. The US Forest Service, the
American Chestnut Foundation, and the University of
Tennessee have been conducting research, hoping to produce a
blight-resistant American chestnut.

Chicken skin: goosebumps.

Chicken wobble: a neighborhood party in which boys or men steal a
neighbor's chicken and invite folks over for supper. The stolen

chicken is then fed to the neighbor, who is unaware that he is eating his own chicken. Also goat wobble.

Chifforobe: tall, stand-alone furniture that serves as a closet.

Clabbered: milk that has begun to sour, thicken, and curdle.

Clean: all the way, completely.

Clod: a lump or chunk of earth.

Commence to: start; to begin.

Conjure ball: same as hair ball. A mass of hair formed by a witch and used for witchcraft. Sometimes found in the straw beds or feather pillows of those who have passed on.

Contrary: cantankerous; to contradict.

Cross: to speak harshly; to act cranky.

Crossways: odds, disagreeable, at cross purposes.

Croup: barking cough.

Daub: smear, streak.

Davenport: sofa, couch.

Dinner: lunch.

Disbelieving: doubting, skeptical.

Dutchman-pipe: climbing vine, also called pipe vine, native to central and eastern North America. It bears heart-shaped or kidney-shaped leaves and purplish-brown tubular flowers resembling a curved pipe. Medicinal properties.

Fancied: imagined.

Feather-legged: a craven, cowardly person.

Frog-drowner: hard rain.

Get shed of: be rid of; be free from.

Git: get.

Give out: to fail, break down, tire out.

Granny woman: midwife, to assist in the delivery of a child.

Grave house: crude structure house erected at the time of burial to shelter the dead from rain, snow, and wind.

Hawkweed: related to sunflower; previously used to treat lung ailments, specifically whooping cough.

Healer: a person with the gift of healing or the capability to impart health to another.

Hitty: a children's novel about a doll written by Rachel Field and published in 1929. *Hitty* won the Newbery Medal for excellence in American children's literature.

Homecoming: annual event when former members of a church gather for a reunion.

Idey: thought or opinion.

Jes: just.

Joe Pye weed: perennial wild plant with medicinal value in treating urinary disorders.

Keeled: fall down suddenly from illness or death. Also, to push something over.

Kilt: killed.

Light out: to leave quickly, in a hurry.

Like a martin to a gourd: focused, zeroed in, headed straight for something, undeterred.

Low-count: a person of questionable character; lazy, lacking in good morals.

Lung balm: a tea made from the bark of the black cherry tree.

Marring: impairing the quality of; blemish.

Mash: press down hard, flatten. Also a mixture of malt, water, and grain fermented in the process of making liquor.

Melungeons: "free people of color"; tri-isolates; people of mixed Indian, White (European), and Black ancestry, located primarily in Southwest Virginia, East Kentucky, and East Tennessee.

Mite: a bit; small amount.

Mountain boomers: small red squirrels who move very fast.

Mucckly: free-spirited; heedless of others and of propriety.

Mulligrubs: sulkiness; despondency; vague unwellness.

Muster: to call forth; to summon.

Nary: not a one; none; any.

Outlanders: outsiders to the mountains; strangers.

Pearling: search for pearls. The Tennessee River and its tributaries host some 102 species of mussels. A pearl button industry was established in the Tennessee Valley beginning in 1887, 272 producing buttons from the abundant mussel shells. Button production ceased after World War II when plastics replaced mother of pearl as button material. Pearling was a favorite sport for young people prior to the dams and environmental changes that have reduced the mussel population in the rivers.

Plumb: complete, thorough, done, absolute.

Poke: paper sack.

Poke salat: perennial plant known commonly as pokeweed. In the spring the leaves are edible for making poke salad (salat) but must be boiled first. The berries are sometimes made into wine. The root has medicinal purposes.

Popeye shiners: ray-finned fish. Minnows spawn in the spring or summer.

Possumhaw: deciduous holly located in the southeast, with bright red fruit and dull green toothed leaves.

Puthery: hot, sweaty, sultry, humid weather.

Quare: queer; mentally unbalanced; senile; defective; oddball.

Rightly: exactly; correctly.

Scouring: to clear an area, or to look closely.

Seer: person credited with extraordinary moral and spiritual insight who can sometimes predict the events to come.

Shitepoke: long-legged, like a heron.

Shumake: sumac bush; bark used to treat burns; blossoms and fruit used for medicinal tea called sumacade.

Slack-twisted: lacking in courage: someone who feigns excuses to escape military duties.

Slanchwise: at an angle.

Smelt: smelled; inhaled.

Snakeroot: poisonous perennial herb, native to eastern North America; sometimes used for medicinal purposes.

Sobby: soaked; soggy; thoroughly wet.

Squallering: crying; hollering.

Staunched: stopped; restricted.

Stewed: worked up; annoyed.

Stick/s: a contingent of paratroopers tasked with a mission.

Sulky: bad-tempered; resentful.

Sull, sullup, sulled: sulk, act or become sullen.

Supper: evening meal.

Sware: swear; curse; express frustration; promise.

Swoll: puffed up; expanded; distended.

Thimbleberries: purple-flowering raspberry; seedy fruit that surrounds hollow core resembles a thimble.

Trodding: walking in a heavy-footed, focused fashion.

Vex: irritate; annoy; provoke; torment; trouble; distress; worry.

Warsh/ed: cleanse.

Whore bath: using a sponge or wash cloth to wash underarms and privates from the sink in lieu of a soaking bath.

Whupped: whipped; thrashed; beat; shoved; rushed. Also very tired.

Witchwood: American mountain ash (*Sorbus americana*), which is native to the highest peaks of Southern Appalachians. No relation to white ash or green ash, this relatively small tree (40 ft) is also known as the "rowan tree," from its European cousin (*Sorbus aucuparia*). The mountain ash is rumored to be the tree on which the devil hanged his mother. Deer, birds, and other wildlife enjoy its red berries.

Worriment: worry; be troubled; distraught.

Book Clubs and Readers' Guide

1. *Hitty: Her First Hundred Years* is a children's novel written by Rachel Field and published in 1929. It won the Newbery Medal for excellence in American children's literature. The book and Maizee's Hitty doll play an important role in the plot of *Mother of Rain*. Why do you think Hitty became such a vital part of Maizee's life both as a child and then again as an adult?

2. Burdy has a vision about Maizee that she can't define until she finds Maizee cutting herself. Leela-Ma later finds that Maizee has cut herself out of all the family photographs. What symbolism can you find in Maizee's actions?

3. After her mother's death, Maizee's father sends her to live with Doc and Aunt Leela. Do you agree with Maizee's father's decision to send her away? How do you think both the tragedy of her mother's death and her father's reaction affected Maizee?

4. Leela-Ma has never had children of her own. When Maizee is sent to live with her, how does Leela-Ma reconcile her joy at finally having a child with her grief over the loss of her sister? How do you think Leela-Ma's conflicting emotions influenced Maizee?

5. What is revealed about Burdy and Leela-Ma's backgrounds? How do you think their relationship influenced their actions? How much do you think our feelings toward others influence our decisions and actions?

6. Zeb knew that something was wrong with Maizee, at least in the early days of their marriage. Do you agree with his decision to join the army? Do you think Maizee's health, or her ability to raise a deaf child alone, was something he considered when he deployed?

7. Burdy has a gift that she calls the "curse of knowing." Have you ever had a gift or talent that felt more like a curse? How did you deal with it? Do you think that Burdy could have used her gift differently to save Maizee?

8. Maizee clearly suffered from some form of mental illness. Of the people closest to her, two of them are doctors or healers. Do you think the people closest to her understood the seriousness of her illness?

9. In chapter 29, Maizee says, "I knowed Zeb was dead before the telegram came." If Maizee knew Zeb was dead, why do you think she refused to attend his service without a body?

10. Maizee develops her own way to communicate with Rain. Why do you think she didn't bother explaining to him that his father wasn't coming home?

11. Some identified Maizee's illness as "baby blues" or postpartum depression. What do you think were the first signs of Maizee's mental illness? Did her problems run deeper than postpartum depression? Do you think perceptions of mental illness have changed since the time of this story? Are there better resources today than there would have been in Maizee's time?

12. The people of Christian Bend have their own hierarchy system and often look down on those they consider beneath

them. Give some examples of this. Why are they quick to point their fingers at Kade Mashburn whenever trouble arises?

13. Leela-Ma says,"There are times when the best thing a person can say is nothing at all. Rain taught us that." Has there been a time in your life when you've learned the importance of being silent?

14. The author chose to tell this story from the different perspectives of the main characters. Did this approach help you understand the characters better? Did you identify better with any of the characters? If so, which ones?

Conversation with the Author

1. What inspired you to write Mother of Rain?

Karen Spears Zacharias: While attending the South Carolina Book Festival as a panelist, I carved out the time to hear Michael Montgomery's compelling presentation about his work on *The Dictionary of Smoky Mountain English* (Knoxville: University of Tennessee Press, 2004).

I bought the book and read through it several times. As I read, I could hear the voices of my Aunt Cil and Granny Leona. I wanted to write something that captured the voices of my childhood.

But the character of Maizee has been with me ever since Andrea Yates, the Texas mom, killed her five children. Yates was the stone in my pocket that I kept turning over as I wrote Maizee's story.

2. Burdy Luttrell is an eccentric character—Melungeon, prophet, and healer woman. She is an outsider in the community, but she is central to the story. What inspired her character?

KSZ: Several years back, while attending Mercer University Press's Author Luncheon, I met Dr. Brent Kennedy, author of *The Melungeons: The Resurrection of a Proud People* (2nd ed.; Macon GA: Mercer University Press, 1997). Dr. Kennedy and I spoke about our connection to the land and the people of East Tennessee. My own grandmother, Leona Lawson, and her family identified themselves as Black Dutch.

I began my research with Dr. Kennedy's work but have also visited with Jack Goins and read his work, *Melungeons: Footprints from the Past* (self-published, 2009). Burdy was, undoubtedly, taking shape then, but she really presented herself as I conducted research at the Center for Appalachian Studies & Services at East Tennessee State University, and listened to the oral histories.

3. *The setting, time, and place of the novel is an essential aspect of the story, influencing the characters and their distinct dialogue. What made you choose rural East Tennessee for the setting of this novel?*

KSZ: I think the remote mountain setting lends itself to the isolation that women who suffer mental breakdowns during pregnancy feel. Having witnessed as one of my dearest friends suffered the onset of mental illness during the third trimester of her first pregnancy, and then again with her second pregnancy ten years later, I had some inkling of the illness that compels a mother to kill her children. Thus, the remote setting becomes a metaphor for how little we have advanced in the treatment of mental illness that arises during pregnancy. I hope this story helps raise awareness about the nightmares such women have endured and overcome.

4. Mother of Rain *is your first novel. Was it difficult to break away from your previous journalistic style of nonfiction writing, or did finding your voice in fiction come naturally?*

KSZ: My fiction voice actually came naturally to me. I feel like I have known Maizee and her people all my life. It was just a matter of sitting down and listening to their stories.

5. *Maizee's early love of reading is an integral part of the story when she discovers the book* Hitty: Her First Hundred Years. *What led you to include Hitty as a character in this story? Do you share a similar love of reading?*

KSZ: I grew up in a military family, which meant that every two to three years, I was changing schools. I attended several different elementary schools, so, yes, books were the place I found companionship. The first "big people" book I read was Madeleine L'Engle's *A Wrinkle in Time*. She remains a favorite. I keep a copy of her *Irrational Season* on my desk and read from it almost daily.

My other constant companion in childhood was a cowgirl doll that my mother had given me. I loved that doll. She was Gail of the West and modeled, I think, after the TV star Dale Evans. I gave that doll to my beloved Thelma, who cared for me and my siblings after our father was killed in Vietnam. Thelma tried to get me to keep the doll—she only had one child, a son—but that doll was the most precious gift I could offer Thelma when she left us for another job. For children who experience the loss of a parent or a sibling at such an early age, I think a doll or favorite stuffed animal can be a great comfort. Such a companion allows them opportunity to express the grief that adults sometimes deny children.

Contact the Author

If you would like Karen to speak to your book club, church, or organization, please contact her at zachauthor@gmail.com. Karen also enjoys hearing from readers. Feel free to drop her a note. Find her on Facebook or Twitter: @karenzach.

Acknowledgments

Mercer University Press made me an author when they published my first book of nonfiction, *Benched: The Memoirs of Judge Rufe McCombs*. I am grateful that they considered this debut novel worthy of publication. Hugs and humble thanks to Marc Jolley, Marsha Luttrell, Mary B. Kosowski, Jenny Toole, and Candice Morris, one of the hardest-working crews in publishing. And thank you, Kelley Land. Your insights are keen. This is a better book because of you.

When my daughter Shelby Zacharias earned her Masters in English at George Mason University, I was proud as a peacock, but I had no idea then how useful her degree would prove to be for me. Maizee's story is as much Shelby's debut novel as it is mine. It was Shelby I sought out when I became wrapped up in this story like a calf in barbed wire. Shelby untangled the mess I had made and helped me create a work of grace that I hope will resonate with women everywhere. Mama loves you, Miz Shelby. Thank you, honey, for doing what Burdy asked you to do—rescuing Maizee.

This work was compelled forward by the following works: Michael Montgomery, *The Dictionary of Smoky Mountain English*; Jack Goins, *Melungeons: Footprints from the Past*; Dr. Brent Kennedy, *The Melungeons: The Resurrection of a Proud People*; and the historical collections at the Archives of Appalachia at East Tennessee State University. Without their assistance, Maizee's story and so many others would remain untold. Thank you.

Special thanks to Mrs. Overall of Chattanooga, Tennessee, who shared her stories of growing up deaf. Thanks also to Beulah Campbell of Crossville, Tennessee, for her remembrances from the 1940s. Thanks to Bill and Lois Thurman for offering me one of their fine roosters, and to all the other fine folks in Crossville who shared their stories with me. Also, thanks to Captain (Retired) Eddie Wofford of Navarre, Florida, for his assistance.

I give wild river thanks and great love to Lee Smith. Lee intimately understood Maizee's story and believed in my ability to tell it. She never wavered in her encouragement to see this story to publication. Amy Greene and Todd Johnson graciously read the manuscript and generously lavished praise upon the work. My humblest of thanks to them. And to two of my favorite authors Ann Hite and Michael Morris, for their constant encouragement.

A big cry of katydid thanks to Rick Wallace, Tammy McCullough, and Debbie Johnson for reading early drafts of the manuscript and offering valuable insights. Big hugs to all of you faithful booklovers (yes, you, Kathy Patrick and Pulpwood Queens), librarians, and Indie Booksellers who have been a constant source of encouragement to me throughout my career.

The friendships and prayers of so many blessed me and sustained me as I finished Maizee's story and buried my own mother, Shelby Mayes Spears. Thank you for your many kindnesses through the dark days of Mama's illness.

Bright yellow sun thanks to Gordon and Pam Wofford of Crossville, Tennessee; Brent and Lisa Baldwin of Lebannon; and Jerry and Patti Burke of Murfreesboro for giving me shelter among the oaks and hickories, nourishment in the form of catfish and turnip greens, and plenty of belly laughs.

Linda Spears Barnes prays mountains to move and, by golly, mountains march. I love you, Sister Tater.

For Tim, my ain true Zeb, and our children, whose candid feedback always makes my books better. Thanks to dogs Portia, Poppy, and Poe for quietly taking turns keeping me company in my office as I worked. And great love to Sullivan for being the best distraction ever. Granny loves you big as the morning sky.